EYE OF
VENGEANCE

JONATHON KING

EYE OF VENGEANCE

DUTTON

DUTTON
Published by Penguin Group (USA) Inc.
375 Hudson Street, New York, New York, 10014, U.S.A.
Penguin Group (Canada), 90 Eglinton Avenue East, Suite 700, Toronto, Ontario M4P 2Y3,
Canada (a division of Pearson Penguin Canada Inc.); Penguin Books Ltd, 80 Strand, London
WC2R 0RL, England; Penguin Ireland, 25 St Stephen's Green, Dublin 2, Ireland (a division
of Penguin Books Ltd); Penguin Group (Australia), 250 Camberwell Road, Camberwell,
Victoria 3124, Australia (a division of Pearson Australia Group Pty Ltd); Penguin Books
India Pvt Ltd, 11 Community Centre, Panchsheel Park, New Delhi—110 017, India;
Penguin Group (NZ), cnr Airborne and Rosedale Roads, Albany, Auckland 1310, New
Zealand (a division of Pearson New Zealand Ltd); Penguin Books (South Africa) (Pty) Ltd,
24 Sturdee Avenue, Rosebank, Johannesburg 2196, South Africa

Penguin Books Ltd, Registered Offices: 80 Strand, London WC2R 0RL, England

Published by Dutton, a member of Penguin Group (USA) Inc.

First printing, May 2006
10　9　8　7　6　5　4　3　2　1

Library of Congress Cataloging-in-Publication Data
King, Jonathon.
　Eye of vengeance / Jonathon King.
　　p.　cm.
　ISBN 0-525-94953-4
　1. Journalists—Fiction. I. Title.
　PS3611.I58E97　2006
　813'.6—dc22　　　　　　　　　　　2005034514

Printed in the United States of America
Set in Galliard

PUBLISHER'S NOTE

*This is in memory of Will Williams, my first editor,
a crusty newsman with a velvet heart.*

EYE OF
VENGEANCE

/ Chapter 1 /

He'd had the hooded binoculars up to his face for forty-five minutes, but still his eyes were not tired. His eyes had never been tired. He could hold this position, prone on the roof, forever if he had to, because if that's what had to be done, he would do it. He was looking south, the direction they would come from. Only when another filthy pigeon lighted on the fourth-floor ledge and pecked at a loose piece of gravel, or when yet another journalist with a camera or a notepad in her hands arrived below, would he move his eyes away from the lenses. Shitbirds and reporters, he thought. Couldn't always predict when they'd arrive, only that they always would.

Everyone else was in their place. The jail guards across the street were uniformed and waiting. The detention sergeant was at the gray intake door, a cigarette butt in his mouth, his thick arms crossed over his chest, waiting. The transport team, he knew, was en route, their man shackled in the back of the van. Everyone was in place for the eight AM transfer of the prisoner.

He checked the shadow pattern one more time. He was sweating lightly in his black cargo pants and long-sleeved shirt. The heat was already rising in the early Florida sun. He registered it, gave the humidity and heat ripple a second thought in his calculations of the shot, but dismissed it. At this range it would not be a factor. He readjusted his baseball cap, worn backward, like the punk kids, but for reasons they would never get. He and Collie had been the first ones to sew black terry cloth on the inside of the band to capture the sweat and keep it out of their eyes. Collie was one of the few men he liked to talk to. Collie would understand.

At seven forty-five he spotted the white van six blocks away, waited for it to catch one more stoplight. He used the binoculars to confirm the decal on the front, and then moved back to his weapon. For the tenth time that morning, he sighted the scope on a spot six feet above the second step of the staircase leading to the gray door. The magnification was so sharp he could see a wisp of smoke from the sergeant's Marlboro drift through the crosshairs. He shifted his right sighting eye to survey the approach of the van. Then he closed it and opened his left to check his flank. It was one of the odd physiological advantages he'd had as a sniper in Iraq and on the SWAT teams he'd been with. He not only had great focus sight, but also excellent peripheral vision. Most guys sighted with one dominant eye, leaving them blind to the field on their closed, weak-side eye. It was OK when you had a spotter next to you, but when you were alone, it made you vulnerable. He could spot with one eye and check the field with his other. He was a switch-hitter. And he could work alone.

In the street sixty feet below, the van slowed and he heard the clanking sound of the automatic gate as it rolled back. The reporters crowded toward the entrance and were kept back by a jail guard, who corralled them with outstretched arms. The shitbirds just love the perp walk, he thought. They'd always yell out to the prisoner for some kind of statement. Like what? He's going to confess right out there on the sidewalk? Shit.

The van passed through the gate and pulled to a stop next to the staircase and he went back to the scope. Red brake lights flashed in the lens. The sun glinted off razor wire as the gate closed. The uniformed driver got out and went to the back, joined by his partner. They opened the van's rear double doors and out stepped the man. He was dressed in jailhouse orange. Only his wrists were cuffed, so he climbed out easily. He was a big man, over six feet tall, but stood with his back slightly bowed, his thick shoulders rolled forward like a yoke.

He followed the man's bald head in the crosshairs. All three men disappeared between the van and the staircase, but he kept the scope moving in the anticipated time of their steps. When the white patch of Steven Ferris's scalp slid into the sight, one hundred and fifty yards away, the shooter took a measured breath. Eight inches up the first step. Eight inches up the second step. The crosshairs were on Ferris's profile, matching each rise. The shooter heard nothing and felt only the pressure of his index finger on the cold metal of the trigger. When Ferris reached the top step, the jail sergeant took a final drag on his cigarette and flipped it away. He opened the gray door and appeared to look into Ferris's face and say something. The shooter's crosshairs were on the prisoner's right sideburn and Ferris seemed to peer up at the sergeant and mouth the last words he would ever speak.

The rifle recoiled into his shoulder like a firm but playful punch, and he did not have to watch as Ferris sank like a bag of water suddenly cut loose from above. The sniper knew that there was now a hole the size of a dime burrowed into the man's brain, the bullet killing him before he could even blink at its impact.

"Smoke check," he whispered.

/ Chapter 2 /

"I don't know why I always have to open my big mouth," Nick whispered to himself.

It wasn't because he didn't know better. He'd been in the newspaper business for a dozen years, had read the same old stuff a thousand times, let it get under his skin and then popped off to some senior editor and gotten his own ass in trouble again. It wasn't that he forgot the lessons, just that he was too foolish to heed them.

"Good morning, Nick," Deirdre Smith, the city editor, said as she slid past him to get into her own office door. She did not make eye contact. She knew better than to make eye contact. It was one of the lessons *she* never forgot. Instead she stowed her purse, tapped the spacer key on her computer, which was always booted up, and avoided him even though he filled up her doorway, standing there with the metro page in his fist, leaning into the frame. After tapping a few keys to see how many e-mails she had to answer and probably wishing to God he would just go away, she finally sat down in her chair, elbows on the desk, hands clasped under her chin. "How can I help you, Nick?"

Management training, he thought: *Ask if you may assist the employee in some manner. Let them know that you are a partner and that you are there to help them.* She smiled her fake smile. He reflected it back with one of his own.

"Man, I hope it wasn't you who changed the lead paragraph in my story last night, Deirdre," Nick said and then laid—didn't toss, but laid—the front page of the section down in front of her. In retrospect, it wasn't the best way to start. But he was proud of himself for the not-tossing part.

She picked up the paper as if she didn't know which story he was talking about and pretended to read it for a few seconds.

"Well, first of all, it was a great story, Nick. And it got lots of raves in the morning editors' meeting," she said from behind the page. "We all really liked that detail you put in about the number of cigarette butts in his ashtray by the BarcaLounger. You've got such a great eye, Nick."

More management training. *If possible, compliment the employee on a task well done before addressing problems with job performance.*

"But yes, I did do some tinkering. I thought you missed a major point, which you mentioned much deeper in the story, about this guy's military past," she said, looking into his face with that cardboard smile. "I thought it belonged in the lead."

Nick took a breath and looked at the bulletin board behind her desk and then quoted from memory the deadline story he'd filed the night before:

" 'Despondent over the loss of his job as a longtime city park manager, a Dania man killed his wife and two teenage children Wednesday and then patiently waited, chain-smoking cigarettes, until police arrived before firing a shotgun under his own chin, authorities said.' "

The city editor glanced up at him with an obvious look of mock confusion wrinkled into her brow. It only pissed him off more, and she knew it. He took the paper from her desk, rattled it as he read.

" 'In a grisly display of firepower, a former Vietnam commando killed his wife and children with a pistol Tuesday and then as police arrived fired a shotgun into his own face, officials said.' "

The editor laced her fingers and cocked her head, just so.

"I think this version is a bit punchier, Nick."

"Punchy? Christ, Deirdre," he said, losing it again. "This was a domestic murder-suicide. The guy used an old Colt revolver and a shotgun for bird hunting, not an AR16.

"He fought in Vietnam thirty goddamn years ago! You think I didn't look it up? He was honorably discharged. The guys down at the VA clinic never heard of him. None of the VFW support groups did. His neighbors had known him forever. The city employed him for the last dozen years and then fired his entire department. He wasn't some psycho dressed in camouflage creeping the suburban hedges for North Vietnamese regulars. He got downsized and lost it. Why put in that veteran of Vietnam stuff? You guys love that knee-jerk shit. This had nothing to do with Vietnam or his military record."

This time he flipped the paper back onto her desk.

The city editor just looked over her folded hands at him, eyes still bright, eyebrows still high like they'd been painted on in the happy department at Mattel. She never argued with reporters. The newsroom was not for arguing anymore.

"Was Mr. Madison," she said, looking at the paper, "a Vietnam veteran?"

Nick said nothing.

"Was he armed with two guns?"

He stayed silent, knew what was coming.

"Did the authorities attribute the killings to him?"

This time she waited.

"Yeah," he said.

"Then we printed the truth, Nick. You can ask the staff attorney upstairs. That's our obligation."

He bit the inside of his cheek, working to keep his mouth shut, when one of the assistant news editors stuck his head inside the door and said,

"Excuse me for intruding. Uh, Nick, we got a shooting over at the jail. We gotta get you out there. Somebody said it might have been some kind of escape attempt."

Nick nodded and looked back to the city editor.

"Death calls," he said, turning to go.

"Nick," she said, stopping him as he started through the door.

"Yeah."

"Larry Keller called me this morning from over at the courthouse," she said, lowering her eyes, her voice going quiet. She wasn't good at being emotional. "He told me that Robert Walker was released early from the Lee County road prison last week."

When she looked up it was Nick who turned his face away.

There was a tightening of lips, a clench in jaw muscle that he knew could transform his face into a portrait of anger, frustration and guilt all at once. He'd seen it in the mirror after Keller had called him first with the news as a courtesy.

"I'm sorry, Nicky," Deirdre said.

Nick took a couple of deep breaths, through his nose, not wanting her to notice. He knew sympathy was not her strong suit, and it wasn't in him anymore to accept it. People in the newsroom knew about the deaths of his wife and daughter. They knew that he had been sent as a breaking news reporter to cover yet another fatal car wreck, only to arrive at the scene and recognize his own family van. They never brought it up. He never brought it up.

"Do you need some time off?" she said. "A couple of days?"

"I had a year off, Deirdre," Nick said, sounding sharper than he meant to. "I need to get back to work."

"That's what I thought," she said and then turned back to her screen, dismissing him with her shoulder.

Nick stopped at the open door, shook his head and let a grin pull at the side of his mouth. He turned back, unwilling to let her get a leg up on him.

"That lead change still sucked," he said. The city editor just raised her hand and flicked at him with her extended fingers.

/ / /

The *South Florida Daily News* city room is a huge expanse of open space divided only by waist-high partitions. From above it must look like one of those rat mazes. Nick figured the idea of offices without walls was to elicit both a sense of personal space and open communication and camaraderie. Shared goals and all that. The designers probably didn't figure in the nascent e-mail culture. Now most of the gossip and innuendo and communication happened on the wires that ran through the ceiling and connected to every computer. Reporters never massed at the coffee machine or at one guy's desk to discuss strategy or to make fun of some management decision to create a "shopping mall reporter" position. Now everyone kept their heads down and whispered through the wire. Scorn to the guy who stood up and voiced an opinion out loud. The heads were particularly low as he left the city editor's office, a sure sign the others had heard his voice bombing the boss, some with embarrassment, a couple with pride and a few more hoping he'd get canned so they could apply for his crime beat. By the time he made it back to his pod, an assignment editor was already waiting for him.

"Nick, you probably ought to get over to the jail. They're saying a guard was shot by some inmates trying to break out."

"Yeah, I heard," he said, sitting down at his desk and picking up the phone. When the guy nodded and walked away, Nick waited until he was gone and then put the phone down. He pushed his chair back and pulled his wallet from his pocket and flipped it open to the photograph. His girls. The twins when they were still in elementary school, ribbons of different colors in their hair. His wife, smiling, like only she could, long ago, before that look of pure happiness in their marriage began to fade. His eyes blurred, only for a second. Deirdre knew Walker was the man driving the car that killed Nick's family, and the visage of the man strolling free in the streets rose in his head and Nick snapped the wallet shut. "You won't just walk away," he whispered and took out his own cell phone.

Nick punched in the cell number of the sheriff's communications desk sergeant, whom he had known for years. They always spoke cell to cell, both of them wary, and both of them knowing that their organizations could easily track their calls in and out of their respective buildings. Nick never wanted to put his sources at risk, or let his own people know what he knew until it was time.

While he waited, a photo editor hurried up to his desk. "Nick, you going over to the jail? We got a photographer over there already who was staking out some perp walk. Now we hear they've got an officer down and the guards are beating the hell out of the prisoners who are trying to heist a van in the sally port."

"Yeah," Nick said, waiting for the sergeant to click on his cell phone. The editor nodded and hustled away. Nick was shaking his head. News was always nothing but gossip until you checked it out, but even the so-called professionals were still human and loved that need to know something first and then go spread it. The chirping in Nick's ear stopped.

"Yo, Nick. A little slow on the uptake these days, heh?" Sergeant Jim Langford's voice announced on the other end of the line.

"Hey, Sarge," Nick said. He'd never blocked the caller I.D. on his cell, wanting his contacts to choose whether to answer or not. It always gave them the option of an unspoken *No comment.*

"What's jumping? The rumors are flying that one of your own might have been wounded over at the jail."

"Shit, Nicky. Would I sound so bright and bushy-tailed if it was one of ours? Hell, no. Somebody made a hit on some pervert who was being transferred in for court. Prisoner was dead before he hit the ground, from what I hear."

"No shit?" Nick said, scratching down Langford's words on an empty notepad in front of him. "The word rolling through here was that a guard got hit."

"Ha! Donny Strock was standing right next to the guy and caught a little blood splatter, but according to the boys down there, the shooter got what he wanted, one clean head shot, and that was it."

"Where was it, Jim?" Nick said, trying to see the scenario in his head. He was familiar with the layout of the jail and the attached courthouse. "This wasn't some kind of Jack Ruby thing, was it?"

"No. No. It was outside, Nicky. Just as they were walking this asshole up the steps to the rear intake door. The security gate back there was already closed. It was a long-distance shooter is what the guys said."

Nick knew from covering too many perp walks the layout of the jail's sally port. They always kept the reporters and photographers out on the sidewalk. The automatic gate was always closed before the bus or van guards even opened the doors and led the prisoners out.

"Any I.D. on the dead guy, Sarge?" he said.

"You ain't quoting me, right, Nicky?"

"Have I ever?"

"I hear it was that asshole who raped those two little girls a few years ago and then killed them when they threatened to tell," he said and then went silent, trying to remember the name, just like Nick was.

"Come to think of it, that was probably one of your stories, wasn't it? The woman was homeless and sleepin' in the park?"

The communications guys were notorious for scanning the newspapers for crime stories, mostly to laugh at how the department put out the news versus the way they knew it really went down. Since Nick talked to them every day, they especially liked to stick him when he got it wrong. They also paid attention when he got it right.

It didn't take Nick three seconds to come up with the name of the killer: Steven Ferris.

"Yeah," Nick said. "He was one of mine."

"Well, somebody just saved the taxpayers some money. We'll be toasting the shooter over at Brownie's tonight."

"Have one for me, Sarge," Nick said. "And thanks."

Nick hung up the phone, stuck a pad into his back pocket and started for the elevators, synapses clicking, trying to set up the scene in his head. One of the most notorious pedophiles and child murderers in area history had been assassinated on the jailhouse steps. How do you play that? It was bound to go out on the front page. He remembered the reaction to his stories three years ago, the fear in the neighborhoods. Schoolgirls swept off the street and killed on their way home. People would remember. Nick was going to have to put Robert Walker aside, shift him into that corner in his head where he had been festering for all these months. Nick had just begun to believe that he could control him, keep him back in that dark spot. But now Walker was out walking the streets and the memory was loose.

He stopped at the assistant city editor's desk on the way out.

"I'm going over to the scene. It's a shooting, but my source says that no guards or cops were hurt," Nick said. "It might have been a prisoner. I'll call you guys when I find out something definite."

"No cop-shooting?" the editor said, letting a tinge of disappointment slip into the question.

"No."

"No jailbreak?" The guy was hoping at least for plan B.

"No."

"Trigger-happy officer?"

Nick was walking away.

"I'll call you guys when I find out something factual." He thought he was being nice. OK. Maybe he did emphasize the word *factual*.

He went directly to the editorial research room around the corner and got the attention of Lori Simons, who was experienced enough not to flinch when reporters called her office the morgue or the library instead of the research center.

"Hey, Nick, whatcha need?"

"Hi, Lori. I need everything you can search up on a guy named Steven Ferris, pedophile who killed two little girls about four years back."

"I remember that one. You did one of your big Sunday pieces on him, right?"

Nick smiled at her institutional memory. Computers don't make people smart, people make people smart.

"That's the one," he said and then lowered his voice. "He might have just been shot to death over at the jail. Can you send the stuff straight over to my queue? I'm going over to get some confirmation."

Lori was tall and thin, with long feathered blond hair and blue eyes. Nick had always liked her because she was bright and eternally positive. After the accident, when he'd come back to work, he'd been drawn to her. It was that positive force, he told himself. She came over to the counter that fronted her room of computers and bookcases and fact books and jotted down the name.

"It shouldn't take me too long, Nick. You want all the court stuff too, right?"

"Yeah, anything you can find," he said, thanking her and turning to go.

"Good luck," she said, watching him walk away. "On the confirmation, I mean. If it's the guy I'm remembering, nobody's gonna be shedding any tears."

Nick waved over his shoulder and went straight to the elevators. On the ride down he recalled a line that an old-timer homicide detective had delivered to him when he was just starting out: "Even the bad guys got a mom, kid."

Somebody's always going to cry.

/ Chapter 3 /

Out on the street, Fort Lauderdale's morning commuter traffic was still heavy. The main county jail was only a few blocks away on the other side of the river. Nick decided it was easier to walk. He'd stopped being in a hurry to crime scenes years ago. He'd gone to enough of them to know that the bodies would still be there, as if he needed to see another body. The immediate area would be cordoned off by the responding officers, so you weren't going to beat them before the yellow tape went up and get some kind of close-up and personal view. And if friends and neighbors and possible eyewitnesses were what you were after, they'd all still be hanging around, at least the ones willing to talk or wanting to be quoted.

He climbed the pedestrian stairway of the Andrews Avenue Bridge. From the top he could see a television news truck already pulled up onto the sidewalk three blocks to the south. When he got down and made it within a block of the rear entrance of the seven-story jail, he slowed and started observing. Camera guys were up against the chain-link gate to the sally port, trying to get shots through the wire mesh. They would consider themselves lucky if they could get a telephoto of a blood pool or, even better, a shot of the medical examiner guys picking up the body and loading it into their black van. The newspaper's camera guys would be doing the same, afraid somebody else might get a shot they didn't have even though they knew no photo editor was going to put fresh blood on the front page. But better to be safe and get the gore shot than have some boss ask you why you didn't get it.

Bridge traffic going north was backed up, the omnipresent rubber-neckers slowing to see what they could see and tell everybody at the office when they got in. Nowadays, they'd probably call it in on their cell phones: *Hey, Jody, I'm down on Andrews and there's a bunch of cops and television guys. What's up? Did you hear anything? I mean, wow, the traffic, ya know?* It was the electronic version of the backyard fence, instant and without boundaries.

Oh, and Jody? Tell the boss I'm gonna be late, OK?

As Nick approached the growing bubble of press, he recognized the TV reporters from Channels 7 and 10. They had done lots of crime scenes together over the years. It was a fraternity of odd undertakers.

"Matt. How's it goin'?" Nick said to the Channel 10 guy.

"Hey, Nick," he answered, nodding in the direction of the gate. "They got somebody down at the bottom of the steps to the back door. Gotta guess that it's a prisoner or they wouldn't still be standing around letting the body lie there."

Nick looked around and found the *Daily News* photographer. She was on one knee at the far edge of the fence, a camera body up to her face. He walked over to join her.

"Hi, Susan."

"Figured you'd be here," she said, not bothering to look away from her viewfinder.

Nick bent down. From her vantage point he could see a long lump shrouded with a yellow sheet at the base of the staircase. He always wondered why they used bright yellow, making it obvious to anyone and everyone that a corpse was lying there. It stuck out, a happy color surrounded by the dark green and blue of uniforms and gray con-crete and black van. While the camera guys focused on that, Nick stood up and began searching the faces of the officers, trying to recognize someone he knew, someone he could call later to get an inside edge on information.

A couple of the jail guards were standing together off to the side, smoking, either as a nerve salve or just taking advantage of an unscheduled break from the inside. Four uniformed road deputies were huddled near the still-opened back doors of a detention transport van. Nick knew that the vans usually carried anywhere from two to eight prisoners from the city jails around the county or from state prisons when an inmate needed to show up for court. The main downtown courthouse was right next door, attached by an elevated walkway. It made it easier and quicker to transport defendants back and forth to hearings and legal appearances.

At first Nick found it odd that no one was at the top of the steps guarding the door.

"Anybody been in or out of the door?" he asked Susan.

"Not since I got here," she said, standing up. "Maybe they're afraid of it."

Nick gave her a quizzical look. He'd been on assignment with Susan before. She was very good. Once they had responded as a team to a late-night homicide down by the city marina. At first it looked like a drive-by, but in the wrong neighborhood. The cops were surrounding a nice Lincoln Town Car with the driver's window blown out and were particularly closemouthed about the I.D. of the dead man slumped over the wheel inside. Susan snapped a shot of the license plate of the car just before the arriving detectives covered it with a dark towel. She called the plate numbers in to research and they matched with a prominent casino tour boat owner. The paper got a damn nice exclusive of a mob-style hit on a high-profile businessman. Mob hits were something that rarely happened in Florida. Since the days of Al Capone and the high-flying Miami Beach of the late 1920s, Florida had been considered "open territory" by the northern mobsters. Since no one mob owned it,

real!

they didn't have to kill each other. So to have someone capped Chicago-style was page one.

"What do you mean, afraid?" Nick said. "Of the door?"

She lifted her digital camera to him and started flashing through her previous shots and stopped at a bland photo of the wall just to the left of the doorframe. She zoomed in on a pattern of discoloration she'd noticed on the beige paint.

"Blood spatter?" Nick said.

"You got it. And from the height on the wall, it looks like somebody got head-shot," she said.

Nick looked back at the door in the distance, figuring, and shook his head.

"You've been at this too long, Susan."

She looked at him and grinned. "You got that right too."

Unlike a shooting in a city neighborhood or in a shopping area, there were few witnesses to talk to on this one. Reporters were milling around, no one to quote. It wasn't like you could get the guy from the house next door to say what a nice, quiet neighbor the deceased was and how you never think it could happen right here on your street. A four-story medical office building was directly across the street. Two blocks away was a donut shop where courthouse workers even now were slipping in and out, blowing on open cups of coffee and giving only a cursory glance at the growing huddle of news folks. Nick swore he could smell the aroma of 100% Colombian in the air and was con-templating a quick trip down there when Susan called his name.

When he turned to her, she nodded her head toward the portico and then raised her camera to her face. Two men had stepped out of the gray door and were standing on the top landing. The first guy out was tall and so thin that his dark suit coat hung from his shoulders as if on a hanger. He had a full head of black hair and stood with his hands in his pockets. He turned his back to the group of reporters and looked down at a slight angle at the blood pattern on the wall and then seemed to tuck his elbows into his narrow hips. He looked like a six-and-a-half-foot-tall exclamation point and stayed that way for several seconds. When he finally turned, Nick watched him give the gathering a short stare-down.

"Hargrave," Nick said to Susan as she snapped off photos. "Sheriff's homicide unit. If he's the lead on this, we're gonna be hard up for information. He hates the press. Did you get a shot of the sneer?"

"He was looking up," Susan said.

"Huh?"

She moved the digital viewer away from her face and held it over again so Nick could see a close-up of Hargrave's face: high cheekbones so sharp they threatened to split his skin, a thin mustache that barely covered a harelip and gave his mouth the impression of a perpetual sneer, eyes so dark they appeared black. He'd transferred in from somewhere in the Northeast. The other homicide guys Nick knew said he rarely spoke. He had yet to even answer a phone call from Nick on a story.

But Susan was right. The press was all at street level. Thirty yards away Hargrave was four feet above them on the landing. Yet, when he'd turned from the blood spatter he was not looking down at them. Caught on camera, his line of sight went up and behind. Nick turned and scanned the building across the street. It was typical South Florida stucco, painted some pinkish earth color with tall reflective glass on the first floor and three rows of windows above, all of them shut. At the roofline there was an attempt at some ornate scrollwork in a complementary color and an antenna of some sort rose into the sky behind it. A physical shift of the press pool caused him to turn around and reporters and cameramen began pressing and then pushing their way to the gate. Over their heads Nick could see Joel Cameron, official spokesperson for the Sheriff's Office, walking over toward them, a single sheet of paper in his hand. Press release, Nick thought, straight off the printer.

Unlike the scenes of the media mob on scripted television and movies, no one yelled out some stupid *What happened?* question. They all formed into a half circle. The sound folks got their microphones up front so they could record. Cameron waited until everyone was set. They'd all been through it before.

"Alright, guys. Here's what we've got so far," Cameron began, reading from the news release:

"'At approximately seven fifty-five this morning shots were fired at the county's downtown jail facility in the eight hundred block of South Andrews Avenue during a routine transfer of detainees.

"'One man was fatally wounded as the detainees were being brought through the main jail's secured north entrance. The location of the shooting is not accessible to the public and no member of the public was in any way endangered.

"'The Sheriff's Office is presently investigating the shooting and the name of the deceased is not being released until notification of next of kin.'"

Cameron took his eyes off the sheet, folded it and took a deep breath, knowing through experience that it wasn't nearly enough for the media machine and now he'd have to start tap-dancing to both the obvious and the unanswerable questions.

A television guy in the front asked, "Joel, we heard a report on the radio of an officer down. Were any officers or detention deputies wounded?"

"No," Cameron said. "No law enforcement or detention deputies were injured."

"How many shots were fired?" asked another.

"That's still under investigation."

"Was it a drive-by?"

"That's still under investigation."

"Is that the dead guy back there?" asked a newspaper reporter from Nick's main competition.

Cameron took a long breath, let the question sit there while the group went quiet with professional embarrassment.

"Well, we don't usually put yellow sheets over their faces if they're still alive," said Cameron, raising his eyebrows, while the rest of the news folk tried to hide their sniggering.

"Yes, that's him, Jean. And the M.E. will be removing the body as soon as the investigators are through."

Jean was known for stating the obvious at crime scenes, and took an unspoken derision from her street cohorts for being a bit ditzy. But everyone also knew she probably had an editor who demanded a source for every line she wrote. If she stood here and watched the body lie outside for three hours she would still have to quote an official saying the body lay out here for three hours.

While the others tossed questions at Cameron that Nick knew would not be answered, he focused on Hargrave. At times the detective would move out of sight, blocked by the transport van. Then he would step back into view. Nick watched him kneel next to the body, lifting the sheet as the M.E. rolled the man halfway over, then back. He was watching when Hargrave stood and said something into the ear of his partner and both of them looked to the street, but up, eyes again focused high behind the press gathering. Nick whispered to Susan and then backed out of the group, facing forward, watching Cameron as Jean was asking if police had any suspects in the shooting. When Cameron turned to shake his head at her, Nick slipped behind a news truck and then dodged through traffic to the other side of the street.

/ / /

The building was the Children's Diagnostic Center and took up most of the block. Offices were on the upper floors, clinics on the first. Nick made his way around the river side, cut through a narrow split in a six-foot ficus hedge to the back and started looking for a fire escape or maintenance ladder to the roof. Less than a dozen cars were parked in the back lot, all bunched close to a rear entrance. Not much cover, he thought, but fewer windows on this side. Halfway down the length of the building there was an interruption in the facade, an alcove with a tow-away sign and the front end of a Dumpster sticking out. Deep in the corner was the ladder he was looking for. It was one of those metal pipe jobs bolted into the side of the stucco. The first rung was five feet off the ground. Why do they do that? Nick thought. Who is that gonna stop other than some overweight burglar who can't do a pull-up? The ladder climbed up to the top edge and curled over onto the roof, and so did he.

The flat expanse up top was empty. Gray crushed stone and that instantly recognizable smell of sun-warmed tar. Nick was standing up in the open, realizing he hadn't thought this through. If he was correct in thinking the detectives were looking up here for a bullet angle, why the hell was he not thinking the shooter might still be up here? Dumb-ass.

He looked out at four big air handlers, spaced evenly across the twenty-yard length of the building, none of them tall enough to hide a man. The antenna he'd seen from the street was speared into the middle, guy wires spread from out for support. When he was confident he was alone, he looked carefully around at the graveled surface and saw no footprints. The surface wasn't made for it, but he still stepped carefully as he made his way across to the front roofline. Nick had never messed up a crime scene in his life and this would not be a good time to start, if he was reading this right. Six feet from the ornamental roof edge he crouched, peering over the top to see if he could spot the sally port fence across the street. The razor wire was north. He crab-walked to his left, looking for anything not to disturb: cigarette butts, pieces of fabric, ejected bullet casings. He rose and took another peek. Middle of the entrance. He flexed a little taller so he could see the heads of the other reporters below. By now they'd been herded to the left and right of the gate entrance and two orange-striped traffic barricades had been set up. From this point he could also see the gray door to the jail, too far away to see the blood spatter, but a perfect alignment. A downward angle. Was this the spot they were looking at? Some deputies and M.E. assistants were still moving around the van. The yellow tarp was still on the ground. Hargrave and his partner were gone.

Nick crouched back down and studied the smooth roll of the concrete ornament edge. Does a sniper leave scratches where he rests his weapon? Maybe an amateur would. Does a gunman leave a depression in this kind of stone? A knee print? An elbow? He lowered his face down to the surface, using the morning angle of the sun to try and spot some depression. He scooted on the balls of his feet and palms of his hands, nose down, first six feet to the left while checking the concrete edge for scratches, and then squinting at the stone for a change in shadow, then back. A second before it happened, he thought about how he might look to someone quietly coming up behind him.

"Freeze, asshole!"

Nick had to admit, even as a cliché, the words—yelled with a deep and hard voice—do make you freeze. They are cop words. And even though they are heard on television and in the movies more than on the real streets, real cops watch TV too. Stuck on all fours with his butt in the air, he had to be hopeful. After the initial shock, he started to turn his head.

"I said don't fucking move," the voice said, big and very male. There was a heavy crunch of gravel now sounding behind him.

Nick kept his nose down. His palms were flat on the roof surface. A vulnerable position, to say the least. He heard more footsteps moving closer and rolled his eyes up and forward to see the edge of the roofline. Still no scratches, only open air, four stories up. Could you survive a forty-foot jump? Or a forty-foot fall after someone kicked you over the edge?

"It's the reporter, Sergeant," a smaller voice said. Nick recognized it as Cameron's.

"I know what the fuck it is," the other voice said.

The crunch of the footsteps was now directly behind him. Nick lifted his right hand and pointed up and back, at his right rear pocket.

"My I.D. is in my wallet, sir," he said into the smell of tar rising into his nose. "I'm Nick Mullins, from the *Daily News*."

"Good for you," the voice said. "I told you NOT TO FUCKING MOVE!"

Nick froze the arm and took a deep breath. He was now in a three-point stance, the sharp edge of a stone digging into his left palm. For some reason he had not registered the heat before. Now it was like he was hovering over a stove, waves rising into his shirt. He could feel sweat forming on his back. A line trickled across his rib cage. He wondered silently if sweat from someone lying up here waiting to shoot could be retrieved, if it could be used as a DNA marker.

"I can confirm that, Sergeant," he heard Cameron's voice say. "It is Mullins."

The sergeant said nothing. His footsteps came closer and to Nick's right. Out of the corner of his eye he caught a part of a thick-soled black shoe. The sergeant did not touch Nick's wallet and moved off to his right. Nick sneaked another look, trying not to move his head as the man continued to step south. The shoes were shined brogans, cuffed trousers, legs too short for Hargrave. Nick's shoulder was starting to sting now from the effort of holding most of his body weight. The stone in his palm was making its way through skin. The sergeant passed behind him and then wandered north a few steps. The sound of slow-moving traffic floated up from below. Above there was a soft chop of helicopter blades, getting louder. In the absence of a good I-95 morning wreck, the news pilots had responded to the shooting.

"Excuse me, Sergeant," Nick said, trying not to sound facetious, but knowing that he had never been good at not sounding facetious in such circumstances. "May I please stand up?"

Cameron had not tried a second time to come to his aid.

Another few seconds of silence passed.

"Yeah, alright, reporter. Stand."

Nick rocked back on his heels and stood slowly, palms out and away from his sides. Better to acquiesce. He turned to the sergeant first, a thick man, his girth around both the waistline and the chest. Straw-blond hair. Fifties and with eyes that somehow showed mirth and disdain at the same time. Those eyes cut over toward the back of the roof. Against the sky stood the exclamation point. Hargrave dressed in black. Cameron was next to him.

"You are disturbing a possible crime scene, Mr. Mullins," Hargrave said in a voice so soft that at first Nick started to ask him to repeat himself but then realized he'd heard every word distinctly.

Nick still had his hands out from his sides, palms toward them, a perfect opportunity to shrug his shoulders and look stupid. Hargrave ignored the gesture and started walking to the edge of the roof.

"You may remove yourself, Mr. Mullins," he said in the same clear quiet voice. His dark eyes had dismissed the reporter and gone on to more important matters, looking out across the street and then down, lining up a sniper's shot.

Nick knew his time on the scene was over. The burly sergeant took a step closer to him and flipped his extended hand in the direction of the service ladder like he was shooing an errant barnyard animal.

Nick avoided making eye contact with Cameron as he went. He'd worked with the press liaison for the last couple of years and they'd normally gotten along. He was almost to the ladder when Hargrave's quiet voice stopped him.

"Mr. Mullins?"

Nick looked back. The detective was now down on one knee, still looking out toward the jail, his long wiry frame seeming oddly bent.

"Did you find anything?"

The question confused Nick at first and he couldn't respond. Hargrave turned his dark eyes on him.

"Pick anything up?" he said.

"No," Nick said. "I wouldn't do that to you guys. I've been around long enough."

Hargrave nodded before he looked away, but said nothing, so Nick did the same and silently walked back to the ladder.

"Jesus, Nick," Cameron whispered as he passed him.

Nick peered over to the ground before swinging his leg to the top rung of the ladder, and saw two uniformed deputies below along with Susan, who was standing out in the parking lot a respectful distance from the cops. He faced the building and started down and could hear the shutter clicking on her camera. He turned his head and looked at the telephoto lens she had up to her face and stuck his tongue out. She smiled under the viewfinder and shrugged. From the final rung he jumped the last few feet to the ground and when he turned, the deputies were giving him that deadpan look they must be taught to use in the police academy. Nick didn't know them and they could tell by the khaki pants, the oxford shirt and the notepad in his back pocket that he wasn't one of them.

"Morning, fellas," Nick said. "Nice day for a shooting, huh?"

They looked into his face like he was speaking Mandarin, then at each other and then up at the roof, where Cameron was just mounting the ladder to come down. Nick walked over to Susan, who was looking at her digital display.

"Get a good shot of my ass while I was on the way down?"

"Hard to miss," she said. "But that's all I got. You could have at least waited for me to come around so I could get up there with you."

"Sorry," he said. "Guess I wasn't thinking. Just going on a feeling that it wasn't just the weather those guys were staring up at from that spatter spot."

She was packing away her telephoto lens.

"Find anything up there to prove it was a sniper?"

Nick shook his head, as much at her skilled perception as at her question. She'd probably been ahead of him all along.

"Clean," he said, looking away from her instead of giving her the satisfaction of knowing that he was impressed with her deduction. He turned his attention to the double glass doors that led into the clinic. Witnesses? Just inside, Nick could make out the figure of a small man hovering, taking furtive looks out in the direction of the cops. Cameron had just made the last rung and stopped, trying to figure the easiest way to make the last leap.

Nick sauntered as best he could over to the doors and when the little man saw him coming he hesitated, like he was going to scramble back inside, and then changed his mind and stepped out the door to meet him. Nick tried to look official and it worked.

"Good morning," he said.

"Yes, sir. Good morning."

His name tag said DENNIS and he was dressed for work: dark slacks and a polo shirt with one of those sky-blue hospital smocks over it.

"Mind if I ask you a question?"

"No, sir. What's, uh, going on?"

"Well, there was a shooting across the street this morning," Nick said.

"Yes, we saw all the news trucks and traffic from the front windows," the man said, looking over Nick's shoulder to the uniformed deputies who were now talking with Cameron.

"So these guys"—Nick nodded behind him—"were checking out your roof."

The man nodded as though it would be pretty routine for a handful of cops to be crawling up the side of his building.

"Did anyone inside see anyone back here this morning when you all came into work?"

"Just you people," he said, finally looking into Nick's face. "I figured there was something going on when I got here, but, you know, since your man didn't say anything, I just went straight inside."

"You mean just a few minutes ago, Dennis?"

Nick knew to always use the familiar first name if you could. It sometimes loosens them up.

"Oh, no. Like, before eight."

"Before eight you saw one of these guys?" Nick said, nodding back at Cameron and the cops.

"No. Not one of them. One of your, like, SWAT people, coming off the ladder."

The little man again looked over Nick's shoulder. Cameron was heading their way.

"What did this guy on the ladder look like?" Nick said, trying to keep the urgency out of his voice, knowing his interview was about to end.

"You know, dressed in black with this equipment bag and stuff slung over his shoulder. Scared the hell out of me at first, you know, coming off the roof like that. Then he kind of just waved to me and then walked on by. Later, when I was inside and people started seeing stuff happening over at the jail, it, you know, made sense."

"Can you describe this man, this SWAT officer, Dennis? I mean, was he tall, short, white, black?"

Skepticism started growing in Dennis's eyes, then went into the wrinkles of his small forehead. "Are you with the police?" he said.

"Oh, no," Nick said, trying to look surprised that he'd been mistaken. "I'm with the *Daily News*, Dennis." He offered his hand. "Nick Mullins. Just trying to figure out what happened this morning." He could feel Cameron move up behind him.

"Did this officer have any identifying marks on his, uh, uniform? You know, like the big yellow letters on his back or some kind of insignia on his chest or hat?"

"No. Not that I can recall, exactly. I just sort of assumed after the commotion outside . . . ," the little man said and then looked again over Nick's shoulder.

"Nick. I need to talk with you."

Nick turned to face Cameron, again feigning surprise.

"Oh, Mr. Cameron," Nick said. "This is Dennis, Mr. Cameron. I was just interviewing him."

Nick could see the shadow of confusion cross the little man's face.

"Mr. Cameron is with the Sheriff's Office, Dennis. They might want to talk with you also, but could I get your last name and your title at the clinic first, Dennis?" Nick said, taking out his notebook and pen.

But Dennis was already starting to back away, maybe a little pissed, maybe just a little confused. And Cameron was turning Nick in the other direction with a subtle hold on his elbow.

"Jesus, Nick," he said. "What the hell were you doing up there?"

"Just reporting, Joel."

"You just happened to leave a press briefing to take a walk on a roof?"

"Well, it's obviously a spot of interest for your guys," Nick said, nodding up toward the building.

The press officer said nothing. It was a game reporters played with public information officers. Cameron had been at it for a while. Nick had been at it longer.

"Does Detective Hargrave think the shooter fired from up on the roof?"

"That's under investigation, Nick. You know I can't tell you that without telling everyone else in the pool, man."

"That's a pretty tough shot, Joel. Seems a long distance for some street slob trying to do a little vigilantism."

"Nobody said it was a vigilante."

"Nobody said it was a sniper yet either. But you've got the body of a prisoner over there and some pretty precise blood spatter on the wall and nobody else injured or wounded, which deals out the scattershot gangbangers."

"Nobody said it was gangbangers, Nick."

"So the victim isn't a gang felon?"

"I didn't say that."

"Nobody said it was an asshole pedophile who killed two little girls either," Nick said and watched for the quick twitch in the corner of Cameron's mouth that always gave him away.

Both of them stopped the dance for a silent few seconds. Cameron put his hands in his pockets and looked at the ground. Nick put his notebook away and started spinning the pen in his fingers like a miniature baton and watched the top of the ladder where Hargrave and his partner had not yet shown themselves.

"Nick," Cameron finally said. "How did you know to go up there? Were you tipped off?"

This was what they called trading information. It was a subtle agreement to give each other what they had. The only rule was truth. But it worked with certain press officers, the ones with personal integrity and the ones who trusted that Nick wouldn't burn them with the other media. Cameron was one of the few.

"No," Nick said. "It was just a guess based on your guys lining up the shot and the spatter pattern that our photographer caught with the zoom."

Cameron nodded. "And the pedophile thing?"

"Just a tip, Joel. Nothing insidious."

Cameron shook his head. He knew Nick had made contacts over the years. He also knew he'd just made a bad bargain.

"You'll confirm if I get anything first, right?" Nick said just to make sure.

Cameron kept shaking his head, this time with a grin. "Yeah, I'll confirm. You just can't use my name."

Nick returned the grin, slapped the press officer on the shoulder and walked away.

Back out on the street, the media gang was peeling away. But the camera guys were still there. And two remote television news trucks were still on the sidewalk. That meant the body was also still there and hadn't been moved and nothing with more violence or potential for blood had hit the police scanners in South Florida this morning. They were all waiting for the shot of the body bag being loaded into the medical examiner's black SUV, the shot that would inevitably lead the local news.

Nick made two stops on his way back to the newsroom. First to the coffee shop on the ground floor of his building, where he picked up a large with cream and sugar and then stood in the lobby letting the caffeine hit the back of his brain for a few minutes. When half the coffee was gone, he rode the elevator up and went the back way to the library and talked quietly to Lori.

"I shipped a bunch of stuff to your queue, Nick," she said. "Was it him?"

"They're not letting it loose officially yet," he said. "But I think my source is good. What I want to do now is get some kind of an M.O. thing going. Can you do a search first locally and then nationwide on shootings, homicides that involved rifles and that might have been described as sniper-type shootings?"

Lori was writing on a pad. "Pretty broad, but yeah, we can do all the South Florida media. National is going to take some time. We can do most of the online newspaper archives and the Associated Press stuff. How far back do you want to go?"

"Two, three years," Nick said. "No, make it four."

She looked up from her pad over the top of her frameless reading glasses. "You've got an editor's approval on this, don't you, Nick?"

In the corporate world of news gathering, computer search time was money. Somebody had to be held responsible for every dime spent. Nick knew that. Lori knew that.

"Yeah," he said. "Deirdre."

Lori was still looking over her lenses. "My ass," she said.

"OK. I'm grandfathered in," Nick said.

"My ass again," she said, this time grinning.

Nick just looked at her with his eyebrows up, surprised.

Lori shook the pad at him and smiled. "Off the books," she said. "For now."

Nick almost winked, but then thought, Don't do that. That's what Carly would call "weird Dad stuff."

"And speaking of books," Lori said, bailing him out, "I've got that Van Gogh book that you said Carly might like." She bent under the shelf and came up with a big picture book he'd commented on weeks ago.

"How's she doing, anyway?"

"Better," Nick said, taking the book and wondering about the coincidence that they'd both thought of his daughter at the same time. "She'll love this, Lori. Thanks."

On the way back through the rat's maze to his desk, Nick kept his coffee cup up to his face. Maybe no one would interrupt him at midswallow. But before he got to his chair an editor for the online edition of the paper asked if he had anything new on the jail shooting and could he please file something so they could put it up on the website. Nick just nodded. In another era newspaper reporters had a daily deadline: Get the best and most accurate story you can by nine or ten o'clock tonight so it makes the morning's paper. Only the wire service and radio reporters had to make several updates during the day, leaving them little time to dig deeper into a story. But in a time of website mania, every daily reporter was in competition on an hourly basis. File what you have so the office workers sneaking looks at the news on their computers at their desks can follow your shifting speculation all day.

Nick hated it, but played the game.

He sat down and called up a blank file and wrote:

An inmate being transferred to the county's downtown jail was killed by an unknown gunman at 7:55 this morning, police said.

The prisoner, whose name was being withheld by the Sheriff's Office, was the only person injured during the rush-hour

shooting as he was being walked into the rear of the jail build-
ing in the 800 block of South Andrews Avenue.

A Sheriff's Office spokesman said the shooting took place
after a van transporting several prisoners was inside a closed
gated area just a block from the county courthouse. Investiga-
tors were unsure how many shots were fired, said spokesman
Joel Cameron, and officials would not speculate on a motive
for the killing.

"The shooting piece is in," he called over his shoulder to the online editor when he finished. It had taken him eight minutes. A lot of nothing, he thought. But it'll hold them off for a while.

He took a long sip of coffee and then called up his e-mail message inbox and started at the real work.

Lori had sent him several files and he opened up the one titled *YOURFERRIS*, figuring it to be the story he had written on Steven Ferris just four years ago.

THE PREDATORS AMONG US
By Nick Mullins, Staff Writer

They walked hand in hand on the street, two little girls, one in green-and-white sneakers, the other in pink shorts, sisters strolling home after school.

When they were stopped by a soft voice, it didn't startle them—it was familiar. When they turned to the big doughy man with the kind smile, they felt no fear—they knew him. When he invited them into his green pickup, they didn't panic—they'd been in his truck before.

In the full sunlight of a warm afternoon, two little girls looked into the face of evil, and didn't recognize it.

The public now knows the face of Howard Steven Ferris, 30, who police say confessed to the abductions and killings of Marcellina Cotton, 6, and her sister Gabriella, 8.

We know their bodies were found in the attic of Ferris's Fort Lauderdale apartment. We know, according to his confession, that his sole motivation was to sexually assault them.

But if the allegations are true—which only a court can determine now—do we really know Steven Ferris?

And what of the other 300 sexual predators identified and released from Florida prisons? What of their dark motivations and urges? How do you recognize evil coming, and what can we do about the men who bring it?

The habits and methods of child molesters are no secret. Law enforcement has worked off a general but clear profile for years.

The more that is learned about Ferris, the closer he fits that outline. Detectives could have picked him off the pages of their own investigative handbooks.

The story went on to describe how Ferris, a part-time construction worker and handyman, had come across the two girls and their mother in a local park. They had been living out of their car for several months. Nick had interviewed the mother, who could not find work and was in South Florida alone. She was cooking the family meals on the grill of the campsite and at night she made up an impromptu bed of blankets and pillows made of clothes packed in pillowcases in the back seat for her daughters while she slept in the front. She said her pride had kept her from going to the homeless shelters and community aid programs. She was doling out her savings in order to pay the monthly fee for the camping space. Restricted to only one month at a time, she would drive off for the minimum three days, parking on the streets, and then come back and pay again, taking yet another spot for another month. The woman said she had specifically picked this park because it was close to an elementary school and that she had enrolled her daughters there using the address of a friend who had put them up for a time until her boyfriend had demanded they leave. The mother said she wasn't afraid of living out in the streets as long as her daughters were near. At night she could reach across the seat back and touch her girls and hear them sleeping in the dark. She considered the park safe. And then Steven Ferris had found them.

Like a predator, Ferris had singled out their weakness. Hanging out in the park where children often played, he read their situation and then struck up a conversation with the mother when she had trouble starting her car. Could he help her? He knew something about engines. He fixed some loose spark plug wires. Later, investigators couldn't say whether Ferris had pulled the wires in the first place.

Another evening he showed up with food and treats for the girls. Another time he gave them all a ride to the grocery store. He made himself familiar. He made himself look safe.

Nick remembered the interviews he'd done with teachers and the principal of the elementary school, their recollections of the girls, how bright and eager they were to learn and be with the other children. The way the older one was so protective of her sister. The description of what they were wearing on their final day.

As the girls were walking to the park which they now considered home, Ferris pulled alongside in his familiar truck. He told them their mother had gone out to look at a house they might move to. He said she'd asked him to give them a ride. Maybe the girls were reluctant, but they knew him, had ridden in the truck—with their mother—before.

Ferris took them to a small house less than three miles from the park. He knew it was the younger girl's birthday and promised a cake. But once inside, he molested the six-year-old in a bedroom. When she began to cry, her sister came to her aid. Ferris killed them both and then hid their tiny bodies in the attic of the house. When they failed to show up at the park, the girls' mother went to the school and police were called. She immediately identified Ferris as a man who had befriended them. It took a day for detectives to track him down. They found him in the small rental house and interviewed him for an hour. They read him like a book and returned the same afternoon with a search warrant.

Nick had gone to the crime scene. He had been there when the two small body bags were carried out, just like the rest of the press. But for this one he could not tear his eyes away. He remembered the look in the lead investigator's eyes when he later told Nick he would never forget the feeling of realizing that the bodies of those girls had been lying right above him as he'd listened to Ferris deny he had even seen the children. Nick remembered thinking they should not let detectives or police reporters who have kids of their own go to crime scenes involving the deaths of children. He remembered interviewing the mother, even though he knew she was still in shock, her eyes swollen, the pupils enlarged and glossed by sedatives and some internal message that kept trying to convince her it wasn't so. He remembered hating Steven Ferris.

Nick scrolled down through the story, past the history he'd dug up on Ferris: the arrests for loitering, the multiple laborer jobs, the interview with the girlfriend who had left him after she'd caught him in her daughter's room but had never reported it, just cursed him and kicked him out.

None of that had come out in court. Ferris's trial had been emotional and sensational. Nick hadn't covered it. That assignment belonged to the court reporter. But Nick had slipped into the courtroom on several days, squeezing into the back rows and watching the back of Ferris's head as he sat at the defense table. One day the little girls' mother, who could not stand to sit inside, was in the hallway on a bench and recognized Nick as he quietly left during testimony.

"Mr. Mullins," she said and stood.

Nick stopped and looked at her face, trying to read whether she was indignant or angered by something he had written. "You are the reporter, yes?"

"Yes, ma'am," Nick said, taking two steps closer to her.

When she put out her hand, he closed the final gap and clasped her fingers softly.

"Thank you, sir," she said. "For the way you treated me and my girls in your stories."

Nick was silent, not knowing how to react, seeing her eyes again, clearer now, but still holding a pain that would be there forever. Nick knew even then that whatever went on in the courtroom would never ease her pain.

"They were beautiful children," he remembered saying and then had excused himself and walked away.

Now he knew the pain personally. Loved ones dead. A child you could never hold again. The urge for vengeance. Robert Walker.

Within days of the start of Ferris's trial the predator was convicted by a jury that would later recommend the death penalty. The judge had agreed. Nick shook the scenes out of his head. He remembered each detail, but today's story wasn't so much about Ferris as it was about his killer.

He moved on to the other stories Lori had sent him. There was a hearing that the newspaper's court reporter had written months after Ferris's conviction. An appeals court had ruled on arguments raised over the prejudicial nature of the trial itself. Several people in the court-room gallery had worn buttons on their shirts and blouses adorned with photographs of the dead girls. Ferris's lawyer argued that the crowd and the photos had influenced the jury. Though the prosecution argued that members of the public had a right to attend the proceedings, a panel of judges disagreed.

"Here, the direct link between the buttons, the spectators wearing the buttons, the defendant, and the crime that the defendant allegedly committed was clear and unmistakable," read the document handed down by the three-judge appellate court panel. "A reasonable jurist would be compelled to conclude that the buttons worn by members of the gallery conveyed the message that the defendant was guilty."

Lori had sent another quick story that quoted a defense attorney who claimed the conviction should be thrown out. Another hit on the computer came up with only a single line: "Convicted murderer Steven Ferris sits mute as lawyers argue for a new hearing for the man who was given the death penalty for raping and killing two sisters, 6 and 8, three years ago. Ferris is currently serving time and no decision by the court was reached."

Nick recognized the line as a caption that must have run under a photo that appeared with no story. He wondered how he could have missed it. He checked the date it ran: January 21 of last year.

Nick had not been aware of anything during that month or the February after that. He'd been on an extended leave of absence. Death in the family.

He refocused on the screen and called up the next mention of Ferris. But with continued delays of the hearing dates, each story got smaller and was placed deeper on inside pages until they were barely noticeable.

Nick knew that information about court hearings and calendar calls wouldn't make the paper. He switched out of the stories and called up a website from his favorites list on the Internet: Florida Department of Corrections. From here, he could enter Ferris's name and date of birth and find out where he had been held in the prison system. While he was waiting, his phone rang.

"Nick Mullins," he answered.

"Hey, Nick. It's Lori. I've got some court docket stuff on Ferris that I got online. The last entry was a request by defense to show cause for a change of sentence that looks like it had been delayed a couple of times."

"Let me guess," Nick said. "Rescheduled for today."

"Two in the afternoon in Judge Grossman's courtroom," she said.

Nick could hear the tinge of disappointment in her voice that she hadn't been ahead of him.

"Was that in the clips?" she asked.

"Nope. Hell, the guy was off our radar for almost a year," Nick said, as much to himself as Lori. "Can you print that stuff and send it over?"

Nick knew that to get into the court's docket database you had to have a subscription. Most attorneys did. Most large newspapers did. It was expensive. But Nick also knew you could still do it the old-fashioned way. The case notes are public record and anyone with an interest in Ferris could have walked into the court records office and checked out the file. From there you could get the date of his next appearance and set up your own appointment for a morning shooting.

Nick thanked Lori and went back to his DOC search and in five minutes had an electronic sheet on Ferris. His most recent home had been the South Florida Reception Center. Before that he'd been up in Tomoka Correctional, a maximum security prison near Daytona Beach.

Nick sat back and took another long sip of coffee. He was gathering string. Piecing stuff together. Speculating? Yes. But not out loud. Hell, even though he trusted his source at dispatch, confirmation that the dead inmate was Ferris was still in the wind. And at this point Nick didn't even know if the shooter was targeting anyone specific. Maybe the sniper was just some whack job out to pop a bad guy, any bad guy, and knew the sally port was where prisoners were off-loaded. But the picture was still in Nick's head, the roofline looking down into the fenced yard, the distance, the single blood spatter. No way, he decided. There were probably half a dozen prisoners down there. All this guy wanted was one shot. One preselected victim.

Nick called up an old file on his computer, a huge list of telephone numbers he'd collected over the years. He was the kind of reporter who recorded nearly every substantial contact number he'd gathered over the years. Each time he finished a story, he'd copy the numbers from his notebooks or cut and paste them from his computer notes and put them on the bottom of this list. There were hundreds. He knew he'd never use eighty percent of them ever again, but times like these kept him at the habit.

Using a search function for Ferris's name on the computer, he found what he was looking for in seconds—Ferris's father's and brother's names and their telephone numbers. The father had been in West Virginia three years ago and hadn't been much help. But the brother lived here. The cops would have the same numbers and at some point they would call to inform next of kin. Nick knew if he got some family member on the line, he'd have a good chance of confirming it was Ferris who was now lying in the morgue. He picked up the phone and started to punch in the number for the brother, then stopped. David Ferris's address, in a mobile home park only twenty minutes away in Wilton Manors, was typed in next to the number. Nick checked his watch: eleven o'clock. He was not pressed for time. No other stories were breaking. He'd made a dozen of these calls before. After the ones in which he was the first person to tell a relative that a son or wife or brother was dead, it always left a soured lump of guilt in his gut. He hung up the phone and logged off his computer.

"We're still waiting on the identification of that shooting victim at the jail," he said to the assistant city editor as he walked by. "I'm going out. But I'm on my cell."

Nick made sure the editor had heard him and waved the phone and got a nod from the guy.

You tell somebody his brother is dead face to face if you can, Nick thought as he rode the elevator down.

/ Chapter 4 /

Don't hesitate, he told himself, sitting in his car outside David Ferris's double-wide, watching the curtains in the window just to the right of the louvered front door. Nick had driven up Federal Highway, practicing the words he'd use when the brother of the dead man answered the door: *Excuse me, Mr. Ferris, I hate to bother you. I don't know if you remember me, Nick Mullins from the* Daily News. *I did some stories about your brother a few years back?*

Liar, Nick thought. You don't hate to bother him when there's a good chance that his brother has just been shot dead. You're after a story. You need a comment.

Hello, Mr. Ferris. Nick Mullins from the Daily News. *I'd like to verify if you've heard from the Sheriff's Office concerning your brother.*

The straight-out-in-their-face technique was at least honest.

Oh, and by the way, if you have heard, could you please spill your guts to me on how you feel about this news for two hundred thousand strangers to read in tomorrow's editions?

When he'd arrived in the correct block, Nick pulled into the entrance of the Palms Mobile Park and checked the address on his pad. But after the first left turn, his memory served him. He eased down the narrow street past Flamingo Trail, Ponce de Leon Court and Anhinga

Way. Speed bumps between each block jounced him, and palm trees, all with too-thin trunks and browned fronds, leaned precariously at each corner. Nick once noted that trees did not like to thrive in trailer parks. Maybe it was the cramped space that wouldn't let the roots spread. Maybe the cheap owner associations refused the expense of fertilizers and care. Maybe, as with the natural instincts of animals, they somehow knew better than to grow in places that always seemed to be magnets for tornadoes and hurricanes.

Nick had turned onto Bougainvillea Drive, gone all the way to the end and parked in front of the dusty turquoise-and-white trailer. He then turned off the ignition and made the mistake of letting the quiet form around his ears. When he was a rookie reporter in Trenton, two weeks on the job, the Marine barracks in Beirut had been bombed. Every reporter on the metro desk was given a list of six names, families who had lost sons and husbands and daughters. All had to be interviewed within two days. He had done the same thing years later after 9/11. And he still hadn't learned to avoid hesitating.

He finally picked up the pad from the passenger seat and opened the door. Before stepping out, he took off his sunglasses. You don't ask a man if he knows his brother is dead and not have the balls to show your eyes. He put the pad in his back pocket.

There were no other cars in the drive. The carport, little more than a sheet of tin supported by poles and tacked to the roof of the trailer, was filled with a full-sized washer and dryer, rusted at their edges. A chaise lounge was missing two plastic straps. And water-stained cardboard boxes containing God knows what were stacked alongside the front of a sheet-metal utility shack. Nick kept checking the curtains, waiting for a movement that would tell him someone was inside who didn't want to talk to him.

A woman opened the door just a crack before he could step up onto the metal grated stairway. Nick lowered his eyes, just for a moment, and then looked into the light-colored eyes that peered out.

"Good morning, ma'am. I'm looking for David Ferris. Is he home, please?"

The eyes continued to look out and the crack widened, letting sunlight give blueness to their irises.

"My name is Nick Mullins, ma'am, I'm a reporter for the *Daily News.*"

"I know who you are," the woman said. Her voice was neither accusatory nor contemptuous. Nick took it as a good sign.

"Have I met you before, ma'am?" Nick said.

"You interviewed my husband about four years ago, right here on these steps," she said, opening the door wider, her hand high on the edge of the jamb. The sun glinted off thin strands of blond hair that dangled in front of her face like a spider's web catching light. She was a small, thin woman dressed in a flower-patterned smock and loose matching pants, the kind of outfit a nurse would wear.

"Yes, ma'am. I'm sorry," Nick said. "I, uh, I don't recall your name."

She just nodded, offering nothing.

"David isn't in, then?"

"He just called, Mr. Mullins. They got ahold of him on his cell phone at work. He's on his way home."

Nick looked down again, as though he understood.

"He's still at the Motorola plant, then?" he said, recalling the reporting he'd done on the earlier Ferris stories.

"We're both still working, Mr. Mullins, trying to pay off the lawyer's bills," she said, only now letting an edge into her voice.

Nick shifted his weight. He was still standing below her, looking up now into her face. He thought he'd remembered her being in her mid-twenties on the documents he'd dug up on the Ferris family. But the crow's-feet at the corners of her eyes and the pull of skin from her cheekbones did not fit that age. He felt somehow responsible, but could not leave it alone.

"Was the phone call about Steven?" he finally asked and she simply nodded in the positive and looked off into the distance behind him.

Again Nick let silence surround them, second-guessing whether she was relieved or saddened. He finally took a step back.

"May I wait for David to get here?" he said.

She fixed her dry blue eyes on his. "He doesn't want to talk with you, Mr. Mullins. Enough has been said," she said. "I know that people can't understand it, why he stood up for his brother after what he did to those children. I don't know that I even understand it."

She looked down for the first time, a crack in her show of defiance.

"But David still loved his brother, sir. And now we have a funeral to plan." Nick nodded his head again, this time in deference, and continued stepping backward.

"I'm sorry, Mrs. Ferris," he said and then closed his lips around the air that had started behind his teeth before he could say, *Thank you.*

By the time he opened his car door, she was gone. He climbed in and the spiral wire of his notebook caught the fabric of the seat. He had not taken it from his back pocket.

/ Chapter 5 /

On the way back to his desk Nick made his obligatory stop at the assistant city editor's pod.

"I have an I.D. confirmation on the dead guy at the jail," he said.

The editor rolled back his chair while his fingers were still on his keyboard, reluctant to leave unfinished a sentence for a budget line item that would have to be presented in yet another news meeting at noon.

"OK, great, Nick. Anybody we know?" he said, finally bringing his head and a grin around with the final word.

"Yeah. It's a guy they put away a few years ago on a double homicide and rape of two elementary school sisters."

"No shit?"

"Yeah," Nick said, knowing he'd finally gotten the guy's attention. "He was coming back into court for a hearing on a change of sentencing and it looks like somebody from the outside popped him."

The editor's name was John Rhodes. He'd only been at the *Daily News* for a year and had been told early that Mullins had an attitude, most of it coming after a car wreck that involved his family some time ago. He was told to walk lightly with him. But he'd also learned quickly that when Mullins brought something to the editors' desk, the guy would have nailed it down.

"No shit," he repeated and looked around to see if anyone else was within earshot and sharing the news of the minute. "How long ago did this guy do the . . . uh, murder the kids?"

"Four years," Nick said. "Only the sentencing was in litigation."

"So people are gonna remember, right?"

"Yeah, John. People will remember."

"OK, yeah, sure. Whadda you think, Nick. Page one?"

"That's your call, man. I got some more people to talk to," Nick said and then nodded his head toward Deirdre's office. "Tell her it's Steven Ferris. I already got the clips from the library."

Rhodes got up as Nick started to walk away. "Hey, does anyone else have this?" he said.

Nick turned around but didn't say anything.

"I mean, you know, do we have an exclusive here?" Rhodes said.

"They're just sources, John. I don't know who else they talk to," Nick said and went on to his desk. He wanted to ask what the hell difference it made if some other news outlet knew Ferris's was the body now being shipped to the morgue. He wanted to ask when "exclusive" had become the value of a story. But he'd said those things before. Maybe he was learning to keep his big mouth shut.

Morgue, Nick thought when he sat down and logged into his computer. While the machine booted up, he called the medical examiner's office, bypassing the switchboard by using an inside extension to one of the M.E.'s assistants.

"McGregor," the deep baritone announced after eight rings.

"Hey, Mac. Nick Mullins. Sorry if I pulled you away from something disgusting and violated."

"Nick? Nick?" said McGregor, making his voice sound like he was perplexed. "Nick, ahhhh. Sorry, I'm having a hard time coming up with the last name. Do I know you?"

Nick smiled into the phone.

"OK, Mac. So you must be working on this dead inmate with the head wound, right?"

"Did I say that, Mr. Nick? I'm not sure I said that. You know this call may be monitored for quality assurance purposes."

"Jesus, Mac. Did they come down on you guys again for leaking stuff to the press?"

"Come down on us? Christ, Nicky, we even had to do a goddamn hour-long seminar with the county attorney on right to privacy and HIPPA laws and then sign a fucking waiver sheet saying we attended and understood 'all materials presented,'" McGregor said, his legendary sarcasm back in his voice. "I can see 'em waving that damn thing in court and pointing at us: 'We told them, they didn't listen, sue them, not the state.'"

"OK, well, I wouldn't want to get you into any trouble, Mac," Nick said and then waited for what he knew would come.

"Up their arse," the baritone growled. "It's a free country. I'll say what I want, when I want. What do they think they are? British occupiers?"

Nick always listened to McGregor's Scottish rants. The guy was three generations removed from Edinburgh, but wore it like an honor.

"Yeah, Nicky. We got your white male, six feet, two-twenty if he's an ounce, dressed in tailored prison orange and a single bullet just missed his bloody ear hole by an inch."

"Who's doing the autopsy?" Nick said.

"We're a bit in the weeds over here, lad. So the old man himself is going to take this one, but he won't get to it till late tonight. Why don't you come on over about midnight? Bring a snack. You two can swap stories like old times, eh?"

"Thanks, Mac. I might take you up on that," Nick said.

"No thanks needed from you, Nicky. I haven't said a word." Nick heard the chuckle in the voice before the connection clicked off.

So the old man, Broward M.E. Dr. Nasir Petish himself, would be doing the autopsy in one of his peculiar "dead-of-the-night" sessions, as the seventy-three-year-old pathologist called them. Nick thought of the last such session he'd attended, snuffed the memory out of his nose and put off making any plans for his own evening. Now he had a story to write. He still had calls to make to the Department of Corrections and at least get their "No comment." He'd get the prosecutor who had won Ferris's conviction. He'd get a line on a couple of jurors in the murder trial from the court reporter who covered it four years ago. And he'd have to try to find the mother of the little girls, though he knew it would be difficult tracking someone who had been essentially homeless. He'd start with the prosecutor, who might know a way to contact her. He picked up the phone. The always-present deadline was creeping past midday.

/ Chapter 6 /

Michael Redman was at his makeshift table, breaking down the rifle he had used most of his adult life to kill dangerous human beings who did not deserve to walk this earth. "Break down," though, was perhaps the wrong term for Redman. He could no more "break down" his weapon than he could break down his right arm. He handled the bolt from the H&K PSG-1 with just the tips of his fingers, feeling the weight and shape and the touch of finely crafted metal against his own skin. The smell of the Shooter's Choice cleaner was as fond to him as perfume; a certain signaling sifted like smoke through his head when he used it to clean the rifle after a kill. It signaled an end. The final act of taking care of business. It made him relax, often for the first time in weeks.

He had taken the door off the adjoining bedroom and laid the heavy plank across two nightstands, creating a wide bench on which to work. The only light was from the street lamp outside, seeping in through the window he faced. He liked the dark. You didn't have to see so much in the dark. And you could feel more—the breeze across a sheen of sweat, the soft vacuum of silence that cupped your ears in the quiet, the weight of a careful footstep on a hallway floor. Michael Redman liked those sensations. Many times they had kept him alive.

Redman caressed the bolt like a lover's hand, wiped it down and set it next to the silencer he had removed from the barrel. He knew he would have to rezero the H&K before he used the suppressor again, but it had done its job this morning. Hell, the few reporter shitbirds that had gathered for Ferris's perp walk hadn't even flinched when his round fired. No one heard a thing except for the splat the bullet had made when it entered the edge of Ferris's sideburn and burrowed through his head. The only sound was that of his lifeless body crumpling to the staircase steps, dead at the second of impact, an unavoidable blessing for someone who had deserved worse. Sometimes justice was swift but not always compensative, Redman thought. But that was not the gunman's choice. He did only what he was trained to do, maybe born to do.

Redman attached a rod guide into the breech of the weapon and then with the folding rod ran a brush up and back once through the barrel. One push through for each shot fired. And there had only been one. In the dark, he let his mind drift back to Falluja and Ramadi. He had been a law enforcement sniper for ten years, six before that in the Marine Corps. He had told friends that the only reason he'd joined the National Guard was to take advantage of the access to military gun ranges when he was traveling. He never expected to get called up to another war at age forty-six. But they said they needed his talent, his training. They attached him to a forward Marine infiltration squad. Let him pick his own high ground, always in a building, rarely one that seemed stable after the early bombing the cities had taken. The spotter they'd partnered him with was active duty and had rank. Their squad was good at close-quarter tactics and always cleared the building before they set up. High ground was a precious commodity over there. Enemy snipers coveted them. On occasion, Redman would hear the quiet spit of the clearing team's silenced handguns or a muffled grunt, the sound of something heavy and soft and lifeless being dragged on the floor above. But when the spotter called him up, he never saw a body, just the drag marks leading to another room or behind a partial wall. Redman would set up with an optimum view of the streets below. By daybreak, the Marine units would begin to move into the city. The spotter would use his binoculars to sweep both streets and buildings. Their orders were to safeguard the advancing troops. When the spotter called out a target, be it a man in a window, a shawled figure moving carefully in the street or some thin-limbed kid struggling to carry the weight of an AK-47, it was Redman's job to kill.

"Take the shot."

He didn't ask questions. After the first four months, he stopped adding the number of times he slid the brush through his weapon's barrel. He was very good at his job. But unlike his police work, he never knew the dead, whether they were innocent or evil, dangerous or just unlucky. After the brush, Redman squeezed some Shooter's Choice on a soft swab and ran it through the barrel and asked himself, Would Collie have done what I have done?

His SWAT friend, his only true friend, Collie always had a way of working the bugs out of Redman's head after a shoot, sitting in a bar washing the vision of blood down your throat. He'd grab Redman by the neck with those Vise-Grip fingers of his and say, "Moral courage, man. We do the job that no one else will do. We make the hard choices. And don't you think any different, Mikey. It ain't the lieutenant. It ain't the sheriff. It ain't the range master. When your finger is on the trigger, buddy, you are ultimately the man. It's your moral courage that lets you pull it."

Would Collie have pulled those triggers in Iraq? Redman couldn't find the answer and it ate at him. But he'd sworn it would be different when he got home, and today he had known his target, he knew the man was deserving, knew he'd exacted a moral vengeance for two little girls whose innocence had been stolen. Collie would have pulled this trigger.

Redman closed his eyes while he worked, his fingers moving with the precision of motor memory in the dark. He wondered what the newspaper story would say in the morning. He wondered if Nick Mullins would get the assignment, if the only journalist he trusted would get it right, would understand.

/ Chapter 7 /

The last call Nick made was to Joel Cameron. It was just after eight o'clock and his story was finished and ready to move on to the editors and copy readers. He had named Ferris and given a full background of his murder trial and the rapes and killings of the children. The bulk of the story was on the dead man. The main question of the piece was the identity of his shooter. Nick had left three phone messages for Detective Hargrave, knowing they would never be returned. He'd watched the six o'clock news on three local television channels and all were still reporting that the name of the dead inmate had not been released. His own editors had voted to keep Ferris's name off the newspaper's Internet site so they could scoop the competition. Every newsgroup monitored each other's site. It had become laughable how one group now bragged that they got their story "up" on the Web ten minutes before the other.

Nick tried out his "he'll still be just as dead tomorrow" line on Cameron when the information officer started to whine after Nick told him he was naming Ferris in the morning paper.

"Shit, Nick. The other guys are going to be all over me that I wasn't being fair by treating everyone the same."

Cameron's defensiveness was yet additional confirmation that Nick had the right guy.

"So just don't confirm it, Joel. I've got it and if anybody gives you a hard time, you can honestly say you didn't give it to me," Nick said.

There was a silence. Cameron was thinking. Always a danger, Nick thought.

"But you won't give it out for the eleven o'clock television guys just because I do have it, right? That was our deal."

"Yeah," Cameron acquiesced. "But Hargrave's still going to be pissed."

"He'll get over it, Joel. And while I've got you, is there anything more on the shooting that you are giving out? Caliber of the bullet? Search warrant issued at the house of a pissed-off relative of dead girls? Anything more from our friend across the street who saw a man dressed in a SWAT uniform coming down off the roof?"

"Shit, Nick. You're not using that, are you?" Cameron said.

"Actually, no," Nick said. "I'm holding back on that for some later development. You might pass that on to Detective Hargrave—my cooperation, that is."

Cameron was quiet for a beat. "All we're giving out is on the most recent press release, Nick. That's it."

That was little more than nothing. Nick had read the release and spiked it on his desk.

"OK, Joel. I'm outta here. Talk with you tomorrow."

"Word of advice, Nick," Cameron said before clicking off. "Walk careful with Hargrave. He's not like the other homicide guys."

Nick had already seen that in the detective's eyes. He wouldn't be the kind who sat around the desks in the squad room and hashed out his theories with the others. Not once had he written anything down, either while he was inspecting the blood spatter or up on the roof. His were the kind of eyes that absorbed everything and then let those images turn and twist in his head until they started to fit. Nick knew Hargrave's kind. They were the ones who burned out quick, or were damned good because of the experience they gained by not giving in.

"I'll try not to piss him off, Joel," Nick said and hung up the phone.

/ / /

Nick pulled into his driveway at nine, only fourteen hours since he'd left this morning. He turned off the engine and sat in the quiet, trying to set aside the scenes in his head, his internal speculations on who might have dressed in black, positioned himself on a roof and killed a man who was already sitting in prison for life and still carrying a death sentence. And that was if Ferris was indeed the intended target. Suppose some incompetent rifleman had meant to hit the jail guard? Suppose Ferris had just stumbled in front of a bullet? Nick took a deep breath and closed his eyes.

"Don't take it into the house," he whispered to himself. "Don't do this to her too."

When he got out, he fixed a smile onto his face and unlocked the front door. When he stepped in, his daughter was sitting cross-legged on the living room floor with a thousand-piece jigsaw puzzle laid out before her, half done. The sight stopped him, like always now when he encountered Carly sitting or standing or twisting a strand of her hair in the exact same way that her twin sister had done. Ghosts, Nick thought. Will I always have to live with ghosts?

"Hi, Daddy. I've been saving all this side for you," Carly said in her nine-year-old voice, sweeping her hand over the yet-undone side of the puzzle. She tossed her silky limp hair aside and gave him that face, the mischievous one with the raised eyebrows and the smile made without parting her lips.

"Oh, saved it, huh?"

Nick walked over and reached down with both hands and his daughter took them on cue, and with a firm grip, he lifted and tossed her up with one motion and then caught her against his chest and she wrapped her legs around his waist and squeezed.

"You didn't just slow down so you could stay up later?" he said into her ear and then kissed her cheek.

"No way," she said, leaning back with her hands now locked behind her father's neck. "I could have done your side easy."

"I know you could have," Nick said, starting to move in a tight circle, beginning the spin he knew she expected, and her eyes got wider and brighter and the fake smile he'd carried in became unconsciously real as they went around together. They were both laughing when Elsa interrupted.

"*Buenas noches*, Mr. Mullins," said the small elderly woman, wiping her hands with a dish towel. "You need something for your dinner, yes?"

Elsa was Bolivian, a grandmother to two young boys, the sons of her immigrant daughter. A decade ago she came to the United States to take care of her grandsons and earned extra money by taking in the children of working parents as a daytime sitter. Kind and matronly and endlessly patient, she had looked after both of the Mullinses' girls from the time they were babies as their daytime nanny. While Nick and his wife worked, Elsa cared for the girls along with her older grandsons in her daughter's home. By the time the boys were old enough to be home alone, Elsa had fallen in love with the girls, and they with her. Nick offered her a live-in position and after the accident she stayed, although Nick had never asked her to. She took it almost as a duty to watch over him and Carly, to protect the child from her dreams and to protect Nick from himself.

"Just a sandwich, Elsa. Please," Nick said and carried his daughter to the small kitchen table.

"Wait, wait, wait," Carly said, squirming from Nick's arms. "You have got to see this, Dad."

When she skipped from the room, Nick sat heavily in the chair near the patio slider and looked out onto the spotlighted pool. The aqua glow rose like a tinted bubble from the water. Nick liked the softness of it on his eyes. After the crash, at the bottom of his breakdown, he'd spent nights staring out into the light, sipping whiskey for hours and trying to let the color wash out the images of white, bloodless skin and torn metal from behind his eyelids. The booze had let him sleep. But the next night he would be back. It had gone on for months until finally he made a decision to stand up and live, for his remaining daughter, and went back to work. Still, on days when he was tired and let down his guard, the lure of slipping into the pale blue light forever would come over him.

"Mr. Nick?" Elsa said and the words snapped him back. When he looked over at her, she was eyeing him and propping up the corners of her mouth with her thumb and ring finger, making a smile. It was her job to warn him when the "grouper" face appeared. The child psychologist had warned him that his own sadness could overtake and eventually empower his daughter's grief. It was something he needed to stay conscious of. When Carly came back into the room with a sheaf of papers and an unframed canvas, he had regained his smile.

"Ta-daaa!" his daughter announced, holding out the canvas, upon which a brightly colored and finely textured painting had been produced. Nick studied the work while Carly posed and held it with the corners balanced in her palms. He felt her watching his eyes. But this time he did not have to pretend. The colors were pastels of pink and orange, the lines soft and flowing.

"It's beautiful, C!" he said, using his pet name for her. "Are these wings?"

"Yes. And here in the corner."

"How did you get that texture in there? That's really cool."

"It's that resin stuff you got me. They showed me how to use it at school, and see, you can peak it just so or really raise it up if you want," she said, pointing out sections of the painting that rose delicately off the canvas.

They propped the painting up against a napkin holder on the table and while Nick ate, Carly showed him homework, her graded papers, and explained in detail how Meagan Marts had been such a pain correcting her and the other girls on the bus that morning when they were discussing what lip gloss was made of. Nick listened. He had set up this nightly ritual on the advice of a divorced friend whose wife had left him. It was invaluable, the friend said, to keep in touch, to keep a semblance of normality, to stay sane.

Elsa had made him one of her famous Bolivian chicken salad sandwiches. Nick couldn't tell the difference between the chopped celery or spring onions, but he truly loved the battle of tastes between the seedless grapes and the rainbow chiles. While father and daughter talked, Elsa stayed busy washing and wiping and straightening a kitchen that Nick knew was already spotless.

"OK, Carlita," Elsa finally said. "It is very late, yes, Mr. Nick?"

Elsa had that wonderful trait of being the boss while using the right phrases to make the man think he was still in charge.

"Elsa's right, babe. Time to get ready for bed," Nick said. "You go, and I'll come in and read."

With a limited amount of preadolescent huffing, his daughter left the room.

Nick spun his chair back to a view of the pool. A random breeze fluttered across the surface, causing the refracted light to dance on the far wall.

"How was she today?" he asked without looking over at Elsa.

"*Yo creo que es mejor*, Mr. Nick," Elsa said. She too was looking outside through the window over the sink. "She is very smart, though. It is too much to see inside her head."

Nick just nodded, but Elsa went quiet and he turned after a moment to look at her. She was again folding and refolding a dish towel in her hands, her eyes on the floor now. Nick knew something was bothering her, but let Elsa decide when to tell it.

"She call me Lindsay today," Elsa finally said. "While she is looking for something in the office room she say, 'Lindsay, do you know where the, the thing for the paper staples is?' and I just say, 'No,' like I no hear Lindisita's name."

Elsa was clearly distressed, but Nick was caught between smiling at her attempt to relate the Freudian slip or crying at Carly's use of her sister's name.

"It's OK, Elsa," he said. "I will tell the counselor when she goes for her session."

The housekeeper turned the towel in her hand. Nick looked back out into the light.

"Dad? I'm ready," his daughter called from her room.

"Can you make me some coffee, please, Elsa?" Nick said as he walked through the kitchen.

"You are going out again?"

"After she's asleep," he said. "I'll lock up before I go." Nick did not turn to see Elsa's reaction. He knew she would disapprove. He'd promised to give up the late-night forays into the streets for the sake of a story, both to his wife before and to Elsa afterward. Now he was again going back on that promise.

In his daughter's room, he knelt down in front of the bookcase, searching for a title. Carly was already in bed and had slid over against the wall to give him room to stretch out in his usual position. Nick had taken the second twin bed out of the room after two months. He'd replaced it with a desk and an additional case of the girls' favorite books, some that had been packed away in the garage.

"I've got the Harry Pottter over here, Dad," Carly said.

"I'm looking for something else, C. One of my favorites."

Carly didn't complain, just pulled a stuffed tiger closer to her and waited for him to find a thin, worn volume from one of the lower shelves. He finally lay down on the outside edge of the bed and turned away from the nightstand, where he knew a family photo of the four of them looked out upon his back.

"*We Were Tired of Living in a House*, by Leisel Moak Skorpen," he announced and then peeked over from the side of the opened book to see his daughter's reaction. She rolled her eyes but still smiled.

"Alright, go ahead," she said, giving him permission.

Nick read the book aloud, pausing to give both of them a long look at the accompanying artwork on each double page. It was actually a long, lovely and mischievous poem about two brothers and two sisters who get scolded for misdoings at home and their adventures finding another place to live—a tree, a pond, a cave and the seashore—before finally returning home to their parents to live in a house.

When he finished, Nick closed the book and turned off the bedside lamp and waited in the silence. He could tell by her breathing that she was still awake. Before, he'd always read to the girls from a rocking chair set in between the beds and when he was done he'd continue to rock, the low creak of the runners sounding in a rhythm that would eventually put them to sleep. He found he could no longer stand the sound and had thrown the chair out.

"Was someone killed today?" his daughter's voice finally, quietly broke the silence.

Nick just closed his eyes. Unfortunately, it was not an unusual question from Carly. She was a bright girl.

"Yes, honey," he said.

"Did you write about it?"

"Yes."

"Will I read about it in the newspaper?"

"I'm not sure you should be reading the paper, honey, with all your schoolwork and stuff. You should really concentrate on that reading."

He had never encouraged his daughters to read his work, but Carly had taken more to it since the accident, and the counselors had suggested he let it go instead of trying to ban her from the practice.

"Did it make you sad, the killing?"

"No, Carly. Not really. I was just trying to find out how it happened. That's my job, to report what happened. You know?"

The girl stayed quiet for several moments.

"Why do you ask?" Nick finally said.

"'Cause you always read that book when you're sad, Daddy."

Jesus, Nick thought. He tried to look into his daughter's eyes but couldn't make them out in the dark room. The kids are too smart for you. You can't overestimate their perception. And you can't hide.

"I know, baby," he whispered. "It just makes me feel better."

He touched her hair and she whispered back, "Me too."

When her breathing went soft and rhythmic and she was finally asleep, Nick carefully rolled off the bed and left, closing the door gently behind him.

/ Chapter 8 /

Nick didn't call the medical examiner's office until he was in the parking lot.

"Would it help you to decide if I told you I was right outside?"

He had called Nasir Petish's cell phone. The doc's midnight autopsy was only just beginning and though the physician had known Nick for several years—they shared an appreciation for Jameson's whiskey and Cannonball Adderley's saxophone—the physician still fell back on administration rules against press access. At least for the first twenty seconds of each conversation.

"You are in my parking area?" Petish said, his East Indian accent flicking high at the end of every sentence.

"Yeah. I figured you'd be up late with this one," Nick said, leaving the assistant M.E.'s heads-up out of it.

"And what you listening to out there, Mr. Mullins?"

"The Adderleys and, uh, George Shearing at Newport," Nick said, quickly rummaging through his collection to see if he actually had the CD in his car.

"Is that the one during which Mr. Adderley comments on the influence of a young pianist named Ray Charles?" Petish said.

"Yeah," Nick said, coming up with the CD, "that's the one."

"Bring it in, if you will, Mr. Mullins."

Nick went around to the loading dock area where the M.E.'s vans and black Ford Explorers were parked. A light mounted above the double-door entrance bathed the raised deck in an orange-tinted glow. One of the doors opened and a small man with tea-colored skin and wire-rimmed glasses ushered him in.

"Thanks, Dr. Petish. I appreciate this," Nick said, shaking the man's offered hand.

"Ahhh. No thanks are necessary, Mr. Mullins, for nothing that has been given, yes?"

Nick grinned into the smiling face of the physician and nodded his understanding of the terms. He was never here. No comment. No attribution. He raised the CD and handed the plastic square to the M.E., who scanned the back intently. Petish carried a perpetually charmed look on his face despite his blunt speech and grim profession.

"Ahhh, yes," he said. "The one when Nathaniel still, as you say, had his lip. I like this recording very much."

The doctor read through the playlist as they passed through an area of wheeled gurneys and shelves of supplies and then down a wide corridor to his favorite examining room. Inside, the walls were concrete block and painted white with the kind of paint that was shiny and smooth and left an almost plastic texture, the better to wipe clean. The floor was done in gray with similar paint and Nick noted the drain located in the middle. There were two stainless steel tables in the room. Only one was occupied.

Ferris had been heavily built, with powerful arms and thin hips in the way of a farmer or factory worker. Nick remembered the yokelike shoulders and the way they'd slumped during his trial. His freshly shaved skull was now gone from the ears up. Petish had already started with the bone saw.

The M.E. slipped the CD into a portable player on a high shelf and set the music at a low volume and then snapped on a new pair of latex gloves. He almost always began his autopsies by sawing through the skull bone in a circular fashion and then lifting the top portion to reveal the brain inside. The sight did not bother Nick. He had attended autopsies before. The clinical atmosphere was actually a lot less disturbing than the open wounds and aftermaths he'd seen on the streets.

"As you can see, Mr. Mullins, the deceased has considerable damage to the brain from a single wound."

Nick moved with the doctor as he positioned himself at the head of the table and turned the dead man's face to the right. A small black hole appeared to be neatly bored into the exact line where his high-cut sideburn had once been.

"It was a very high-velocity round and would most likely have snapped the head in this direction," Petish said, mimicking the movement by grasping the dead man's stiffened neck and jerking it toward one pale shoulder. When he turned Ferris's head back the other way, an exit wound four times the size of the hole on the other side yawned ragged and blackened with dried blood in the area of the jaw.

"Any way to guess the caliber?" Nick said, letting the doctor make an assumption instead of making it himself.

"Yes. A .308, if I am not mistaken," Petish said while sneaking a peek at Nick and smiling at his raised eyebrows. "Oh, they recovered the round, Mr. Mullins. I am good, but certainly not that good."

Nick instinctively reached for a notebook from his back pocket, but then simply scratched a spot on his thigh, recalling Petish's rules.

"If the marksman was only just lucky, he could not have been more accurate," Petish said. "To enter the skull from this point and the expansion of bore diameter damage as it enters the brain would have the effect of instant cessation of all motor and neurologic response."

"Dead before he hit the ground," Nick said.

"Precisely," the doctor said as he pointed out other discolored spots on the body.

"My external examination of the deceased shows a number of bruises both anterior and posterior. Some very old, some more recent, but none that would have been administered in the last few days," Petish began as if he were reading into a report recorder.

"Jailhouse jostle," Nick said, thinking of the status Ferris would have had at MDCC as a child molester.

"Possibly," the M.E. said as he positioned a scalpel over the body's chest and began making his incisions.

Nick concentrated on the tattoos that Ferris had obviously gotten while he was inside. Serpents in dark ink that now stood out on the pale insides of both forearms. Somewhat crude but detailed enough to see the fierceness of eyes and sharpness of claw. Nick wondered if Ferris had paid a prison artist to do them so he could project his toughness or whether it was an expression of what was inside his head.

Petish worked quickly and meticulously, cutting away inside the chest cavity, with deft strokes slicing the connective tissue of major organs and carefully weighing each before unceremoniously dropping them into a five-gallon bucket on the floor nearby. In the air, the Adderley brothers played a buoyant riff of 1930s blues in stark juxtaposition to what was going on at the table. Nick asked an occasional anatomy question and watched as the doctor took tiny samples of the organs and slipped them into test tubes for later microscopic examinations.

"Don't you think that hole in his head makes a pretty good case for cause of death?" Nick said, only half joking as the physician pointed out a darkened portion of lung tissue, snipped and bottled it.

Petish looked up for the first time. "Really, Mr. Mullins. Have you known me to be anything other than completely thorough?"

Nick kept quiet but had to turn his head away when the doctor removed the lower intestines from the corpse. After the weighing, the M.E. misjudged the bucket below and one end of the colon caught an edge, flipping a stream of liquid through the air and against one wall.

Those who thought they'd witnessed autopsies by watching *CSI: Miami* were missing this part unless they had scratch-and-sniff TV. The odor was nearly intolerable. But Nick was bothered more by the growing disdain he was building in his head by going back to the serpents and then recalling Ferris's crime scene: the little house, the small body bags. Instead of the scientific atmosphere he usually held to at these proceedings, he could feel a hate building. *Fucking deserved it* was on his lips when Petish said, "There it is."

Nick stepped closer to look at the cutting board that Petish had lain on top of the chest and realized the M.E. had Ferris's heart out and was snipping an artery with a pair of scissors.

"What? He had a heart attack," Nick said and then realized his voice was much too anxious.

Petish shook his head with a look of smiling exasperation. "No, no, no, Mr. Mullins. Yes, you can see the hardening of the artery here. But no. I was speaking of the recording."

He was now pointing the scissors at the CD player and the band was just launching into "We Dot" and Cannonball had just made reference to a young man named Ray Charles.

"Ha!" said the doctor. "A young man. Yes. Did you hear?"

/ / /

It was three AM when Nick shook hands with the doctor, minus the latex gloves, and made his way across the darkened parking lot. A false dawn was showing in the east and even though he knew what time it was, and could feel the dry tiredness in his eyes like a parchment on his irises, the possibility of daybreak encouraged him. He got behind the wheel and sat for a while in the quiet, trying to gauge the anger he was still holding for the dead man inside. Why be pissed at a guy who took one through the brain and had just been eviscerated in front of you? Hell, wasn't that enough? But Nick was transferring and he knew it.

The face of the man who had killed half his family was the one he'd wanted to see on that table.

He'd almost gotten over it, the anger, the raw feeling for revenge. Or at least he'd pushed it back into a dark spot in his brain so he could get back to work, get back to Carly. Then he'd heard last week that Robert Walker was out. Then he'd called in a marker with a friend at the Department of Corrections and Parole to find out where Walker was living. He knew that he'd put his own ass in trouble if anyone found out that he was stalking the man. But he shook off the argument and started his car, rolled down the window and let the moist night air sweep in around him as he started east along a route and a destination he now knew by heart.

/ Chapter 9 /

Nick slowed and drove down Northwest Eighteenth Terrace, past Highsmith's Tool & Die on the corner, past Willow Manor, the oddly located Cuban nursing home where the poorer old folks went to die. He turned off his headlights and slid down warehouse row with only his parking lights on. Under the dirty white cast of high streetlights a handful of cars, a couple of pickup trucks and some delivery trucks were parked in front of the line of corrugated steel buildings. He stopped two blocks down and then backed into a spot next to the big Dumpster in front of Flynn's Awnings and Rain Gutters. From here he could see across the roadway to the painted green door of Archie's Tool Sharpening Shack and still use the Dumpster as cover. He turned off the ignition and listened to the ping of cooling metal for several minutes until the silence wrapped around the car, and then he reached for the coffee. He had stopped at an all-night 7-Eleven and bought the twenty-four-ounce cup, loaded it with cream and sugar and also bagged two donuts as an afterthought. He started on the chocolate glaze and sipped at the steaming cup and checked the end of the street. If a police sector car came through on the overnight shift, he would have to explain himself. But he'd done this three times since tracing Walker's work address and no cops had come by yet. It was probably just off their regular radar, but this week it had become the late-night center of his. He checked his watch—four fifteen—and made sure the alarm was on and then stared out at Archie's sign and before the first donut was done, he fell asleep.

/ / /

He dreamed the dream he always did, the one where he is sitting back in the third seat of the family van while his dead wife is driving. His dead child watches vigilantly out a side window, counting the lighted deer she spies among the Christmas decorations. Carly is at the other window, trying to outdo her sister. It is dark outside. "The girls," which is what he calls all three, are out cruising through the local neighborhoods on Christmas Eve. In snowless South Florida, the garishness of the colored displays seems profoundly out of place, lights strung in palms, the white-wired deer bending their heads and munching at grass that is eternally green. The girls are laughing at some observation Carly has made about a deer that has lost the electrical current from all his bulbs but the single red one at his nose and a broken strand running down one leg. But Nick is in the back, realizing that his wife seems oblivious to the fact that she is driving in a constant loop, around and around the traffic circle near their house, going nowhere, seeing the same houses, the same deer, over and over.

Nick doesn't see deer. He stares out of his dead daughter's window and sees the headlights of a pickup truck cresting the hill that rises up over the interstate. He has to twist his head around and look out back as his wife continues the circle and he sees the headlights grow larger and brighter. Nick can feel the apprehension coming into his throat but cannot speak. He cannot move his legs or arms to crawl over the back seat to pull his daughters to him, to shield them from what is about to occur. He cannot shout to his wife to warn her. He cannot tell her to speed up or slow down. In the dream he can only watch the synchronization of the circular movement and the oncoming truck, a speeding straight line of light coming to match the slow orbit of his family. Nick feels the hot tears slide down his cheeks even before the impact.

Eeeep, eeeep, eeeep, eeeep.

Nick's eyes flashed open and at first he thought the noise was the high-pitched bleating of an ambulance and then realized the sound was coming from his wrist and then reality shook his brain loose. He was in the parking lot, next to the Dumpster, the sky lightened enough to have turned off the overhead lamps, his coffee long gone cold. He took a deep breath and rubbed his hands over his face and was not surprised to find moisture there. It happened each time. He was no longer mystified by the dream or the emotion. Nor was he one step closer to accepting it.

He sat up straight and surveyed the street. An additional delivery truck, maybe two, had arrived. At a bay halfway down the block, he watched the movement of a single man bending to pick up a ball of trash, or a wayward piece of hardware, or a half cigarette butt that might be used later in the morning. Then his eyes moved automatically to Archie's and the empty spot where Robert Walker would park his F-10 pickup and then the beige color of the truck Nick had memorized forced him to focus. He watched Walker slowly approach, not speeding, never speeding, and then carefully pull into the open spot. Only then did Nick check his watch. It was six fifteen. Not a minute late or early, like Walker knew exactly how fast to drive to roll into that spot at the perfect moment, every day, Monday through Friday. Intersection of time and place.

When the truck's brake lights went out, Nick watched the man's head move slightly down, gathering things from his front seat. When Walker opened the door, the interior dome light came on and added color and dimension to the man. He stepped out, tall and heavyset with a mop of straw-colored blond hair sprouting from under a ball cap. He was wearing his work uniform, blue pants and a short-sleeved white shirt with the name ROBERT stitched across the breast pocket. Nick knew this even from a distance, because he had been up close and personal with Robert Walker.

The day after Nick learned of the release, he staked out the house where Walker lived before the accident, even though he knew the sight of the man would dig open the scar. On the second day he watched him pull into the driveway in an old pickup truck, the profile unmistakable, the face unforgettable. Nick stayed in his car parked across the street. The third day he did the same thing at the same time, early evening, when Walker was obviously arriving home from work. This time the truck pulled up next to Nick's car and Walker rolled down his window.

"Mr. Mullins?" Walker said, his voice raspy and slow. "You can't do this, sir."

Nick just stared into his face, saying nothing.

"I called the Sheriff's Office, Mr. Mullins, and they said you can't just park outside my house and harass me."

Nick remained silent.

"I'm sorry, Mr. Mullins. I said that a hundred times, I'm sorry about what happened. But you can't stalk me like this, sir. I did my time."

Nick had almost spit out in anger that the street was public property and he would do any damn thing he wanted to on it. He wanted to scream in the man's face that his lousy eighteen-month sentence was nothing. Nothing! The manslaughter conviction was a sham. It had been a homicide, and Walker knew it! Instead he just stared at the man's face until he rolled his window back up and drove away.

Last Thursday one of Nick's friends with the department warned him that they couldn't ignore Walker's complaints about him parking outside his house. So Nick found out where Walker worked and was required to show up each day during his probation, and now this was where he came at six fifteen in the morning.

Nick watched Walker holding a lunch box and thermos in one hand while he locked up his old truck with the other. Was there booze in the thermos? Nick thought. Could he catch him violating his court order to quit drinking? Walker had refused a Breathalyzer test at the scene of the accident, and they drew blood from him after he was hospitalized. By then his readings weren't over the legal limit. There was no documented proof to make a DUI charge, but everyone knew that was bullshit when they did it three hours after the fact. Now Nick watched him walk to the door of Archie's and work a key into the lock and then step inside without once looking back over his shoulder. Nick wasn't sure if Walker had noticed him parked across the way beside the Dumpster. So he waited until he saw the blinds open in the only window to Archie's, and hoped the man was looking out and knew that someone watched him, that someone would never forget.

/ Chapter 10 /

Michael Redman was peering out the glass door of the rented town-house, watching for the delivery truck that would fill the newspaper racks across the street. It was seven in the morning and he'd timed the stubby-looking guy who pulled up in the step van around sunup and stuffed the day's news into the honor boxes and collected the quarters. Redman could have watched the television news last night and seen their coverage of the shooting, but he had no use for that. There was only one story he wanted to see, only one journalist who would tell the truth.

When the silver-sided van rolled into view, Redman took a step back from the door. No sense being more obvious than he needed to be. He'd taken this place back from the main roads and near a corner where a canal split the flat land and separated two equally boring housing developments. He'd signed a year lease with a fictitious name knowing he'd skip out on it in a month at the most. He was surprised, though, that his old stomping grounds had felt so comfortable. He didn't have to map out the routes and time out the distances to the interstates and account for bridge openings and all the other exigencies that might hamper his movement or possibly his escape. Redman had worked these streets as a sheriff's road deputy for several years. When he moved onto the department's SWAT team the surveillances and the detailed mapping of troubled neighborhoods only intensified. That knowledge and training aided him now. Just like when he used to do undercover INTEL gathering, he would have to be careful out in public. Some of the criminal lowlifes he'd dealt with then were still out here. And now he also had to stay cognizant of the law enforcement personnel who might remember him. So he tended to move only at night. Shopped for food at three AM in the twenty-four-hour grocery, pumped his own gas after midnight, had the local phone company install a DSL line while he was out and made sure all of his lethal equipment was locked in a storage garage signed for under yet another alias. During the day he stayed in, doing research and setting up his next target. The *Daily News* archives had made that so much easier for him. He could even do a search that would highlight all of Nick Mullins's bylines. The man had a gift for writing about the evil assholes in the world that deserved to die.

Redman stood at the door waiting anxiously for a full five minutes after the deliveryman had pulled away before slipping on his dark windbreaker and then walking out to the honor box with a handful of coins in his fist.

By Nick Mullins, Staff Writer

On his way to try to overturn his death sentence, a convicted child murderer and molester instead walked into his execution yesterday as he entered the Broward County Jail in downtown Fort Lauderdale.

In a blatant morning shooting as commuters drove by on Andrews Avenue, Steven Ferris, convicted three years ago for the murder and rapes of a 6-year-old girl and her 8-year-old sister, was killed by a single bullet fired from somewhere outside the fenced compound just before 8 AM, said Broward Sheriff's Office spokesman Joel Cameron.

"One man was fatally wounded as the detainees were being brought through the main jail's secured north entrance. The location of the shooting is not accessible to the public and no member of the public was in any way endangered," Cameron said.

Police authorities would not confirm the identity of the dead man, but the stepsister of Steven Ferris, Charlene Ferris, said that the Sheriff's Office had called to inform her husband, David, of his brother's killing. David Ferris, who attended each day of his brother's jury trial in 2001, was unavailable for comment.

"David still loved his brother," Charlene Ferris said. "And now we have a funeral to plan."

On Thursday sheriff's officials would not speculate on the motive for the shooting but said they had not yet ruled out a random drive-by or that a shot meant for one of the other inmates had simply struck Ferris by chance. But other sources described Ferris's wound as being precisely placed to kill instantly. The ammunition used, a .308-caliber round, is commonly used in high-powered rifles. Less than two hours after the shooting, investigators were inspecting the rooftop of a building directly across from the jail compound. Spokesman Cameron would not comment on the possibility that someone may have taken the deadly shot from that position.

Assistant State Attorney Mark Sheffield, who originally prosecuted Ferris and was due in court today to defend the death sentence, received by the convicted murderer, said:

"I believe we would have been able to withstand the defense challenge that Mr. Ferris did not deserve to go to the electric chair. I don't know how anyone familiar with the case, in which a man hunts down two innocent children, rapes and murders them, could accept anything less. But obviously, after what has occurred, there will be no further action by this office."

When contacted late Thursday in his office, Ferris's defense attorney, Jake Meese, said:

"This is a tragic situation. We were prepared this morning to show that Mr. Ferris did not receive a fair sentencing three years ago and that he was deserving of an equitable resentencing. The man never got his day in court."

Meese was Ferris's attorney at the time of his conviction and had presented his defense over a two-week trial to a jury of twelve that convicted Ferris of two counts of murder and two counts of sexual assault of a minor under the age of eleven.

The rest of Mullins's story was on the inside pages of the A section and reiterated the background of crimes that Ferris had been guilty of. Redman had read those accounts a dozen times. When he got back inside, he flattened the newspaper out on his door-panel table and reread the beginning. He was only mildly surprised that Mullins had named the caliber of the sniper round he had used. But that was standard ammunition. No way to trace it unless they obtained the weapon, and there was no way they would ever take his weapon. Redman was also stopped by the quote from the defense attorney. What an asshole. Never got his day in court! Ferris should have been strapped into Old Sparky and electrocuted. Redman didn't have a broad-brush dislike for lawyers. He knew they were just doing their jobs, and some did them professionally and ethically. They'd studied and trained and worked their way up the line, just like he had, and some were damned good. He'd had a pretty damned good one himself when the PBA represented him before the shooting board after he was involved in the death of a suspect after a SWAT operation. But come on, Ferris never got his day in court? This guy didn't need to spit out that old cliché. Whose ass was he kissing? He knew what he was defending. He had to be thinking good riddance.

Redman shook his head and carefully cut the story out with a razor blade, then folded it and placed it in a manila folder before putting it into the back half of an accordion file. Reports, he thought. Always hated writing up the reports afterward. In Iraq, his Marine spotter did all the reports. Redman only fired the shots, and then sat alone back at the goddamn dusty tent barracks and let it grind on him, not knowing whose lives he'd taken that day. This time he knew. And the next one he would know too. Redman rifled through the accordion file, split into two parts; the back half were missions accomplished, the front half were possibilities. He pulled three jackets from the front and on the door he spread out three manila envelopes. The first thing he did was take out the newspaper printouts and then he began to read.

/ / /

Nick was back home by the time his daughter got up for school. He was at the kitchen table looking through the sports pages when Carly shuffled across the tile floor, her eyes half opened and puffy with sleep. Her small high voice scratched out, "Morning, Daddy," and he pushed back his chair and let her climb onto his lap.

"Hey, sweetheart. How'd you sleep?"

"OK."

"Good," he said and let her head rest warm and scented with sleep into the crook of his neck. He said nothing for a full minute, letting their hearts talk in silence.

"Big day today?" he finally said.

"Not really."

"I thought you were doing those FCAT exams."

"Pssst," she said, coming more awake, at least enough to start injecting cynicism into her voice. "Those things are easy, Dad. And it's boring to just sit through the whole time."

"Well, I'm proud that you're such a brainiac, but you still have to go to school," Nick said, bouncing her just a bit with his knee.

"I knowwww," Carly said with that omnipresent nine-year-old whine.

"So let's get moving," Nick said, bouncing his knee higher.

His daughter stood, trying to look disturbed, started away and then turned with one of those preteen looks.

"Brainiac? Dad, that is like sooooo old."

Nick watched her spin and walk back toward her room, the sleepy shuffle already replaced by a small bounce. She already had her mother's legs, delicate ankles, strong calf muscles. Her sister had had those long and impossibly skinny legs, her knees like knots in a rope. She'd walked like a newborn colt. Carly's gait was more like a sturdy dancer. Watching the colt might not have made him think of his wife, but watching the dancer made him miss her so much he had to turn his face away. Nick took another sip of coffee and looked down at the newspaper on the table, where he had covered his 1A story with the local section, letting only a touch of red from the masthead show. I'll have to get into the office by ten, he thought. Anything you put on the front page, they're going to want a follow-up story for tomorrow.

/ / /

He was only halfway through the newsroom when one of his fellow reporters said, "Nice story this morning, Nick. Like that lead, man."

First paragraph, always the grabber if you did it right. If you did it wrong, Nick always worried, they'd turn the page on you.

When he got to his desk he fired up the computer and then looked apprehensively at the blinking light on the phone. Messages. He'd learned to hate the messages. Every story had the potential to bring out the nuts. Every sentence was just lying out there every morning for someone to disagree with, poke fun at, provide black-and-white proof that the reporter was incompetent. If you wrote anything even bordering on the political, you took the chance of having the right-wingers blasting you the next morning for your unfair liberal stance and the liberals calling you a fascist. Nick preferred to get it from both sides. It was the only way you could tell you'd been fair.

But crime stories rarely had a political bent, so he was safe from most of the second-guessing. He dialed up the message system and listened to the first call:

"Hello, Mr. Mullins. I read your story this morning and would like to compliment you on your writing. But who gives a shit? The guy is scum and should have been executed the day they found him in that house with those little girls. Why do you guys even waste the ink? Who cares who did it except for maybe we want to give him a medal. Anyway, good riddance." OK, Nick thought, I'll forward that one off to the editorial-page folks. He punched up the next message:

"Hey, Mullins, are the cops going to waste a bunch of time and money trying to find out who pulled the trigger on a guy we all would have gladly shot ourselves? I paid for this man's trial. I paid to have him fed and housed for the last four years in prison. And I would have ended up paying for him to sit on death row for the next twenty while the lawyers got rich filing appeal after appeal. Now I suppose they're going to use my taxes to find his killer. Please. Give me a break."

The next call was from Cameron:

"Thanks a bunch, Nick. You swamped my ass already this morning. Give me a call when you get in. Hargrave is all over me to find out where you got the info on the .308 round. He thinks you might have pocketed evidence from the rooftop and lied to him about it."

"Shit," Nick said aloud. He didn't need the detective to be pissed off. If he could work with the guy, that would be helpful. But if Nick was just going to have to filter everything through Cameron's press office anyway, he didn't think it was worth it. He wasn't going to give up the doc just to pacify the homicide team. He was thinking about a strategy and unconsciously punching up the next message, so the next voice snuck up on him:

"Thank you for your story today, Mr. Mullins. A very thorough job, as usual. I look forward to your next case. Your profiles have been very helpful over the years. I hope this has been as gratifying for you as it has for me. Thanks again."

Nick fielded an occasional compliment call. Rare, but sometimes it helped him get through the others. But the voice on this one had a timbre that made him replay the message. He listened closely to the deep male monotone. "Your next case." Odd for a caller to use a law enforcement term when talking to a reporter. Profiles? Yeah. But reporters didn't do cases, they did reports on other people's cases. And what did the guy mean by gratifying? Nick had never thought of what he did as gratifying. It was reporting and he had always considered it straight reporting. He told himself he was after the truth in black-and-white or as close to it as he could find. Yeah, he knew a woman who sneered at him each time he made that statement: Nicky, there is no truth, only perspective.

Part of that statement was true for him now because the only gratification he could see was if Robert Walker was on the autopsy table. And that was his perspective.

A blinking e-mail notice popped up on his screen, pulling him back to the work. He opened it with a click and saw it was from the city editor: *Come in and talk when you get a chance.*

Right. When I get a chance. It was a polite order and he knew it.

Nick scrolled down through the rest of his messages. Some he recognized as reader comments. The one he was looking for, the information from the library on similar shootings of inmates from around the nation, was down the list.

He ignored the rest and called it up. Lori had left a note up top: *I came up with a few sniper-type shootings. Hope some of these help. I put the Florida events first instead of doing them by time line. I also searched for stories where both inmates and former felons were shot and killed on the outside. I might have generated a lot of drug killings, but I stuck them on there anyway.*

Nick checked the size of the file. Huge. He shook his head and looked at the time Lori had sent him the message: past eleven last night. She'd put in some overtime, and he'd have to take her to lunch or at least order her some flowers or something. But before the thought turned into action, his eye caught a name in the first batch of pages he scrolled through: Dr. Markus Chambliss.

Nick scrolled through the accompanying story, pulled from the archives of a newspaper over on the west coast of Florida.

A prominent San Sebastian physician and former medical examiner, who had once been the target of a police investigation into the death of his wife, was found dead of a single gunshot wound Tuesday, Hillsborough County police said.

Dr. Markus Chambliss, 58, was found slumped over the steering wheel of his car about nine AM in the driveway of his home in Tropical Park. Police declined to say whether they considered the death a homicide or a possible suicide. Chambliss had lived in the quiet suburban home for more than a year, moving there with his girlfriend from northern Florida's Dixie County, where he had once been a suspect in the death of his wife of 26 years, Mrs. Barbara Chambliss.

How the hell did I miss this? Nick thought as he checked the date of the story. Four months ago. The story had run in the *St. Petersburg Times*. Nick closed his eyes. You're slipping, man, he thought. Two years ago that never would have gotten by you. Two years ago nothing got by you when it came to work. He went back to the file and moved down to subsequent stories by the west coast newspaper.

A few years ago Chambliss had been the subject of one of Nick's own big Sunday profiles. When the stories had first broken on the M.E. suspected of killing his own wife, Nick had talked his editors into letting him travel to north-central Florida to do a story on what was already being called the perfect murder.

Chambliss was described as a respected member of the community and a doctor whose reputation was beyond reproach. That's always a clue, Nick had argued at the time. Human beings are always fallible, and he had learned long ago that when you started digging, you could find something on everybody. Now, whether it was illegal, immoral or unethical was in the sorting, but no one was as perfect as the superficial stories first tell you. The editors relented and Nick went and dug. With the help of a contact he had in the Florida Department of Law Enforcement, he was able to get the inside information.

Chambliss had called 911 on the morning of his wife's death, telling a dispatcher that he discovered that his wife had passed away during the night. A rescue squad had responded and they did little more than confirm that Mrs. Chambliss was indeed dead. Knowing the medical examiner on a professional basis, they did not question his request to transport his wife to his office. The doctor did the autopsy himself and ruled his own wife's death as heart failure from natural causes. Case closed. Burial set for the next day. Grieving to begin.

The local cops probably would have let it go. But the FDLE heard of the case and said, *Whoa*. For a man to do an autopsy on his own wife and make an evaluation of death by natural causes might have seemed all right for the rural areas of Dixie County, but that's not the way it worked in Tallahassee. They sent an investigator to town, and Nick had a direct line to the guy. Within a day, Nick was told about a phone records request and the discovery that Chambliss had made three calls during the night to the number of a woman who was quickly determined to be the good doctor's mistress. When she was interviewed, her story was way too well rehearsed, and the FDLE was suspicious enough and powerful enough to have an independent autopsy ordered. A team was called in and the pathologists found a suspicious injection point on Mrs. Chambliss's thigh that was fresh. When questioned, the doctor said that he had given his wife, a diabetic, an injection of insulin at the time she went to bed. Some insulin was found in the house, but because Chambliss had already done an autopsy, had already drained his wife's blood and filled her veins with embalming fluid, the concentrations of insulin—which can be deadly on its own in high amounts—or any other chemicals could not be ascertained. The perfect murder? Possibly.

Nick did the initial stories, reporting the inconsistencies, and then kept track of the ongoing investigation while also interviewing the doctor's grown son and daughter and the doctor's girlfriend. The affair had been long and ongoing. Within two months of his wife's death, the doctor moved into a townhouse with the girlfriend. A special prosecutor from outside the county was assigned to the case. Phone records and financial statements threw red flags all over the field. But the doc sat back and maintained his innocence. Eventually, Chambliss was indicted on circumstantial evidence, and even though both of his children were convinced he had killed their mother and testified as witnesses for the prosecution, the jury could not be convinced to find him guilty beyond a reasonable doubt. He walked.

Nick had reported and written the stories straight up. He too was convinced of Chambliss's guilt, but he left the opinions to the columnists, and the readers, who sent him outraged messages about how the guy got off the hook.

Nick scrolled down Lori's list of follow-up stories. The cops had originally let loose that they were considering the doctor's shooting death a suicide, but crime scene technicians came up with proof that the bullet that killed Chambliss was fired from outside his car and that a high-powered round had penetrated the glass and had struck the doctor in the temple, killing him instantly. No further stories were in the collection that Lori had dug up.

Nick sat back and stared at the screen. He didn't like coincidences. They always made you start spinning off in areas that led to useless dead ends that were mostly a waste of time. But just like the cops, you had to do it so you wouldn't get your ass in a sling for not being thorough. Maybe it was Sergeant Langford's reference to "one of your stories" when he I.D.'d Ferris yesterday morning that made it more nagging. He started searching through his contact numbers for his FDLE source on Chambliss when his phone rang.

"Nick, could you come in to my office for a minute?"

Deirdre. She didn't have to say who was calling. Nick stood and took up an empty reporter's notebook to carry into her office. He knew it looked like he was a secretary answering the call to dictation. That's why he did it. On his way across the newsroom someone called out his name.

"Yo, Nicky."

He looked in the direction of the voice, where Bill Hirschman, the education reporter, was standing under one of the ceiling-mounted televisions tuned to the local news. On-screen was videotape from a position high in the sky over the Broward County Jail. The cameraman had zoomed down onto a rooftop that was empty except for four figures, three men standing, one seemingly crouched over. As the shot pulled in closer, Nick saw himself bent, face down into the roof gravel, his butt still up in the air and posing in all its breadth for the camera.

"Not your best side, Nicky," Hirschman said. "Is that textbook investigative reporting or what?"

Nick just shrugged and smiled. "No stone unturned," he said to the other reporter.

Hirschman laughed. The city editor wouldn't.

Deirdre did not look up from her screen, as usual, until Nick was seated.

"Good morning, Nick. Nice job on the shooting this morning. We really kicked the *Herald*'s ass on that identification."

Nick nodded and said nothing. He did not read the competition's stories until he'd come in and gotten some phone calls out and seen what his own story might have stirred up overnight.

"The other editors really liked your detail on the caliber of the bullet and the placement of the wound. Good stuff."

She didn't say she liked it. She said the other editors, Nick thought, catching her words, studying them like some paranoid. Is she still pissed?

"So what are you thinking about for the follow today?" Deirdre said, moving on. "Are they going to give you anything on the shooter? Do you think they're going to go after someone connected to the dead girl's family? I mean, they gotta be looking for motive, right?"

"I'm trying to track down the mother of the girls through her attorney," Nick said. "It's been a while, but he might still have a line on her. Research also ran her name through the Florida driver's license database, but it still comes up with the same address she had back when the girls were killed, and we already know she hasn't been living there. But I can't see where this woman takes three years to learn how to fire a high-powered weapon and then stakes out the killer of her daughters and drops him with a single shot from the top of a building and then somehow disappears without leaving a trace behind. And that's even going on the supposition that Ferris was the target, which no one in law enforcement has yet to state."

Nick always tried to rattle off the steps he'd taken in reporting and the lines of inquiry he'd already thought out when Deirdre called him in to ask questions that were already obvious to him. It usually stopped her. Today it didn't. She leaned back in her swivel chair and laced her fingers. Nick knew the move as a sign of trouble.

"I want to ask one thing, Nick."

He tried not to show any emotion in his face or body language that would say, *Oh, Christ, here it comes.* But he was lousy at controlling it.

Still, he stayed silent, not falling into the old question for a question, not responding by saying, *Yeah, and what's that?*

Instead he waited her out.

"You got the caliber of the gun, Nick, the .308, which you knew was a high-powered rifle round. You were the one up on the roof, and nice close-up, by the way."

He nodded, wanting to match the grin she was trying to give him, but too obstinate to do it. He was waiting for the other shoe to drop.

"So why is it that the *Herald* used the word *sniper* in their headline *and* in the body of their story and we never even mentioned it?"

She dug the *Herald* out from under the pile on her desk and held up the front page: SNIPER KILLS CHILD MOLESTER ON WAY TO COURT

Nick tried to keep a dry, unflappable look on his face.

"Attribution?"

Deirdre flipped the paper over and skimmed through the story like she was trying to find the line Nick knew was not there. If someone with any authority had called the shooting the act of a sniper, it would have been in the first paragraph of his story. No one called it that, even if it was true.

"Did they contribute that characterization to any source or member of the law enforcement team that's investigating?" he said. "I honestly didn't hear the spokesman or the detective in charge or the medical examiner that did the autopsy use the word *sniper*."

Deirdre finally looked him in the face and if anyone else had been in the room, they would have called it a look of compassion.

"Nicky. I know where you're coming from with your theory of black-and-white news," she said and Nick turned away from the look.

"You're a great reporter because you have the instincts and experience to go after your own suppositions, to prove them true."

"I'm still doing that!" Nick snapped, getting defensive.

Deirdre raised her palms. "I know. I know you are, Nick. But you're not putting it in the paper."

"When I nail it, it'll go in the paper," he said.

"It makes us sound unsure, like we're waiting for someone else to get the good stuff first. It makes us look like we're afraid to pull the trigger."

The heat was up in Nick's face now. He could feel the flush in his neck, the hot tingle on the edges of his ears.

"Is that why *we* never called Robert Walker a drunk driver in print, Deirdre?" Nick said through his teeth. "Were *we* waiting for someone else to get the goods on that guy after he killed my family? Why didn't somebody go and dig up that guy's background and pull the goddamn trigger in print?"

Now she couldn't hold his eyes. She knew the arguments he'd had with the paper's management after the accident that killed his wife and daughter. She knew Nick had tried to get the editorial writers to paint Walker as a drunken killer. But they had refused, citing journalistic standards and telling him to wait until after the trial. She knew it had hurt him.

"That situation was different, Nick. That was personal. You're an employee. It would have looked prejudicial."

"But you want me to call this guy a sniper on the front page before we know who or what he is," Nick said, trying to make the statement sound smug, but that emotion was no longer in him.

Deirdre just looked down at her desktop.

"I'll keep chasing what happens next," Nick said, getting up. "You'll get the truth in my story at eight."

As he turned to go, Deirdre couldn't help herself, as if her comeback were so ingrained in her psyche that it was like an involuntary muscle response:

"The truth is in the—"

"Yeah, yeah," Nick interrupted. "The eye of the beholder."

He didn't turn around, just kept walking out the door.

/ Chapter 11 /

When he got back to his desk, Nick started to call up the list from research but only got back to Dr. Chambliss's name when his phone rang.

"Mr. Mullins? This is Brian Dempsey. I'm a lawyer representing Margaria Cotton, the woman whose children were killed by Mr. Ferris four years ago that you wrote about in the paper today."

Nick was instantly wary. Lawyers, by profession, are not impartial. They do what they need to do to help their clients. A reporter never talks to an attorney without thinking, What's his motive?

"Yes, Mr. Dempsey. What can I do for you, sir?"

"Well, Mr. Mullins, against my advice, Ms. Cotton would like to meet with you."

"Great," Nick said and then quickly toned down his exuberance. "I'd lost touch with her, Mr. Dempsey, and didn't have a contact number or I certainly would have interviewed her for today's story."

Nick could hear the lawyer's hesitation in the beat of silence.

"Ms. Cotton has tried very hard to keep her life private after her tragedy, Mr. Mullins. But I felt duty-bound to pass on your request to speak with her and again, against my advice, she would like to meet with you first."

"First?"

"Yes, Mr. Mullins. Investigators from the Sheriff's Office are also interviewing Ms. Cotton today in my office, at one o'clock this afternoon. She would like to speak with you first."

Nick looked at the huge clock on the wall, omnipresent in the newsroom to remind everyone of their daily deadlines. It was nearly eleven.

"OK. At your office, then, Mr. Dempsey?"

"No. Ms. Cotton would like you to come to her home. She's awaiting your arrival. When you're through, I hope you could give her a ride to the Sheriff's Office in time for the detectives, if you would."

"Absolutely, sir."

The attorney gave Nick the addresses of both Cotton's home and his law office.

"And please, Mr. Mullins," he said before hanging up, "I hope you can appreciate the delicacy of this matter."

Nick could not come up with an answer to the statement before the line went quiet. He looked up again at the clock. Cotton's address was less than twenty minutes from the newsroom, thirty even if traffic was bad. He closed the research file in front of him, stuck his reporter's notebook in his pocket and told the assistant city editor that he was going out on an interview and could be reached on his cell phone if they needed him.

Standing at the elevator door, Nick could feel an electricity in his blood. You're not supposed to get giddy when you're going to talk with a woman whose children were raped and murdered. But he still gave up on waiting for the elevator and took the six flights of stairs to the parking level, two steps at a time.

/ / /

Nick looked at the address on the page of his notebook one more time and then slowly rolled up Northwest Tenth Avenue. The houses were single-story and all seemed to be painted a dusty color—pale yellow, powder blue—and even the white ones gave off a hue of bone. The yards were mottled with patches of dirt and the green grass seemed to have been robbed of its chlorophyll. The macadam road surface had been bleached a soft gray by the sun. Nick always wondered at the ability of poor and neglected neighborhoods to dull even the effects of the bright Florida sunshine. Postcard photos were never taken here.

The number he was looking for was not visible on the house where it should have been. He drove past two more before spotting an address painted above a doorway and then put the car in reverse and backed up, subtracting by lot. He pulled into the two-strip concrete drive in front of a dull beige clapboard home that must have been built in the early 1960s. But the roof was newly shingled. There was a potted red geranium on the front step and the porch had been swept clean. When Nick raised his hand to knock, the inside door opened before his knuckles touched wood.

"Good morning, Mr. Mullins," the woman's voice said.

"Ms. Cotton?" Nick said, though he still could only see her dark figure in the shadows of the room.

"Please," she said, pushing open the screen door for him to enter. Nick took note of the thin forearm, mottled as much as the grass yard, with patches of pink marring the naturally dark skin.

"Thank you, ma'am," Nick said, taking two steps into a darkened living room where the odor of medicine and potpourri battled one another.

When his eyes adjusted he could see the features of Margaria Cotton's face and small figure. They had changed over the years, pulled perhaps by the gravity of grief, as if every bone and every centimeter of skin had been attached to a weight. Her shoulders were slumped, her back, which had been proudly stiff when she sat in the courtroom for Ferris's sentencing, was bowed forward. Her cheekbones were sharp, but in the way of malnutrition versus some role of fashion. Nick, as was his way, preferred to watch her eyes, which still held the intelligence and strength that he had noted three years ago. She did the same, meeting his gaze, not with defiance, but more as a way of showing her confidence and lack of pretension.

"Can I get you something, Mr. Mullins? Coffee? Water?" she said while extending her hand to show him a seat.

"No. Thank you. I'm fine, ma'am."

The woman nodded and took a seat opposite him on a sofa. A low, glass-topped table separated them. Nick noted the stack of newspapers on one end, the *Daily News* and, he could tell by the style of the type, the *Herald,* and at least one out-of-town publication.

"I was hoping to get in touch with you, Ms. Cotton," he began. "I assume that you have heard of the shooting death of Mr. Ferris."

"Yes," she said, folding her hands in her lap. "Mr. Dempsey called me yesterday. And I read it in the newspapers this morning." She too looked over at the papers.

"I read the news every day, Mr. Mullins. I suppose it isn't always healthy to let all that ugliness inside my house," she said, but did not look around herself when she made the comment. Nick, however, took the opportunity to take in the small wooden cross mounted on the wall behind her. It was flanked by the elementary school photos of what he recognized as her daughters. They were the same photos that his newspaper had used during the coverage of their killing. The same computer-stored photos had run in this morning's edition.

"I know it might sound kind of, you know, sick," she said, bringing his attention back to her eyes. "But there is something about the tragedies of others, Mr. Mullins, that helps remind me that I am not the only one suffering."

Nick nodded his head.

"I am sorry about your children, Ms. Cotton," he said, motioning slightly to the photos behind her with his eyes.

"You were very kind to us in your stories, Mr. Mullins. There was a word my minister used for it, I forget . . ." She closed her eyes for a moment, searching. "Compassion. That was it. He said your writing had compassion in it."

Again, all Nick could do was nod. He noted the diction in her conversation. A poor black woman, but one who was educated, maybe even well read. She went out of her way to choose her words in the presence of someone like Nick, only letting an occasional slip of slang enter her sentences. It was perhaps an unconscious habit she fell into when she wanted her listener to be comfortable. Nick did the same thing when he was with southerners, slipping into a minor drawl that did not belong to him. His daughters always noticed and would tell him later that he had embarrassed them. He shook off the recollection and reached into his back pocket. He took out the notebook and drew a pen from his shirt, a signal that he was here to work.

"I'm sorry, Ms. Cotton. I don't want to sound simple here, but in your position, these years later, I was calling to find out what your reaction to Mr. Ferris's death might be."

The woman went quiet for several moments, but Nick had learned long ago not to give up on any interviewees other than politicians when he could see in their eyes that they were forming an answer to his questions, testing a reply in their mind.

"I'm sorry, Mr. Mullins," she finally said. "I guess I wanted to say relief, or maybe some kind of feel of justice. But I can't say I have that. I have long given judgment up to the Lord Himself, and that man is meeting his Maker this very morning on his own terms," she said with a certainty that Nick was always befuddled by with people of faith.

"No, sir, I would have to tell you, Mr. Mullins, that I don't believe that any kind of vision of Mr. Ferris has entered my mind for some time. I believe he was already gone in my mind."

"But you still wanted to see me," Nick said. "Is there something that you wanted to say about the shooting?"

"Only that I was bothered by some things in the newspapers, not yours, of course, that said maybe I or my people might have done something to get revenge for my girls."

"OK," Nick said, without taking his eyes off hers.

"And we did not do anything. I did not," she said, bringing the strength back into her voice that had been there during Ferris's trial.

Nick nodded and wrote on the pad, a nonsensical squiggle that the woman could not see, just to make her know she was being heard.

"Revenge is not in my blood, or my family's blood, Mr. Mullins," she said. "And I cannot think of anyone I know who would have been wanting to kill Mr. Ferris."

"I think the detectives will have to look at any and all possibilities, Ms. Cotton," Nick said. "I would think that's why they want to interview you, ma'am, not because of anything that was put into the newspaper."

He stopped. Wondering why he was defending himself.

"But since I am here, has anyone contacted you, Ms. Cotton? Anyone, say, on the phone? Or anonymously written you, someone who might have sounded like they were doing this on your behalf? You know, like taking action because they felt you deserved closure or something?"

Nick hated even using the word. There was no such thing. Closure. It was a buzzword someone came up with and then it spread like kudzu into the vernacular.

"No, sir," she said, then hesitated, not speaking as she held up the fingers of her right hand, as though stopping time.

"Mr. Dempsey did give me a whole bunch of letters after the trial from folks sending me sympathy," she said after gathering her memories. "Sometimes he still does. I put them all in a box, and I think it's very kind."

"Has he brought you anything recently?" Nick said. The mention of paper piqued his interest. Something written and verified, especially with a postage mark, was manna for a journalist. It was the fuel for a paper trail.

"I can't say I recall the last time," Cotton said. "Might have been in the fall. I am not much for keepin' track of time anymore, Mr. Mullins."

"Any names in the box that were familiar, Ms. Cotton?" Nick pressed, envisioning a list of names, something he could use, something solid he could trace.

"Well, I don't really pay much attention to the names, sir. I read the ones from the mothers mostly," she said and a wistful look came into her face, making Nick feel a twinge of guilt at his grilling. But not too guilty.

"Could I perhaps take a look at the letters, Ms. Cotton? Just sort of go through the names, I mean. I don't want to pry," Nick said, lying. Of course he wanted to pry. It's what reporters did.

"I would have to look up in my closets to find them. I believe that's where I might have stored that box away."

Nick looked at his watch. It was late. They would have to leave soon for her to make her appointment with the detectives. But he didn't know what to ask.

"Ms. Cotton, has anyone related to Mr. Ferris, or even someone who said they knew him, ever come to speak to you or even introduce themselves?"

Nick watched her close her eyes, searching again for a picture of the past.

"His brother," she said, her eyes still closed. Then she opened them. "His brother seen me in the hall outside the court and walked up to me on that day when the jury found him guilty."

"And he talked with you?" Nick said, prodding her.

"He said he was sorry about what happened. I could see it in his eyes, Mr. Mullins, that he was hurtin'."

"You do seem to have that ability, Ms. Cotton," Nick said, making a guess as to why he was here. "To pick up on people's pain."

This time she looked straight into Nick's face, studying it, the creases in his brow, the lines at the corners of his eyes.

"I read about your family, Mr. Mullins. I recognized your name right off and remembered the way you had with your words, that compassion. It was your wife and daughter, so you know how it is when somebody needs that," she said. "Maybe someone else is going to need that now."

Nick looked down at his open notebook. He had yet to enter a word with any meaning or usefulness in his "exclusive" interview.

"Is that why I'm here, Ms. Cotton?" he finally said, not wanting to look in her eyes, not wanting her to see his. "Is that why you asked to see me? Because of my compassion?"

He felt her nod more than saw it.

"I read the newspapers a lot, Mr. Mullins," she said. "Sometimes I can feel people in there, in the words. I learned that by readin' what happened to me, to my family. And like I said, you had that feeling in your words before."

"But not now?" Nick said, wanting her to continue.

"I watched the paper to see when you got back to your job. I have seen your stories now and compared them with before. And if you don't mind my saying so, sir . . . you changed," she said without taking her eyes off him. "The pain changed you."

Nick stared at her, this small black woman, telling him about his heart with a plain open face that did not show sympathy or judgment, or assess fault.

"Compassion," she said. "I believe you are losin' that, Mr. Mullins. And I believe that would be a terrible thing in the end, sir."

/ Chapter 12 /

Nick was still rolling Margaria Cotton's words around in his head when he got back to the office. While he'd been dropping her off in front of the Broward Sheriff's Office, Detective Hargrave and his partner, the big sergeant, had been just getting out of their unmarked Crown Vic. Detectives being what they are, Nick knew they'd check out the driver who was bringing Cotton to see them. Even the stone-faced Hargrave could not cover the look of consternation on his face. The big man had turned around just as they were entering a side door for employees and officers only and given him a sorry shake of his head.

Now, as Nick was making his way to his desk, a sports editor grinned at him and said, "Hi, Nick. How you doing?"

The greeting snapped his concentration at first, and then piled onto Cotton's observation.

"Hey, Stevie. Alright," Nick answered.

Few people in the place bothered to talk to him these days. The sports guy, Steve Bryant, had told him it was because they didn't know what to say after Nick returned to work following the accident. The first few weeks, there were the quiet condolences. He'd nodded, thanked them. But he'd never been a gregarious sort. He'd have an occasional beer with the other reporters after a late shift, would toss a good-natured barb across the desk like the one he'd received from Hirschman about the roof photo. But Steve had confided that if Nick was already intimidating with his intensity before the tragedy, he was downright scary when he'd returned.

Loss of compassion? Like Ms. Cotton had said? A scene from an old movie flashed into Nick's head. A hard-core mercenary is told during a firefight that he's bleeding. The guy's rebuttal: I ain't got time to bleed.

When he got to his desk there was a press release lying in the middle, a one-sheet write-up that had been faxed by the Sheriff's Office as it had been to every news organization in three counties. Cameron had given everyone all the updated information that Nick had already put in his story for this morning's edition, including the caliber of the bullet. While his computer was coming up, Nick answered the blinking light on his phone. Three of four messages were from readers who wanted him to know how glad they were that Ferris had been shot, saving them the cost of another trial "for that animal." None left a name. The fourth call was from Cameron. There was a distinct edge in his voice:

"Nick. Nice job this morning doing an interview of a witness before the detectives could even get to her. Man, you're gumming this one up, pal."

Cameron paused, maybe for effect, maybe because he didn't want to say what he had to say next.

"Detective Hargrave wants to see you himself this afternoon about four. I'll assume you'll be here. Believe me, Nick, it might be a once-in-a-lifetime offer. But I'm going to have to be in the room with you, so ease up, eh?"

Nick replayed the message, twice, and then sat back, thinking it through. Hargrave, the wordless one, the man who always turned his back on the media, wanted a sitdown. Did he think Nick had gotten something from Cotton he hadn't? Maybe he thought she knew the people who had worn the pictures of Cotton's girls during the trial. That would sure as hell be one of Nick's moves if he was looking for someone with motive. There had been news coverage of the trial. Nick would have to call Matt over at Channel 10 to see if their film was being subpoenaed. But most of those video shots would have been of the front of the courtroom, not of the gallery. Hargrave also would have known from Cameron that Nick hadn't covered the trial. He looked up over the cubicles to see if the court reporter was still at her desk. She might have quoted some of the people who'd worn the buttons and had some names and contact numbers. He looked at his watch. It was two o'clock. If the meeting with Hargrave took a while, he'd be pushing deadline later in the day. To be safe he opened up a new screen on his computer and started typing a rough draft of tomorrow's follow-up story, which at this point wouldn't be much different factually from today's, other than planting a quote or two from Ms. Cotton. He could always hope that Hargrave would let loose with something, but he wasn't planning on it.

It took him an hour to bang out 350 decent words that could pass for a Saturday story on its own if it had to. At this point, he'd have to lead with the only fresh thing he had, which was that police were talking with the mother of the slain children in connection with Ferris's killing and the investigation was continuing. Nick knew it was bullshit. The investigation was always continuing and most people with half a brain would know that the cops would talk with the girl's mom. But he also knew that if you phrased it just right, the general reading public would skim it, figure it was close enough to news and give themselves something to gab about at dinner with their friends on Saturday night:

"How 'bout that shooting downtown? The pedophile guy?"
"Yeah, I saw they were talking to the mom of the girls he killed."
"Like she wouldn't have a big smile on her face, eh?"
"Can you believe they were gonna let the guy off?"
"The system is all fucked up, you know?"
"I'd of hired somebody to kill him if I was her."
"Yeah?"

"Damn straight."

When Nick was finished with the draft, he stored it away and turned off the computer. He'd have enough time to stop at the café downstairs and grab a cup of coffee and maybe one of those plastic-wrapped sandwiches and he could eat on the way over to the Sheriff's Office. He hadn't bothered to look at the rest of the research files that Lori had sent. Later, if he got back early, he thought. Right now he was already getting cranked up for Hargrave. What the hell was the guy going to say? Just chew him out? Hell, he could take that without a sweat. He hadn't put anything unethical in the story today, and sure as hell nothing that was going to stink up the investigation. The dead man's name and the caliber of the bullet? The killer knew the name would come out and the bullet caliber was only good in dismissing some of the nut jobs who would call the cops claiming they'd done the shooting. *Oh, yeah? What'd you do him with? A nine-millimeter, you say? Good-bye. Don't call back again.*

No, whatever Hargrave had in mind would be something more than the simple stuff, Nick thought, trying to prepare. But hell with it, he finally whispered to himself, better not to speculate, just let it fall the way it was going to fall.

/ / /

Nick walked through the front doors of the sheriff's administration building at 3:50 PM. As soon as the wash of air-conditioning swept over him he was taking the car keys out of his pocket, fishing the cell phone off his belt, checking to see if he had a pack of gum in his shirt, the foil of which would set off the metal detectors. While he stood in line waiting for his turn to pass through the security screen, he looked up into the huge ornate rotunda. The building had been constructed a few years ago to replace what had been little more than a retrofitted warehouse south of the city. The entryway soared up several floors to an atrium roof that let in the signature sunshine of South Florida. Nick thought it far too ostentatious for a cop shop. But what the hell. Your tax dollars at work.

The deputy on the other side of the electronic gateway nodded as Nick passed through without a beep.

"Where are you visiting today, sir?"

"Media relations," Nick said and tipped his head to the left where the doors to Joel Cameron's department were located. He watched for a change in the young officer's face. Did it change when he was told the press was in the house? But the kid just nodded and was already on to the next person passing through the hoops of post-9/11 decorum. Nick gathered his stuff from a plastic bowl and moved on.

The receptionist just inside Cameron's office recognized Nick immediately, smiled, asked how he was doing.

"Fine, how are you?" Nick didn't come here often. Most of his work was done out in the streets or by phone. If he was meeting an inside source, it was usually done at a designated lunch spot, Houston's on Federal Highway, Hot Dog Heaven on Sunrise. Nick stole a look down the hall into the office. It had the same setup as the newsroom, a smaller version, but the same fabric-covered separators that made you think you had a space of your own. Cameron was at the end of the created hallway, heading his way.

"Thanks for being on time, Nick," Cameron said, moving briskly, not offering a hand or a greeting. He was carrying a legal pad and checking his shirt pocket for a pen. Nick noted that the pad was brand-new, nothing yet on the top page.

"The detectives want us to meet them upstairs in a conference room," Cameron said, opening the door to the lobby and holding it for Nick. "We'll have to get you a pass."

Nick shrugged at Cameron's iciness. The media officer had already told Nick that Hargrave was a hard-ass who never talked to the press, or even Cameron, for that matter. Now he'd been told to bring a seasoned police reporter in for a private meet. Nick knew Joel would not only be nervous about what might be said, but also pissed if he had to explain to the rest of the media types who would be howling if word got out of such an exclusive.

While Nick was passing his driver's license and newspaper I.D. through the bulletproof glass at the admittance office, he said, "So, you gonna give me a clue here as to what's going on, Joel?"

"I can't say that I even have a clue," Cameron said, still not looking Nick in the eye. "If Hargrave wanted to leak something to you, Nick, he should've just called you on the phone like the rest of your sources do."

Yeah, Nick thought, Cameron's pissed.

When the officers inside the security fishbowl passed a temporary I.D. back at Nick, he clipped the badge onto his shirt pocket, listened for the electronic click of the lock on the adjoining door and then followed Cameron into the main offices. They immediately took a right and got onto an escalator rolling up to the second floor. When did they start putting escalators into police headquarters? Nick thought as they rose. The world, my man, has changed.

At the end of a hallway that Nick knew led to the executive offices, Cameron stopped and hesitated at a door just shy of the double entrance to the sheriff's own suite. He carefully knocked twice and then entered, again holding open the door so that Nick would have to walk through first. Nick quickly recognized the room as the conference area where he had once conducted an interview with the sheriff during an election year. Nick had always hated politics, but, as the senior police reporter, it was in his job description to cover the sheriff's race. The only redeeming aspect was that the assignment only had to be done once every four years.

The room was dominated by a long, polished maple conference table and at the other end sat Hargrave and a sheriff's lieutenant Nick recognized as head of special operations. Against the wall behind them stood a middle-aged man whom Nick judged to be a lawyer by the cut of his suit and tie. He had a file opened in his hands and did not look up as they entered, never a good sign, Nick thought. It was Cameron's job to make introductions.

"Gentlemen," he began, a slight catch in his throat. "Mr. Mullins is here as requested. Mr. Mullins, this is Lieutenant Steve Canfield."

Canfield stood up as Nick worked his way down the length of the table on the side opposite Hargrave and offered his hand.

"I believe we've met," he said, "at one news conference or another."

Nick had had few dealings with Canfield but respected him. He had started as a street cop and rose to be commander of the department's SWAT operations and then implemented the first community policing program as a captain in a rough neighborhood in the northwest section of the county.

"It was actually during a training exercise at the abandoned Margate hospital when you were running SWAT, sir," Nick said, shaking the lieutenant's hand. "Probably four, five years ago when I was putting together a magazine piece."

"Yes, I think you're right," he said and then sat.

Nick detected a movement from the mystery man when he had mentioned the SWAT exercise. The man had slightly lowered his file and Nick caught his eyes peering at him over the top edge of the paperwork.

"And you know Detective Hargrave," Cameron said, "who you met the other day."

Hargrave nodded but did not look up from his hands, which were clasped and resting on the table before him. Nick extended his own hand but, instead of presenting a handshake, turned his palm up to show the indentations that were still visible from its time pressed into the stones on the roof of the diagnostic center.

"Yesterday, in fact," Nick said and then withdrew the hand.

"OK, please," Lieutenant Canfield quickly said. "Fellas, let's sit and talk about some concerns."

As they pulled out chairs, Nick could see Cameron's uneasiness as he cut his eyes from the lieutenant to the man still standing at the wall. Canfield picked up on the mood of the room.

"Guys, this is Agent Fitzgerald, who is an observer from a, uh, federal agency who will be sitting in."

Fitzgerald raised his eyes again and nodded. Hargrave stared at his hands. Cameron said nothing, but scratched something onto the pad he'd now placed on the table.

"OK. We all know why we're here," Canfield began.

No one at the table responded. The statement had perhaps caught them all cynically thinking, No, we don't know why the hell we're here. Why don't you tell us?

"Detective, you've got a homicide case that's still fresh. I know you want to work that with every advantage available, and I know you've got your methods.

"Mr. Mullins, you've got a job to do as a member of the press covering this incident and we all respect that. You've been quick to come up with information that you're presenting to the public, and we respect that too."

Both men nodded their agreement to the obvious and let the silence force Canfield into saying something they didn't already know.

"We would normally let these things run their course," the lieutenant continued. "But Mr. Fitzgerald here is now connected peripherally to the case because his agency has been alerted to all shooting incidents in which a sniper might have been involved.

"They have been using a computer-assisted alert system to red-flag reports nationwide and then dispatching agents to observe and be made aware of any, uh, protocols that might match up and be useful to them."

Protocols? Nick was watching the agent to see if the man was going to make any acknowledgment of the lieutenant's useless bureaucratic jargon.

"Sniper shootings?" Nick suddenly said, again using his big mouth to get at least some kind of reaction, juggle things up a bit and see if anything fell. "You're specifically looking at sniper shootings?" He took out his notebook. Deirdre wanted to use *sniper* in the story, she was going to get it now.

The mystery man simply looked up over his file and fixed an unreadable, mannequinlike look at Nick's face.

"I'm not at liberty to say."

Nick loved that form of no comment. "Not at liberty." "I cannot confirm nor deny." "Beyond my purview." Everybody's a lawyer these days. But it rarely slowed him down.

"And the reason you're letting me in is that you put this sniper homicide on a fast track, and you wanna know what I know when I know it instead of waiting to read the paper tomorrow?" he said, since no one else was going to explain it.

He looked across the table at Hargrave, who was still studying his interlaced fingers, but Nick noticed the top edges of his sharp cheeks rise slightly as he suppressed a grin.

"OK. Yeah, Nick. It's on a fast track," Canfield jumped in. "And as soon as Mr. Fitzgerald knows all that we know so he can rule out that this particular shooting has any interest for his agency, he'll thank us and get on with the work he's been assigned to."

That's why Nick liked the guy. Even if he knew Mr. Federal Agency was drilling into the back of his head with his stone-cold eyes, Canfield was going to just lay it out on the table in plain English.

"So you're officially looking for a sniper, not a drive-by, not a random shooting?" Nick said, just to make sure.

"Yeah," Canfield said. "That's official."

Nick was impressed. A sniper and the presence of the feds. This was a new twist on homeland security. He didn't write anything down, he just took a moment to let the admission sink in.

"So the ball's in your court, Nick," Canfield said.

Nick felt Cameron shift in the chair beside him. This was touchy stuff, asking a journalist to divulge information before publication. Nick knew he could easily fall back on the old freedom-of-the-press line and walk away. But he was also too damned intrigued by the exclusivity he would gain by being on the inside. And besides, as far as he knew, he didn't have squat that they wouldn't already have learned.

"OK, Steve," Nick said, using the old first-name trick. "First of all, I can't give up the names of any sources."

"We know that, Nick. We know you've got a dozen guys in the Sheriff's Office that like to talk to you. We know that's where you got Ferris's name and probably the caliber of the bullet. What we need you to tell us is whether you had some sort of early knowledge of the rooftop. We would like to know what Ferris's family might have said to you that you didn't put in the paper. And we'd like to know what Ms. Cotton told you in her interview this morning."

"Geez. Anything else, Steve?" Nick said, talking to the lieutenant but looking at Hargrave.

"Yeah." The detective finally looked up from his hands and asked directly across the table into the reporter's face, "What did the witness from the children's center tell you about a man he saw coming down off the roof before we got there?"

The question caused the federal agent to lower his file to the side of his thigh. Canfield also seemed to move his elbows forward on the table. Nick started to turn toward Cameron, who had obviously reported the encounter to the detectives, but stopped himself.

"You mean the little guy who came into work at eight?" Nick said, already knowing the answer. "The guy said he thought it was one of yours, a SWAT officer," Nick said, turning his eyes to Canfield. "Dressed in black and carrying a bag."

"Did he give you a description of the man?"

The question came from the wall, from Fitzgerald. Nick was surprised by the high, scratchy timbre of the man's voice. He thought all federal agents learned to modulate their voices in training. The man was focused, though, intensely. Nick pictured a flier posted on the bulletin board of the FBI with large black print: SNIPER. *If you see this man . . .*

"No. I was trying to work him when Joel came up to give me a message and then the guy, Dennis was his name, got antsy and walked away," Nick said, trying not to indict Cameron. "Why? Isn't that what he gave you guys? I mean, you've interviewed him, right?"

Hargrave looked up at Nick. "Yeah, we talked to him. Same stuff. Said the guy was above-average build, whatever the hell that means, and had a balaclava covering most of his face. He thought he was white, and I emphasize the word *thought*," the detective said, cutting his eyes over at the fed.

"OK, how about the roof business?" Canfield said.

"Nobody tipped me to that," Nick said. "The photographer I was with noted the blood spatter on the wall next to the steps, lower than the victim's height. I noticed that the cops were looking up and behind us at the crime scene. I just put two and two together."

Hargrave and Canfield glanced at each other. Nick was satisfied that he hadn't used the detective's name as the one whose eyes on the rooftop had given it away.

"OK. The families?"

"I only talked to Ferris's sister-in-law, at her house trailer. She didn't sound like she was terribly crushed by the whole thing, but not exactly relieved either," Nick said. "I got the sense that her husband had been carrying his brother's load for a long time."

"Enough of a burden to want to finish him off?" Hargrave said.

"That wasn't the feel. More like enough to just bury him and try to forget," Nick said, but he was getting tired of the one-way conversation. "Why, did he say something different to you?"

He was talking directly to Hargrave, who hesitated, looked at his lieutenant and then said, "No. We checked him out with his boss and two other workers who put him in the warehouse at the time of the shooting. He isn't a suspect. He didn't say good riddance. He didn't cry. He just asked when he could pick up the body."

Nick jotted something on his reporter's pad. The room went quiet for a moment. The rules were being set.

"Robert Ferris is not a suspect?" Nick said, looking directly into Hargrave's eyes, making sure he was getting the comment straight.

"Not at this time."

Nick knew it was a fallback position, but OK, never say never, he'd give him that.

"OK, Nick. How about Ms. Cotton?" Canfield said, trying to swing the information tide back to his side. "You got to her before we did. What did she tell you?"

"Not much," Nick said, rebuilding the scene in his head. "That she wasn't the kind of person to look for retribution. She's religious but isn't going for that eye-for-an-eye thing."

The heard-that-a-million-times feel in the room was as clear as if all three law enforcement officers had covered their mouths and yawned.

"She said she didn't know anyone who would have done Ferris, and she hadn't had any suspicious visitors or contacts that would lead her to believe anyone would shoot the guy for her."

As he said it, Nick's head jumped to a vision of the box of letters that Ms. Cotton had told him about. He should have looked at them. He should have taken down some names. But should he mention it to this group? Hell, if they'd asked the woman the same questions he had and she told them about the letters, they would probably have the box in the back room already. But just in case he jotted down "go back to Cotton on letters" in his notebook and flipped the page.

"OK, now what are you going to give me?"

Canfield started to say something, then stopped.

Nick looked over at the press officer. "You know," he said. "The reason I came in here, agreed to this trade of information?"

Cameron cut his eyes the other way. *Not my call*, he was saying. *I'm just taking orders.*

"Well, you've already got the brother declared a nonsuspect. That isn't out yet," Canfield finally spoke up.

"At this time," Hargrave said off to the side.

Nick went from face to face. All eyes were down. They always knew more than they told you. Always.

"How about ballistics?" he said, trying to pry something loose.

"You've already got that, Nick. It was a .308. Actually, a Federal Match loaded with the 168-grain Boat Tail Hollow Point," Canfield said.

Nick jotted down the name. He didn't know shit about bullets. But that didn't matter much to his readers.

"Federal Match?" he said, cutting his eyes to the agent, who was still standing. "Does that mean it only comes from the military?"

The agent's eyes lifted and Nick detected a muscle twitch in the guy's jaw as it tightened. OK. If you were a poker player, that was a tell. Did mention of the military trip the guy?

"No, not at all," Canfield said quickly. "It's a round that's on the civilian and law enforcement market. Anyone could buy it."

"Any prints on the casing?" Nick said, working it.

"Never found a casing," Hargrave answered, not looking up until he asked his own question: "Did you?"

Nick let it pass. He knew his reputation would have already been passed to Hargrave. He'd never keep something that vital to a case to himself. It was more than unethical, it would have been stupid. Instead he took the opportunity to nail an attribution for the rooftop site.

"So you're saying the kill shot was taken from the roof?"

Canfield nodded. The creases in Hargrave's brow made it clear he was in pain giving such information to a reporter. Nick let it sit for a moment and then carefully set up his next question, wanting to watch the reaction, see which of the men in the room clenched his teeth the hardest, or breathed deepest, or just got up and walked out.

"So, you're working the angle that it's a military sniper or a law enforcement sniper?"

No one flinched. The fed even controlled his jaw muscle. Everyone was in control, almost like they'd expected the question and rehearsed. Even Nick knew by now that it would be Canfield's job to answer the delicate ones.

"We would be remiss in our duty, Nick, not to pursue all possibilities."

Nick let the standard answer hang in the air for a moment, but couldn't control himself.

"So you guys learned a lesson from the D.C. Beltway, eh?"

This time the federal officer's eyes came up and seared into Nick's. Gotcha, Nick thought.

In the fall of 2002, the Beltway sniper case had scared the hell out of Washington, D.C., and surrounding Virginia when ten innocent people had been killed, shot dead by a cold-blooded sniper from long distances as they were going about their daily lives. One was filling her tank at a gas station. Another was carrying groceries. Another picking up her son at school. In the flurry that built after the second shooting, the rumors and assumptions flew. The speculation, fed by so-called sources from the FBI and both the state and local police departments, was that a disturbed soldier, active or retired, or some rampaging cop was serially wreaking havoc. The shots were too difficult. The skill in striking and then disappearing was too well planned and logistical. The weaponry too sophisticated.

When the killer was finally caught, it turned out to be some teenager firing from the trunk of a car driven by the boy's pissed-off and most likely deranged stepfather. Amateurs. The speculators had been all wrong.

"Like your fellow seers in the media didn't like jumping on that? Like they had some fucking movie playing out," Hargrave mumbled.

"No argument there, Detective," Nick said. "No one's finest hour on that one."

In the following silence, Canfield shoved his chair back, signaling an end to the meeting. Nick flipped his notebook closed. The fed pushed off the wall with one hip, turned without a word and started out the adjoining door.

"OK, Nick. Please keep in touch through Mr. Cameron's office," Canfield said as he stood and offered his hand.

"I will," Nick said, shaking the lieutenant's hand over the table.

Hargrave stood during the formality and met Nick's eyes, his own holding a look devoid of hostility or superiority. The softened lines surprised Nick, and forced his eyebrows to rise in anticipation.

"Check you later," the detective said, a phrase that in one way may have said nothing. But Nick didn't think so. There was a crack in the ice.

"Anytime," he said, taking the man's hand, almost skeletal in its thinness and sharp protrusions of knuckle and bone. But once again he noted the taut cablelike muscles in the detective's forearm. I would not want to be caught in that guy's grip in a dark alley, he thought and carried his own warning out the door.

/ / /

When Nick got back to the newsroom it was almost six PM. It was the busiest part of the day, when reporters had all come back into the house after being out on assignment, when assistant city editors were working line by line to get through each of their charges' daily stories, asking questions, getting clarification, trying to make sure photographs taken during the day were matched up with the right reports and generally busting hump to clear the decks before deadline.

He stopped at the city desk to tell the assistant in charge of the cop shift that he had a story coming as a follow on the jail shooting.

"Yeah, Deirdre said you'd have something," the editor said as he looked through a sheaf of papers that Nick knew was a printout of tomorrow's story budget. Man, that woman was something, he thought, shaking his head, but with a smirk of respect at the corners of his mouth.

"How much space do you think you need?"

Nick knew the question was really eighty percent rhetorical. By this time of day, most of the paper would already have been laid out and story lengths pretty much decided. He also knew the business, this paper in particular, and knew what length would be acceptable and wouldn't put a twist in anyone's shorts.

"Twelve to fifteen inches should be enough," he said.

"Sounds good," the editor said and looked at his watch. "You've got two hours, man. Early deadline because of the breaking stuff coming in late from Miami on the mayor being indicted."

Nick just nodded and moved away. Two hours to compose four or five hundred words. Easy. He might even get home to eat dinner with Carly. That was sometimes the blessing of early deadlines.

"Oh, and Nick," the editor said as he started to walk away. "Call that story VIGILANTE3, and we'll use file art on Ferris again."

Vigilante. Shit, thought Nick. Where did they get that? TV? The *Herald*'s Web page? He hadn't even written the piece and they were jumping to conclusions. Go write the story, Nick told himself. Go home. Keep your mouth shut.

At his desk Nick charged up the computer and ignored the blinking message light on his phone. The top of the story was already in his head and he clicked it off on the keyboard:

> *On the hunt for a sniper with an unknown motive, police yesterday began a widespread investigation to track down the executioner of convicted child molester and murderer Steven Ferris.*

Interviewing members of the Ferris family, the mother of the two children Ferris abused and killed and a witness who may have seen the triggerman Friday morning, sheriff's detectives put their efforts on a fast track to find the marksman who shot Ferris inside the fences of their own jail.

From there Nick rolled through the piece like a simple game of eight ball: quotes from Canfield confirming they were looking for a sniper, all of the statements from Margaria Cotton that Nick thought were relevant, the admission by Hargrave that Ferris's brother was not a suspect. Even if he was being given special access, Nick still wasn't obliged to ease up on his own reporting. He included the quotes from the witness who had seen someone dressed in black and carrying a satchel leaving the roof of the building across the street just moments after the shooting. Even though he knew it would be questioned by the editors, Nick omitted the worker's name. He knew that the guy would freak out if he saw his identity in print and would swamp the paper with complaints that Nick had set him up to be a target of the killer. And who knew if he wouldn't be right? The editors didn't like unnamed sources and Nick would have to explain it, but he figured he was on solid ethical ground.

The other thing he left out was the presence of the federal agent. It wasn't necessarily a favor. Nick still didn't know what agency this Fitzgerald guy was from. And other than following similar shooting reports, he had no idea why the hell the guy was here. The way he'd twitched up when asked about a military sniper made Nick nervous. Were the feds looking for a nutcase off the reservation of a military base? Had someone from the VA with a trigger finger gone wacky? Figuring no other media outlet was even aware of the feds' involvement, Nick decided to work the angle a few days, call a friend at the local FBI office. He might have just put it off as some weapons-tracing program ATF was running, but that wouldn't "fast-track" this specific investigation as Canfield had explained. And he sure as hell wouldn't have prompted the Sheriff's Office into letting a journalist like Nick into the inner circle. Something was humming on a higher level and he put it on his priority list to find out where Fitzgerald had come from.

After maxing out the story at exactly sixteen inches, Nick read it through one more time for spelling of names and attributions, made an electronic copy for himself and with a touch of a button shipped it to his editor. He slid his chair back and looked over at the metro desk to let him know and saw a knot of folks, including his man, an assignment editor and a woman from the photo department having a close conversation. This sort of gathering was always ominous, and ninety-nine percent of the time they'd end their little conclave by looking for someone to do something for them.

Nick pulled his chair back up to his desk and gave full concentration to his keyboard. It was seven thirty. He wanted to go home. He needed to be with Carly. Friday nights had been set aside for movies and popcorn and he'd been mostly true to that. He'd made a lot of those promises after the accident. He'd been guilty of not showing up on Friday nights, working big weekend pieces for the Sunday edition. He'd shortchanged his family. He hadn't been there when they needed him.

When he took a chance and glanced over at the group, the photo editor was shaking her head and walking away. The assignment guy was looking at his watch. And Nick's editor just shrugged his shoulders and headed Nick's way.

"Hey, Nick. How's that piece coming?"

"Pretty close," Nick said. He hated lying. He'd always hated lying.

"Good, man. 'Cause we've got a situation."

Nick pushed his chair back. "Yeah?"

"Yeah. There's a multicar accident out on I-95 down near the Hollywood Boulevard exit and, you know, traffic is hell and backed up all the way to the Dade County line."

"Injuries?" Nick said, letting a forced passivity mask his face.

"Yeah. But we don't know how serious. We've got a couple of reporters on their way."

Nick had done this dance a couple of times since he'd come back to work, and he felt a twinge of sympathy for the guy. But he was a police reporter. It was still what he did and in his business death was a regular staple of the news cycle.

"Those guys will do the scene, Nick, so we don't need you to go out there, OK?" the editor quickly said, trying to soften it. "But we're going to need you to do rewrite, you know, so we can try to make deadline with it."

"Yeah, sure. OK," Nick said, turning his chair and bellying back up to his keyboard. "Just give 'em my extension. I'll take the feeds." He did not look back at the editor's face and instead focused on the screen in front of him.

"And I'll ship this other piece to you in a minute."

"Thanks, Nick. I mean, you know, thanks."

Nick waved him off and let his fingertips start snapping at the keys. He called up a street schematic of the accident location on MapQuest. He tried to visualize the businesses and major landmarks along that stretch of interstate from memory. But the scenes in his head kept jumping back to December, two years ago. *Christmas decorations on the pods around him. Diane Lade with her inevitable miniature tree on top of her computer terminal. An editor's voice: "Nick, we got some kind of wreck up in Deerfield Beach. Somebody T-boned a family van. Sounds like it might be a good story."*

His ringing phone snapped him back.

"Hey, Nick. Kevin Davis—I hear you're doing rewrite?"

"Yeah, Kev. You out there yet?"

"Just got here. Man, the traffic is way backed up. It looks like four or five cars from here. The location is about two hundred yards north of the Sterling Road on-ramp in the northbound lanes. I'll call you back when I get up there and see what's what."

Nick hung up and went back to his screen and tried to block out Christmas Eve.

He'd been wishing only that the night would end so he could go home and help lay out presents for his kids. He was looking for the swirl of blue cop lights and red ambulance strobes. He was walking up to the scene smelling the odor of raw gasoline and burnt rubber and recognized a motor patrolman he knew as a friend but was puzzled by the look on the guy's face. He got a glance at the wreckage in the middle of the intersection. Steel twisting in the shine of headlights. Maroon color. Same as his own van.

"Hey, Nick?" The photo editor's voice turned his head as she approached. "We've got this digital stuff that Lou got from the accident scene."

She laid the printed photos on his desk.

"He's sending them in from his laptop so we can make deadline. Thought maybe they'd help if you, like, needed a visual to put the story together."

Nick nodded, thanked her, but when she turned to go he shoved the prints over to the corner of his desk, partway under a stack of old newspapers.

In between the front of a squad car and the back end of a rescue vehicle he focused on a torn fiberglass bumper that had been split in two and could make out the jagged crease across a University of Florida Gator sticker that his wife had jokingly stuck on their bumper just a few weeks earlier and he felt the constriction, like a knot of physical fear, rising up to choke him. He took three more steps toward the wreckage before his friend the patrolman could get to him and the view opened up to reveal a yellow sheet, that fucking yellow sheet, already spread over something in the road. He could feel someone's arms wrapping around his shoulders, more cops, more hands holding him back, and then he felt the rip of sound and pain that scorched the back of his throat when he started screaming.

"Hey, Nick, it's Kevin," the voice said and Nick realized that somehow he'd picked up the ringing phone without thinking about it.

"Yeah." Nick managed to cough out a response.

"Hey, man, you alright?"

Nick was staring out into the newsroom, seeing something he could not banish from the inside of his head.

"Yeah," he finally said into the phone. "I'm alright."

"OK, this is a bad one out here. They say the FHP investigator is on his way, so we're going to have to wait on the particulars 'cause they want everything to come through him. But from what I can tell we got at least two dead, maybe more. So I think we're going to send Lisa Browne over to Hollywood Memorial to check on victims over there, and maybe she can get some I.D.s from folks there. I'll just camp out here."

"Yeah, OK. That's cool," Nick said. "Give me what you've got so far."

He crooked the phone between his shoulder and ear and put his fingers on the keyboard to take dictation.

"You ready?"

"Yeah," Nick said. "Go ahead."

///

He got home at eleven thirty, came through the front door tired and drained. Elsa was on the couch, lightly snoring as a Spanish-language soap opera played low on the television and flooded the open room with a blue glow. Nick covered her with an afghan and then went to check on Carly. In his daughter's room he stood in the darkness until his eyes adjusted and he could see her pale skin against the pillow, her mom's profile, her mouth slightly open, and he was somehow soothed by the sound of her breath rhythmically sighing in and out. He sat down carefully and reached out and just with the tips of his fingers he moved a strand of hair off her cheek and lightly stroked her head. He used to play a game after the girls fell asleep in which he tried to match his breathing to the beat of theirs and found that he could never keep up with the air that filled and emptied from their tiny lungs. He tried that now, and then curled up on the end of his daughter's bed and closed his eyes with the odor of her comforter in his nose and fell deeply asleep.

/ Chapter 13 /

Michael Redman tried again to close his eyes and sleep. He lay flat on his back, arms folded across his chest, fingers interlaced. His body was on the exact middle axis of the too-soft mattress, his legs stretched out to their full length and heels left hanging just beyond the foot of the bed. His head was square on the flat pillow, facing the swirled plaster of the old-time ceiling. If he could have seen himself from above, he would have recognized a soldier stiffened at something resembling parade rest, or a corpse readied for lowering into the earth.

Redman was determined to sleep this night, like all the other nights that he had been so determined. He'd been staring at the ceiling until he could see with frustrating clarity the patterns of cracks and fissures that were never meant to be seen. Like so many other nights, his peripheral vision had picked up the motion of the moon by the changes in the intensity of its glow against the hardwood floor and the low corner of one wall. He closed his eyes but again that empty, dark, nourishing nothingness would not come. Sleep. He'd lost that ability in Iraq, the ability to see nothing, to think nothing, to succumb to darkness. His ability to stay alert, trained into him for years as a law enforcement sniper, had become his enemy over the months and months of his deployment. He had so envied the young ones, the eighteen-, nineteen- and twenty-year-olds who could fall into their cots, pull the thin blankets over their heads and snore their way into oblivion for hours. As a cop, he'd trained himself to do that only after danger and the need for his service was past, after the crime-scene breakdown, after the target had been neutralized. But in Falluja and Mosul and Tikrit, the danger never really passed.

Iraq put the bug in his veins. He thought it would pass when he got back home, was back in his own bed, thought the resumption of routine in the real world would convince his mind that he could relax. But it never did. Instead it crept through his blood and into the tiny capillaries behind his eyelids and in the dark he would see the robes and *hijabs* and draped blankets float across his line of vision like the vestments of ghosts. And he could never see their faces. The scope only allowed a fragment of a hooded profile, the hook of a nose or jut of a chin.

"Take the shot."

Redman's fingers twitched and he opened his eyes and cut them to the side where the moon glow had painted the far corner of the room. He tightened the muscles in his stomach and swung his legs off the bed and sat up. He had again sweated through the T-shirt he wore. He should have reacclimated to the South Florida humidity by now. He looked over at the window beyond his door-panel desk and saw that it was opened.

In his last few months in Iraq, the night air had been cold like he hadn't experienced since his years growing up in New England. He remembered thinking then that they were right about Florida thinning your blood. He recalled the tent barracks in Ramadi where he'd bunked in for a few nights with a National Guard unit from Florida. He'd recognized some of the cities they came from when the men were introduced. But by then he was used to being vague about his own background. As soon as the others saw the black, hard-sided case that protected his H&K sniper rifle, the whispering started.

"Hey, yo. The grim reaper, man."

"How many notches you think are on that stock?"

"I heard like fifty, man. Guy's the Marines' special weapon."

"Fuckin' like to see him take out that goddamn mortar nest on the north quadrant. Maybe that's why he's here."

"No, that ain't why. I know why he's here," said a red-haired corporal who cut his eyes at Redman and then stuck a cigar in his mouth and walked out.

Redman had pretended not to hear. He remembered envying them and their loose camaraderie, but he stayed to himself. And they noticeably stayed clear of him. He'd watched their Texas hold 'em games from a distance, laughed inside when they told stories from the streets about Iraqi kids who thought the Americans wore air-conditioning inside their uniforms, and kept his head down when they shuffled in after a night patrol, exhausted from the six-hour flow of adrenaline and anxiety. After a few days awaiting his next assignment, he'd purposely worked the mess line and cut the redhead out of a group and sat down next to him. The guy started to get up, but Redman put a hand on his forearm and the grip made the corporal tighten his lips into a line.

"Tell me something," Redman said in a nonconfrontational voice. "How come that cot across from me is always empty?"

Every other spot in the canvas Quonset was filled but one, an unmade bed where photos of a bright, white-sand beach and a *Sports Illustrated* glamour cover of the Miami Heat were pinned to the wall. Just above was a homemade banner that read: ONE WEEKEND A MONTH MY ASS!

The banner's comment was a shot at the recruiting slogan to join the National Guard. Most of these guys, like Redman himself, had been weekend warriors with regular day jobs when they were called up for active duty. Now they'd been in Iraq for more than three hundred days. Redman remembered waiting for the corporal's answer.

"Randy Williams," he'd said, not moving his eyes off Redman's. "Best damn soldier in the unit. Kind of man who'd do anything for you. Share anything with you. Watch your back and keep everybody loose but, you know, alert."

Redman had run two or three faces of guys he knew at home who were just like that, guys on his SWAT detail or duty shift that people naturally clung to, admired, depended on.

"Nobody wants to move his stuff," the corporal had said. "They shipped his personal gear back to Fort Lauderdale with his body, but nobody wants him to be gone."

"How did he die?" Redman had asked in a soft tone.

"Sniper," the corporal had said, looking up, challenging-like. "We were on a daily patrol, broad daylight, looking for IEDs. Everybody was suited up with body armor and headgear. Williams was in the rear, covering our asses like always.

"There was one shot and everybody heard it. But the sound was from so far off, some of us didn't even turn on it. Then Murray started yelling and we looked back and Randy was down. One fucking shot, man. He was still twitching on the ground. Murray got his hand over the hole, but the blood kept running out and nobody saw the exit wound till we turned him. Round went right through his neck, ripped out his carotid. Fucking sniper knew exactly where to hit him. Above the armor, below the helmet. Wasn't nothing any of us could do."

Redman could still recall his own reaction to the story. Ground-level shot, he'd thought, immediately working the angles. Probably taken from a wall or a window as the squad moved by. You had to lead the target, gauge his foot speed, fire and let him walk into it. It was beyond lucky and obviously everyone in the redhead's unit knew it. The corporal's eyes had shifted to the table and Redman waited out the silence.

"They got 'em too," the redhead finally said.

"I'm sorry?" Redman said, not understanding.

"They got snipers too," the corporal had repeated. "We ain't the only ones in the world who can shoot straight."

Redman sat on the edge of the bed, sweating in the late-night Florida heat, remembering the words, watching the moon glow creep across the room, remembering that night in Iraq when he'd tried to rationalize his talent yet again. You take out the ones that might easily do the same to guys like Williams. That's why you do it. But Redman's targets in Tikrit weren't in uniform. And the sniper who killed Williams wasn't just taking out anything that moved like Redman had been asked to do. Redman knew he should rationalize it. In war innocent people get killed for the greater good. But he was sick of not knowing. Yeah, he was a trained killer, but the difference was that back at home, working for SWAT, you acted on intelligence. You knew who you were killing: Bad Guys. When he got back home, he would always know. When he got back, there wouldn't be any questions. Those who deserved to die were the ones who were going to die.

Now he was home and Redman stood up from the bed, stepped over to the table and opened the file once again. On the yellowed newspaper clipping was a mug shot, a photo the *Daily News* had reprinted from the arresting agency. The man's hair was leaning to one side, all tufted and tilting. His chin was up, maybe just because the booking officer ordered him to, but Redman could swear he saw a hint of a cocky grin pulling at the corner of the man's mouth and the light in one of his eyes.

The story detailed how the man had come home, slapped his long-time girlfriend around and then, during an argument, had sloshed rubbing alcohol over her head and body, rubbing alcohol she had used to ease the pain of her sickle-cell anemia. And then the boyfriend whom she thought she loved struck a match and set her aflame.

The story also detailed the man's history of domestic abuse and a harrowing line from the woman's seven-year-old daughter, who described how she'd come to her mother's aid and had to "slap the fire out of my mama's hair." The man's defense attorney had argued that the two were smoking cocaine and the alcohol had simply spilled and caught fire by accident. A plea bargain was struck. Attempted murder. Redman had already looked up the man's DOC file on a computer at the public library. He was already out, after seven years.

It was clearly wrong, Redman thought. The story was perfectly clear and convincing. No rationalization possible. A man tried to burn his sick girlfriend to death in front of her own daughter. In the light from the window he scanned the face again, memorizing the shape and profile. This man deserved to die. He shifted his eyes next to the photo. In Times Roman type, fourteen-point, was the byline that proved it:

By Nick Mullins, Staff Writer

/ Chapter 14 /

Nick spent the weekend with his daughter, trying as best he could to give her his full attention. He still cheated her out of at least half of his conscious thought.

On Saturday morning he got up and found Carly in her usual spot, camped out in her pajamas, legs curled up under her just like her mother used to do and watching cartoons with a Pop Tart and glass of dipping milk in front of her. He made coffee and settled down next to her without saying a word and aimed his face at the screen.

"SpongeBob SquarePants," she finally said after three minutes of silence.

"I know," Nick said.

"Liar," she said, but the dimples in her smooth cheeks gave her away.

He switched the coffee cup to his other hand and pressed his warmed fingers to the side of her face.

"And Patrick," he said.

She looked over into his face and smiled that full smile that had the same warm effect on his heart that his fingers were having on her skin.

"OK, maybe you are paying attention," she said and then, when she saw his expression start to change to that spaced-out, blank look, she quickly added, "What are we going to do today?"

Nick and his wife, Julie, had become aware of both their daughters' abilities to pick up on the unspoken rift between their parents. Nick's attention would spin off into the most recent story he was working on, the priorities of keeping up with an investigation or finding yet another source that he hadn't thought about and then taking a chance that he might best get them to talk by calling or knocking on doors at hours they wouldn't expect. Like on weekends, or the middle of the night, or when he should have been taking one of his daughters to a piano lesson or driving them all to an impromptu weekend getaway. His frequent disappearing acts had strained the relationship, and his vow, after the accident, was to do better by his surviving daughter.

"I am going to take you out to experience the two things that you love to do more than anything," he said, deliberately punching up his voice with enthusiasm.

Carly's face reflected a nine-year-old's version of skepticism.

"Photography and alligators," he said, watching her look turn to confusion. "We're gonna go out to Clyde Butcher's in the Everglades to look at his pictures, which I know you're going to love, and while we're out there I promise you will see some gators lolling around in the water next to his place."

Carly whined, as nine-year-olds will automatically do. Then, maybe after thinking about the picture-taking, which she did love, and the fascination of gators, which were at least different and possibly exciting, she did something that nine-year-olds don't normally do: acquiesced.

With Elsa's help, they put together a picnic lunch of *salteñas,* chips and homemade salsa, and Nick filled a cooler with juice boxes. When they packed the car, Nick tried to coax Carly into the front beside him but was met with a clear statement: "Mom never lets us sit in the front. She says we're not big enough yet, and the air bag would kill us."

Nick did not say what immediately came into his head: *The air bags didn't help your mom or your sister, so what goddamn difference does it make?* Instead he looked into her face to see if she realized what she'd said and then just nodded and put the cooler and a carton of Goldfish in the back seat with her.

Within thirty minutes they'd escaped urban South Florida and were heading west on what was once called Alligator Alley, a name that caused Carly to stare out the side window for at least twenty minutes before getting bored and voicing her opinion that they shouldn't name a highway for alligators if you can't see them lying alongside the road. Nick was going to tell her they'd changed the name to Interstate 75 but decided to keep his mouth shut.

He did try to keep up a conversation about the Everglades, directing her attention to the acres of brown-tipped saw grass that rolled out on the northern side of the freeway and stretched to the horizon. He tried to liken the sight to Kansas wheat fields, spread out and swirling in the winds, but realized his daughter had never been to Kansas. He tried to get her to imagine how the water they could see in the canal alongside was just as deep way out in the grass. "Like an ocean with the stalks poking up from the bottom over every inch."

"So how come the grass is brown at the top, Dad? I mean, jeez, shouldn't it be green if it's growing in water?"

He was never surprised by the logic of a child. Pretty damned simple, Dad, if you quit overanalyzing it. It was one of those things his daughters had taught him.

"Right now the tops are brown because the saw grass is blooming, sweetheart. It's the blooms that are brown."

All he got from the back seat was an "Uh-huh," like she'd accept it even if it was stupid for a plant to have brown blooms. Every few miles, Nick would make some kind of observation, loud enough for Carly to hear, but when he glanced back, her eyes were on a book she'd brought, or the blue GameBoy she and her sister always fought over until they bought a second one. The red one had belonged only to Carly. He noticed that after the accident, she played only with the blue one.

Finally, he gave up the act and let the sound of the car's spinning machinery and whir of rubber on concrete and rush of wind on glass and metal dominate the space. But silence only took his head where he'd sworn not to go.

What was the federal officer doing sniffing around and supposedly looking at similar shootings? Similar to what? The idea of this being a sniper job was getting hard to argue against. The cold precision of that single shot was pretty damned convincing. And both Hargrave and Nick now believed the shooter had climbed up the fire ladder and had prepared the shot, maybe even beforehand. Did the guy have a list of other shootings with the same tag? Professional-type jobs. Preparation. The use of SWAT-style clothing. Did the shooter intentionally wear the clothes to throw off witnesses, make anyone who saw him dismiss him as official? Pretty ballsy. Or stupid.

"Dad?"

Nick was thinking ballsy at this point.

"Daaad?"

His eyes snapped up to the rearview mirror to search for his daughter's expression. It was annoyed, again, at his wayward concentration.

"Yeah, sweetie. You OK?"

"When are we going to get there?"

The inevitable kid question. He looked alongside the freeway for a mile marker.

"Only a couple more minutes and then we go south, honey. We're going to go right along the edge of the wildlife preserve, so I want you to look for the panther-crossing signs, OK?"

"Really?"

"Yeah, just like when you see pedestrian crossings or those deer-crossing signs up north. Out here they've got panther-crossing areas."

Carly thought about it for a moment. "Cats don't walk across the street where you tell them to," she finally said. "They go where they want to so they can hide and do what they want. Remember Dash?"

Dash had been the girls' tiger-striped tomcat. The thing would disappear for days, somehow getting into the house through a torn screen just to eat and then slink back out. The only way you knew he was still around was by the empty food dish.

Nick got off an exit and then turned south on U.S. 29.

"We're not going to see any panthers," Carly said, not with disappointment or cynicism, just a little girl's statement of fact.

"You're probably right, but you'll still see the signs," Nick said and looked back and smiled at her, but she was staring out the window.

The road was flanked by a line of trees on the west and a canal on the east. Nick knew from experience that there was little to see and the arrow-straight two-lane was a boring strip cutting through nowhere. His head moved back to snipers, no signs to let you know where they were, where they would strike next. The D.C. killers proved that. Every so-called expert in law enforcement had blown that one from the beginning, working the old scenarios, searching for connections between victims, some sort of pattern so they could predict the sniper's movements. They took a witness's statement about a white van and went crazy pulling over every white van they could find.

Now Hargrave too had a witness who'd seen a man in black who looked like a SWAT cop. Would he pull over every SWAT cop he could find and question them and their whereabouts on Thursday morning? Maybe he would. Maybe he already had.

"Dad?"

Carly brought him back and Nick chastised himself. Pay attention, man. Don't do this to her again.

"Yeah, sweetheart?"

"Can we stop someplace to go to the bathroom?"

He smiled, had known it was coming all along.

"Absolutely," he said. "I've got just the place. Can you hold on for another ten minutes, sweetie?"

"If I have to. Yes."

In five minutes he was at the junction of 29 and the Tamiami Trail and headed back east, past the airboat ride signs, the Miccosukee Indian village signs. He tried to divert Carly's mind by telling her about how men long ago had built the trail as the first road across the great Everglades by scooping up the dirt and muck and limestone with a huge dredge and dumping it alongside the canal they were creating as they moved forward.

"See the water over here on my side? That's where they dug, and this road is where they piled the stuff."

"Uh-huh."

Nick looked out beyond the canal at the occasional spread of sawgrass meadow spotted by islands of cabbage and silver thatch palms. Then the hammocks of dwarf cypresses, wild tamarind and rimrock pine would fill up the space with a thin greenness. And always there was the heat, bubbling the mixture to a deep simmer. He admired the men who had worked through this relentless nature and wondered if they had ever taken an appreciation of its bare beauty while they tried to tame it.

After another ten minutes, Nick pulled over at a sign reading: CLYDE BUTCHER'S BIG CYPRESS GALLERY. He parked next to the small pond that bellied out from a culvert running under the roadway. The water was dark and coppery and lay like an unrippled tarp around several gigantic water cypress trees, their branches strung with Spanish moss.

Carly got out on the other side while Nick gathered up his thermos, balanced a cup on the roof and poured.

"We can go inside and use the bathroom, baby," he said and when he got no answer he stepped forward and looked over the hood for his daughter. She had forgotten all about her need and was staring out into the near water, her arm outstretched and a slightly crooked finger pointing.

Nick followed the line of her finger and saw the rumpled black nose of a gator cutting slowly through the water, leaving a growing V behind it. The eyes were like two disfigured lumps on the trunk of a tree with their centers buffed smooth and glassy.

"That's a good-sized one," Nick said, injecting a lightness into his voice as he moved around the front of the car to Carly's side. His daughter took a step back, but her eyes did not leave those of the reptile. When the beast took a turn to the south from its dead-on path, Nick felt Carly move up into the side of his leg.

"Wow," was all she said.

Now that they knew what they were looking for, Nick pointed out two other motionless snouts and Carly found two others among the cypress knees poking up through the water.

"Won't they come up and, you know, bite the tires or something?"

"I think they're used to company by now," Nick said. "As long as some idiot doesn't start feeding them from the parking lot, they don't have much reason to come out of the water when people are around."

They stood and watched for a bit, Carly now giggling at each perceived movement. After several minutes she seemed to have her fill and started looking around. The simple wood deck of the studio took her interest.

"Pictures?"

"Yeah, your other love," Nick said. "Let's go in."

When they stepped inside Butcher's studio, Carly's reaction to the large black-and-white photograph of the Big Cypress Reserve had the same effect as her initial spotting of the gator—her eyes froze on the photo. But this time she stepped forward. The frame that greeted them was one of Clyde's shots of spreading clouds building in the limitless sky over the Glades. Their movement and tumble and growth from drawing up the water below had been frozen in his lens. Below was a sheet of still water, reflecting the image of the clouds as if on a hot mirror. Bordering the open pond were marsh grasses and hammock trees, and bisecting it was a small sliver of island. The textures, in pure black-and-white, made the viewer forget even the possibility of color.

Carly stepped even closer and reached out to touch the photograph with the tips of her fingers as she might a sleeping animal. "Daddy," she said. "How does Mr. Butcher do this?"

Nick was looking at the photograph with only slightly less wonder than his daughter. He had always been as mesmerized by the man's skills as she was now.

"He's just very, very good at what he does, honey. He's like an artist, only with a camera, you know, who can see things in a way that other people can't," Nick said, but he knew he too was flummoxed. "Let's look at his other stuff."

Carly uncharacteristically took his hand and they drifted into the gallery, every wall filled with portraits of the wild and majestic Glades, from a small frame of a rare and intricate ghost orchid to a broad, wall-sized print of the moon rising over land no man had stepped on for thousands of years.

Nick had been absorbed by the guy's photos ever since a newspaper colleague had profiled Butcher years before. But only recently had he been drawn out to the studio, to stand and look again. Nick knew Butcher's story. The photographer, already a recognized talent, had been stunned by tragedy when his seventeen-year-old son was killed in a terrible car crash. Butcher and his wife closed in on themselves. And then, in a way maybe he himself could not describe, Butcher slipped alone into the ancient and otherworldly land of the Everglades swamp. He spent days and weeks alone in the pristine wilds with his big eight-by-ten-inch box camera and let the energy of his grief spread out in a place where other people did not reach. Out there he would stand waist-deep in the water, then focus and wait, enduring heat and mosquitoes and loneliness until the perfect moment of light and shadow could be captured. And out here he let his talent, the thing that defined him, grow in spite of his anguish and it redefined him. Nick felt a sliver of that now, and it made more sense to him, and he was pulled to it.

"OK," he finally said to Carly after they'd wandered through the entire exhibit. "Which one do you like best?"

She looked up at him with that delicious look in her eye she used when she knew her father was about to do something she would adore, and then dropped his hand and he had to follow her around a wall to a far corner.

"This one, Dad."

She chose not a photo of the Everglades, but a shot from behind a white-sand dune on one of Florida's empty coasts. The sun was rising, the wind bending sea oats, the tiny ridges of swept sand so clear in relief you swore you could see the individual grains.

Nick studied it, giving the shot his appreciation, but he sneaked a look at the huge dark makeup of a silent river bend draped in a canopy of cypress. His daughter caught the look.

"I like this one because Mom would like it," she said. "It's like her."

Nick quickly shifted back to the seascape.

"Yeah, you're right, sweetheart."

"That one's lonely, Dad," she said, gesturing toward the river that she knew was drawing her father.

"Yeah," he said. "You're right."

Nick had the gallery keeper wrap up the seaside print.

In the car, he took a detour south to Chokoloskee Island and treated Carly to a visit of the one hundred-year-old Smallwood Store, where the original owner's descendants, with the help of the historical society, had maintained the stilted trading post, one of the first in southwest Florida. She touched the old hand-wringer washtubs and the tanned pelts of otters and raccoons still hanging on the walls. Nick read to her from the original ledger that Ted Smallwood had kept in the twenties when his clients paid him in gator skins. Carly especially liked the Seminole Indian dolls, even though she never would have admitted that she was still into that sort of thing. Afterward Nick treated both of them to a stone-crab dinner at a restaurant in Everglades City. The meat of the stone crab claws is the most delicious seafood ever discovered, and having it fresh off the Everglades City docks where the crabbers came in from the Gulf was one of the wonders of the world.

On the trip back across Alligator Alley, it was only twenty minutes before Nick looked back through the rearview mirror to see Carly sound asleep. His cruise control was set at eighty, and he was feeling pretty good about himself. He'd spent the day with his daughter. She'd been relatively pleased with their adventure. He was being the dad he was sure he was supposed to be, the dad he promised to be over and over on moonlit nights when he went to his family's grave site and sat in the grass, and whispered to Julie and Lindsay, "I will do the right thing by her, guys. I will do the right thing by all of you."

When his cell phone rang Nick's shoulders jumped as if a trumpeter had sneaked into the passenger seat and ripped a high C into his ear.

"Jesus!" he hissed and reached over to snatch up the phone. He didn't recognize the number on the readout. He knew no one at the paper would bother him on the weekend, but it wasn't a paper prefix anyway.

He was about to let the cell take a message but then pushed the answer button. Sources, he thought. Can't live with them, can't live without them.

"Nick Mullins," he said, businesslike.

"Mr. Mullins. This is Detective Hargrave."

Mr. Uncooperative, Nick thought. No use for the press.

"Detective. What's up?"

"I'd like to have a sitdown with you, Mr. Mullins. Go over some things that might benefit the investigation."

Despite his reticence, Hargrave knew exactly how to dangle possibilities in front of a reporter. Even if the ploy was new to him in dealing with the media, Nick was sure Hargrave had used it with informants and inmates before.

"I would be more than happy to meet wherever you'd like on Monday, Detective," Nick said.

"You know JB's on the Deerfield Beach oceanfront? Just north of the pier?"

"Yeah," Nick said, picturing the place.

"I figure it's close enough to your home. We could meet there about eleven tonight."

Nick didn't answer. Why would Hargrave know where he lived? And though Nick knew how easy it was to find someone's private cell number, it was unusual for a cop to check out the address and phone of a reporter.

"Detective, I don't usually work on weekends. I like to be with my family."

Nick checked the rearview. The sun was going down in the west behind him. Carly was still asleep, her head flopped to one side against the door panel, her mouth slightly open.

"So eleven o'clock, then," Hargrave said and Nick could picture the man's hatchet face, impassive, unaffected by anything Nick had said. The detective had not called to ask. He was ordering, like he would if Nick were a suspect, or a confidential street source, or an underling. Nick didn't like any of those labels. He was about to get pissed off and open his mouth again but stopped himself. A sentence seemed to slip into his head from the back seat: *You're not the boss of me!* It was the girls' favorite answer to each other when they'd argue and Nick recalled it as being cute. Petty. But cute.

"OK, Detective. If it's that important, I'll see you at eleven," he finally said. Hargrave did not answer and simply hung up.

/ Chapter 15 /

Elsa met him at the door. Always vigilant when her Carly was away, she had watched for the sweep of headlights coming into the drive. Nick checked his sleeping daughter and then got out and opened the back door. He slipped his hand under Carly's legs and as he lifted her from the seat she instinctively wrapped her arms around his neck and lay her head on his shoulder, her eyes still shut. He carried her in as Elsa held open the door: *"Aaayyy, pobrecita, esta cansada,"* Elsa said.

In Carly's bedroom, the covers were already turned down. Nick laid her in her bed, took off her shoes and watched her scrunch her body into the pillows and heard her exhale contentedly. He bent to kiss her forehead, then turned out the dimmed lamp and started to leave.

"Good night, Daddy."

Nick turned back.

"Faker," he whispered and knew her smile was there in the dark. "Thanks for going with me."

"You're welcome."

In the hall, he asked Elsa to make him some coffee and then went out to empty the car. It was ten o'clock when he sat alone at the kitchen table and ate the *salteñas* from the cooler and sipped his coffee. Why did

Hargrave want to meet with him in a seaside bar, of all places? Not in his office. Not with Joel riding shotgun. He had been rolling the possibilities in his head since the detective had hung up and wasn't any closer to a solid guess. It was well out of character for the guy, and Nick kept running the conference-table scene through his head, trying to pick out who in that room had gotten the worst of Hargrave's skepticism and distrust, and decided it hadn't been him.

"You are OK, Mr. Mullins?" Elsa said, breaking the silence with her quiet voice.

"Huh? Oh, yes, yes, Elsa. I'm fine," Nick said, shaking his head back into the present. "We had a good day. But I have to go out again."

The housekeeper pointedly looked up at the kitchen clock.

"I'll lock up when I leave."

Elsa did not bother hiding her worried brow.

"It's OK, Elsa," Nick said. "I'm OK."

"You are going to talk to Ms. Julie and Lindisita?"

Nick had once confided in Elsa, told her of his night trips to the cemetery. He guessed that her heritage, her acceptance of the souls and ghosts of the dead, led her to be wary, but not overtly concerned. She wasn't going to call the loony bin to come take him away.

"You will be home to take Carlita to church, yes?"

Sunday was the one day of the week that Elsa spent with her own family since the accident. Her grown daughter and now teenage grandsons would be expecting her. She'd given so much to Nick, he would never deny her that. But he was also feeling an apprehension in the old woman's eyes. His late nights before the accident. The heavy drinking she had witnessed afterward.

"Yes, Elsa," Nick said. "I will be back."

/ / /

Nick let the valet park his old Volvo because it was the only way at JB's. Nobody in South Florida puts a parking lot on the waterfront, so restaurants and bars were forced to purchase alternative spots for their clientele, and they sure weren't giving it out for free.

Nick took the stub, walked into the restaurant foyer and immediately wished he'd taken a shower and shaved. JB's was an upscale place and the late diners looked wealthy and hip. A scruffy-looking guy in blue jeans and a polo shirt didn't get so much as a look from the maître d'. That was OK by Nick. He figured Hargrave for the outdoor bar and walked right on by the WAIT TO BE SEATED sign and worked his way back. As he stepped out through the glass doors, the live, the slightly sour scent of the ocean washed up into his face and although the smell of low tide was pleasant enough to Nick, he wondered how the to-be-seen people could dine with the odor washing over their food on the humid breeze. He moved toward the bar and let his eyes go first to the corners, where he knew a cop like Hargrave would have his back against a wall. He found him there, sitting on a stool, his thin back straight as a stick, his pointed elbows stuck into the bar top. Nick thought of a praying mantis and then walked over in full view so the detective could see him coming. The burly sergeant was nowhere to be seen.

"Hey, how's it going?" Nick said, never knowing for sure how plain-clothes detectives wanted to be greeted out in the civilian world. He noted that Hargrave did not unlace his fingers to offer a handshake and he slid onto the open stool.

"Sticky," Hargrave said.

Nick thought what multiple meanings that statement held and then fell back on the weather.

"Yeah, pretty humid," he said and listened for a moment to the sound of the surf brushing up onto the sand fifty yards out into the darkness.

"Buy you a drink?" the detective said.

"Just iced tea."

Hargrave's hands hovered over a bourbon glass and with a nod of his head got the attention of the bartender and ordered Nick's tea. Nick had not taken a drink of alcohol since he'd gone on a six-month bender after the accident, but he did not begrudge others their habits.

"Thanks," he said to Hargrave when the tea arrived and they went quiet, both having run out of manners.

"You seem to have some kind of relationship with Ms. Cotton, Mullins. We're the ones that caught Ferris, but she wants to talk to you first. What's that all about?"

Nick waited until he finished ripping a couple of sugar packets and dumping their contents in his tea. A stalling tactic, to get his answer straight.

"Can't say that I know," he finally said. "I talked with her a few times when it happened and then only a little during the trial. She seemed to like the stories I wrote. I got the sense she liked being, you know, respected."

Hargrave took a sip of his whiskey, looked down into the glass. "Yeah, I read your stories. You never called her homeless. The rest of the media kept calling her a homeless woman bringing her kids up in a car."

Nick remembered the arguments he'd had with editors over that.

Hargrave let him think and then said, "She give you anything you didn't tell us about in that room?"

This guy was going to be hard to slide anything by, Nick thought. "Not really," he said, taking a long drink of the tea, trying to judge the guy. Hargrave was pushing this investigation, up late on a Saturday, reworking the already unusual ground of talking to a reporter. Would it hurt to give him the mention of the letters? Would the detective give him anything in return? Nothing ventured, as they say.

"You get the letters she said her attorney kept forwarding on to her? The ones from sympathy folks and people encouraging her?" Nick said.

Hargrave lifted one eye at him, making Nick think maybe something was wrong with the guy's peripheral vision. "No. It wasn't mentioned."

"She said that she had held on to some of them, put them in a box someplace. I figured, you know, that I might go back," Nick said, avoiding Hargrave's look. "Might be some names, maybe some threats against Ferris, you know, 'We'll get that son-of-a-bitch' types."

"We'll have to look into it," the detective said, but Nick could see the mental note-taking going on in Hargrave's head. He'd probably be at her door Monday morning, if not sooner.

He drank his tea. Maybe it was time to get something back.

"So what's with the federal guy at the meeting?" he asked, knowing Hargrave would have checked the guy out with his own law enforcement contacts as soon as he could get out of the lieutenant's sight.

"OK," Hargrave said, recognizing the game of give-and-take. "He's with the Secret Service. Sources say he's down here as security on a political junket, but he's got this hairbrush up his ass about snipers. They say he's got a whole list of shootings that have anything to do with long-distance kills and high-powered rifles."

"They say? Who's they?"

Hargrave let something that might have been a grin come onto his face. "My unnamed sources."

Nick tried to give the information an appropriate "That's interesting" response. But he was thinking about his own list of shooting victims, the one he'd asked Lori to put together. It was still in his computer at work and he hadn't taken the time to look at it all.

"You've seen this list?" he asked Hargrave.

"No. But Fitzgerald's definitely got a hard-on about it. And with all this homeland security shit, that puts the pressure on us to cooperate with him."

"And with me," Nick said.

"The guy's on a timetable," Hargrave said, sipping again at his drink, but Nick could see there was nothing but ice left in the bottom.

"What do you mean?"

The detective again gave Nick another sideways look, while sucking a cube into his mouth and then gnashing the thing between his teeth.

"Jesus, Mullins. Don't you read your own paper?"

"Yeah, but I only believe half of it," Nick said.

Hargrave looked over the top of his whiskey glass as though he were trying to tell whether Nick was serious or joking. Nick shrugged.

"He's Secret Service. The Secretary of State shows up next week for a meeting of the Organization of American States down at the convention center," Hargrave said. "I figure this guy to be part of the advance team, but he's a little too focused on the sniper bit. That's usually taken care of in protocol, part of the overall security plan."

Nick knew about the upcoming OAS confab. Representatives from most of Latin America would be present. Miami was pretty much the gateway to the United States for the Hispanic and Caribbean world now, and the Broward County convention center was north of Miami. Protestors would have a harder time getting there and the center was right next to the Fort Lauderdale/Hollywood International Airport. They picked the site because it meant less travel for the dignitaries and was easier to secure. In fact, Nick figured Deirdre would be pulling him aside to do a piece about that security anytime now. But as a rule, Nick rarely paid attention to politics until it lapped over into his coverage of death or law enforcement. He recalled the time he was asked to write a story about some dustup after the President started using scenes of September 11 in his reelection advertisements. The editors came to him because Nick had interviewed families in South Florida who had lost loved ones in the Twin Towers. He had at least a fledgling relationship with them, along with their contact numbers. Death revisited. It was a shitty assignment, having to call people still emotionally raw and ask stupid questions. But he did it. And everyone he talked to said they were bothered by the use of 9/11 in any advertisement, political or not. Nick had written their responses, and had only the President's press secretary's rebuttal to balance it. The next day his phone and e-mail were filled with angry readers pissing on Nick personally and the "Liberal press" in general for being one-sided and taking a political stand against Republicans. Nick endured until the eighth or ninth call and then spouted off at some condo political captain: "It's not a political story. It's a human story, man. It's about people's feelings. It's about people who lost sons and daughters and family and felt like they just got gouged again. Can't you understand that? It's about humans, not politics."

The guy on the other end of the line just laughed at what he considered Nick's naïveté. "Everything's about politics, young man. You'll learn that."

Nick went back to his regular police reporting that day when the dismembered body of a prostitute was found in a Dumpster only thirty yards away from Federal Highway, and Nick was taken off the political advertisement story.

"You think the Secret Service has some kind of credible threat that a sniper is tailing the Secretary of State?" Nick said.

"Christ, I don't know," Hargrave said, hissing between his teeth. "I'm sure as hell not thinking that my guy is assassinating felons just to warm up for the Secretary of State. But if he finds something to link our guy to whatever he's looking for, I'll take the help. Right now I've got a homicide to work even if no one else gives a damn."

Nick wasn't sure how many whiskeys Hargrave had downed, but the reticent man was showing the pressure. The detective pushed his glass toward the bar gutter and peeled off a few bills and left them as a tip.

"I'll give Ms. Cotton a visit on Monday for those letters, and maybe if I get a look at Fitzgerald's list, I'll let you know."

He got up and slid past Nick without so much as letting his coat sleeve make contact. Nick said, "Thanks," to his back as the thin man walked away.

/ Chapter 16 /

Get in. Kill quickly. And get out without being seen.

Sniper Theory 101. He had learned it and earned it in his first stint with the military, and gave it all up after the first Gulf War when he came home to be a cop.

Out here in the civilian world, he'd also learned intelligence and careful planning and specific targeting and, he admitted, a hell of a lot of patience and frustration had replaced the kill-quickly rule. He'd been proud of his abilities in both theaters before. He had always, in his head, done the right thing. And now, he told himself, he was doing the right thing again.

From the parking lot a block behind a row of street-side businesses Redman sat in the dark van, doing surveillance. His gear was in a bag stuffed in a concealed drop box in the floor. He'd had a welder hang the box under the frame, just behind the rear axle, so he could get to it easily enough. From the outside it was hard to spot, obscured by a low-hanging license plate and a trailer hitch that would never be used. The mechanic had used reverse hinges so the plate door was nearly seamless and difficult to recognize from inside the van. If he was stopped for any reason, he wasn't going to be caught carrying an H&K sniper rifle and try to say he was going deer hunting in the Glades.

With patience, he watched the coming and going of traffic for an hour, long past midnight. He'd already used a night-scope spotter to check the fire escape that led to the roof of the office building he wanted. From the front he knew the business plaque read: MYERS & HOPE, ATTORNEYS AT LAW. But back here it was just as dark and unpainted and weather-stained as all the rest in the line. He'd already spotted the burglar alarm lights on the back door and the magnetic slide bars on the windows. But he wasn't going inside, and no such devices were on the fire escape.

He'd long ago unscrewed the bulbs inside the van, so he held a small Maglite between his teeth and scrambled between the seats and into the back. He opened the drop box, left the rifle and took out a night spotting scope and a laser range finder. If he got caught on a dry run, there would be no sense getting caught with a gun. He might get picked up for attempted burglary, but he wasn't there to steal anything. He got out quietly through the rear doors and clicked them shut.

The fire escape took him to the roof and he stayed low crossing the graveled tarpaper, stopping at an air-conditioning unit that was as big as his van. The thing was humming. It was after one AM, but the air temperature was still in the high seventies. He could feel the heat of the day coming off the roof surface when he went to all fours and crossed to the building's front edge. Down on his belly, he checked the street north and south and then brought the scope to his eye. Across the avenue and one hundred yards down the line, he focused and watched the BAIL BONDS sign twitch through the green glow of the scope lens. A slip to the right and he found another door with its own small letters painted on the glass: DEPARTMENT OF CORRECTIONS. He had always found the locations humorous. The bail bondsman sitting right next door to the parole office. One-stop shopping.

From a computer printout, Redman had the specifics of the felon he called Mr. Burn-Your-Girlfriend-to-Death. Out on parole after doing time for attempted murder, Trace Michaels was required to show up at this office every second Monday of the month. Due up in two days. And a bullet with his name on it would be waiting.

Redman took out the laser range finder, pointed it at the door and checked the distance: one hundred twenty-eight yards. A fish-in-a-barrel shot. And from this far back, he'd be down the fire escape and in his van before people could figure out why a man was suddenly lying on the sidewalk. Redman would be driving in the opposite direction. No reports to fill out. No shit to take from the media. He glassed the building again, thought about a night just like this three years ago.

He and the SWAT team had been after bad guys that night too. The ATF unit out of Fort Lauderdale had turned a pile of investigative tapes over to the sheriff's investigators. On the recordings, three wannabe gun dealers in Deerfield Beach were trying to set up a buy for several 9mm handguns and supposedly an MP5 semiautomatic rifle, the same kind the SWAT members carried. Everyone on the team gathered in the planning room and listened to the men brag to the potential buyer, "We got the firepower, man. And we know how to use them too."

The confidential informant said he wasn't looking for that kind of trouble. He had the cash and just wanted a smooth deal.

"You wanna smooth deal, you be smooth."

The CI and the gunrunners set the sale at a two-story motel just off the interstate. Easy in, easy out. Two hours ahead of time, the SWAT sergeant met with the motel manager and cleared the rooms of other guests with quiet requests over room phones. The team then set up in an unmarked van in the horseshoe-shaped parking lot. Three officers were in the van, watching a video screen. They would send in the CI with a bag of money and a concealed camera and the guys outside would be able to see exactly what they were dealing with. Michael Redman was the ultimate backup. He was in a second-story room on the other side of the horseshoe, directly across from the dealers' room. He set his tripod on top of a dresser shoved four feet back from the window so that no passersby would see the barrel of the sniper rifle. When the team went green-light, he would open the sliding half of the window and have a perfect line on the bad guys' doorway, just in case someone came out shooting. It wasn't likely, but the voices on the tapes had convinced the team that these assholes could talk the talk. They weren't taking chances they might walk the walk.

The team had also rigged the room next to the gun sellers. Like most cheap motels, it had a suite door that connected the rooms. One of the team had disabled the dead bolt, but left the turn knob intact. The bad guys on the other side could throw the bolt, it would feel and sound like it was locked, but two members of the team would simply spin the knob on their side and charge on in. Complete surprise.

When everything was set, the team commander sent in the informant. From the van, half the team listened to the audio and watched the video being transmitted from a hidden camera in the CI's bag. Three men were inside, 9mm in their waistbands. The CI played it pretty cool.

"Hey, man, come on, ya'll. I ain't carryin' nothin', just like you said, man. How come ya'll bristlin' with your personal shit an' all?"

"We told you we know how use what we sell," said the dealer, who called himself Freddy. "You do things smooth, they don't come out."

The CI said he was only there to do business and asked to see the merchandise out on the bed. On the video screen the SWAT sergeant watched six handguns and the assault rifle being placed on the mattress. He made a determination that moment: The team was not going to let those weapons back out on the street. That contingency plan had already been set. When the key words came out of the CI's mouth, the team would move simultaneously. Most of the men in the van were holding their breath when the informant said, "OK. This all looks right. I got your money right here."

The sergeant called a "Go" on his radio. Redman already had his scope on the door and even from his distance he heard the *whump* of the inside suite door as one of the team gave it the shoulder and rushed in on the dealers shouting, "Police, don't move! Police, don't move! Police, don't move."

At the same instant three deputies jumped from the back of the van and headed for the stairs. They were dressed in black with yellow letters across their chests and back: POLICE.

Two team members also burst from the front door of the room next to the dealers' to cover the second-floor walkway. Redman let a breath out and pulled two pounds of pressure on the three-pound trigger. Despite the order not to move, the bad guys did.

The first man out of the dealers' room was a guy with a baseball cap. He instantly wore Redman's crosshairs on his chest. Redman saw that the grip of the man's 9mm was still sticking out of his belt and held off as the deputies on the walkway continued yelling. But Baseball Cap kept going, starting down the outside stairwell as the team had figured, funneling into the hands of the van team. The second man out had his gun in his hand. When he came out the door, Redman put the scope on him. When the guy turned to look at the deputies on the walkway and began to raise his 9mm, Redman fired a .308 WIN boat-tail bullet into the man's chest, one inch below his heart and slightly anterior. It sheared the breastbone as it went in, and the velocity expansion that fans out three inches in diameter around the bullet pulverized the two right chambers of the heart. He was dead within seconds.

That was when Redman heard the reports of the van team's own MP5s. The first man down the stairway had pulled his 9mm from his waistband but did not get the chance to fire. Redman moved the scope down in time to see two blossoms sprout on the man's chest like tiny roses opening in an accelerated-time-flash film.

Voices continued to sound and Redman swung the sights and caught a glimpse of a booted foot leaving the targeting field. He moved his eye from the scope and watched a man leap over the walkway railing and hit the ground. The guy rolled, using his rifle to absorb the shock, and scrambled to his feet: a runner. Up on the walkway, the deputies plowed full into the fourth man who stepped out of the room, tackling him but also losing chase on the runner. Watching the confusion, Redman lifted his rifle, slid on his ass across the top of the dresser and took two steps to the window. From there he had an angle on the runner, who had in his hands the automatic rifle he'd been trying to sell. The parking lot deputies never saw him and Redman called out, "On the fence! On the fence!" as a warning and then swung his scope to the right, steadying the rifle against the window frame. He had a full view of the runner, who had made the chain-link fence and was scrambling up. He watched him throw one leg over and then, straddling the top, sling the rifle up to his shoulder and aim back at the parking lot. Redman's shot was perfect given the circumstances. The boat-tail caught the man just below the left sideburn, half an inch in front of the earhole. He was dead in a millisecond.

In the investigation that follows every time a lawman fires his weapon, the operation came out clean. The SWAT team acted exactly as it had been trained to. They'd done an assessment of the danger and secured the room. They'd assigned adequate overwhelming force. When hostile weapons were identified, and when those weapons became a danger to team members, those members shot to kill. It all went down as it should have under quickly changing circumstances.

Only the media questioned the operation, which, Redman knew, is what the media does. When someone dies by the hand of a cop, journalists seem to be sent out to determine if it was a fair fight. But SWAT officers know it is never a fair fight. It's never supposed to be. It's not a game.

The sheriff was adept at spinning the local media. The public information officers dealt with the reporters they had relationships with. But it had been Redman's fifth killing in the line of duty. The editorial writers, dusty white collars in isolated offices who only watched TV and hadn't been on the streets in years, had their opinions.

Redman could still quote the editorial written in the *Daily News* only two days after the SWAT shooting:

> Since all witnesses to the contrary are dead, it may be impossible to know exactly what occurred in the middle of a darkened motel parking lot last Tuesday. Of course the Sheriff's Office has cleared itself—using its own investigators—but a taxpayer-supported agency that is given the mandate to protect and serve does not have a license to kill as if they were some kind of 007 squad. Deputy Redman has fired the fatal shots on five SWAT unit killings in the last seven years. If the man has a quick trigger finger or a questionable lust for the job, he should be arraigned or at least fired. If he has confused his role with that of the Marine sniper he once was in the Gulf War, that mind-set should not be allowed to roam our civilian streets and given a warrior's impunity.

Redman's lieutenant, Steve Canfield, had taken him aside.

"Don't even read it, Mikey. You've saved our asses a dozen times. They don't know shit about it," Canfield said while Redman sat in front of his locker reading the editorial and quietly boiling. "They're opinionist, man. They make up opinions. None of them are there when the shit is flying. They're still watching the Lone Ranger shoot the gun out of the bad guy's hand. None of them know how it really works, Mike. You remember that, partner."

But Redman never considered himself the lieutenant's "partner." In the first of his so-called quick-trigger killings, his real partner, Marcus Collie, had been the first one in on a barricaded-man call. Within forty minutes the team had surrounded a dilapidated home in an upscale neighborhood, an eyesore that residents had complained about for years. The owner, the neighbors said, was an oddball who'd taken the place over when his mother died. He hadn't paid the electric or water in several months and threatened every city code officer who'd tried to talk with him. When city officers tried to contact him, he threatened to shoot anyone who crossed his property. SWAT was called in. The guy had painted every window in the house black from the inside. There was no opportunity for sniper work. It had to be close quarters. The cops had bullhorned the guy for hours. All they got were more threats. The team then bashed out all four corner windows, tossed in smoke bombs and waited for the guy to come out coughing and sputtering. Still nothing. Finally an entry team was formed. As usual, Collie was on point. Redman, his partner, was behind him.

They took down the front door with a battering ram and went in low, flashlights mounted on their MP5s. Nothing. They went on a room-by-room search in the dark. The third room they encountered was the master bath. Because of the dark, they did not see the water on the floor at the edge of the door. If they'd noticed, they might have figured the guy had closed himself up in there and used wet towels under the door to keep the smoke out. Instead, Collie kicked in the door and jumped to the right. Redman stayed left. No sound. When Collie brought his gunsight around the doorframe, the guy must have timed the sweep of the flashlight, and fired a twelve-gauge loaded with deer slugs into the doorframe where Collie stood. Almost simultaneously Redman swung around and fired a three-round burst just above the flash of the shotgun and the bullets stitched across the man's neck, nearly separating it from his shoulders. Lucky pattern in the dark. But the suspect had been just as accurate.

Redman yelled, "Medical," before he even called, "Clear."

He could only tell that Collie was down. Still, as he was trained, he stepped into the bathroom and ripped the shotgun from the suspect's death grip and tossed it aside. Then he aimed his flashlight on his partner. He did not ask if he was OK because he knew that answer. Collie's breathing was ragged and sounded like a kid sucking the last bits of soda through a straw. Redman went to his knees and tried to search for his partner's eyes in the beam, but one was missing. A gaping hole was torn in his left cheek, and Redman could see broken teeth floating in blood inside.

He might have started screaming, "Man down! Man down!" as was his training, but Redman did not remember afterward. From then on he did not consider anyone a partner. And with Collie gone forever, no one on the team ever took point but him. And no one ever spoke of moral courage.

Redman looked at his watch now and then proceeded to bag the scope and the laser range finder and took an extra few seconds to mock the time it would take to also bag his rifle and pick up a shell casing. He inched backward from the roofline and then walked in a crouch to the fire escape. When he was back in the van, with everything stowed away, he rechecked the watch. He wanted the timing of his exit on Monday to be perfect, nothing left to chance, only training. One shot, one kill.

/ Chapter 17 /

On Sunday Nick spent two hours on the couch watching cartoons with his daughter. He drank coffee and munched on oven-baked crescent rolls and worked very hard against the urge to get the Sunday newspaper from the driveway, and even harder at keeping the conversation with Hargrave from ringing in his head.

He would keep his unspoken promise to Carly not to ignore her on his days at home. He'd done that to his family before. It had been the source of friction in his marriage ever since the girls were born. In the beginning his passion for the work, that he was good at what he did, that he was respected, was a source of pride for his wife.

After the girls were born, he hadn't changed. He'd gotten them through the pregnancy and the postpartum by working only eight-hour days and sneaking computer time on the weekends. But at three months, the twins went to Elsa for day care and once he dropped them off, he reentered the news world. Maybe it was subconscious, the pleasure he got from it, the demands and the people and the streets. It was the only thing he did well, and without saying it, he knew it defined him.

But his wife did change. Her priorities became different. He kept claiming that he understood the mothering instinct and all. He talked a good talk about sharing as a family and how he knew how important it was for him to be part of the equation, but failed to show it. That lack of action was the reason Julie and the girls were riding alone that night, touring the Christmas lights without him. He was out doing death when it came to visit his own family.

"Why does the redhead always have to play the ditzy one?" he asked Carly, who was lying back against his legs, using them as a chair back.

"They can't change every week," she said in that *Duh?* voice so popular in her age group. "The dumb one is the dumb one, Dad. It's preordained."

He laughed. "Preordained? Geesh, kid. Is that the fifth-grade word of the week or what?"

"No. I read it," Carly said, being coy.

"In what did you read it?" Nick tried to match her.

"I think it was in *Messenger*."

"Good book." Nick had introduced her and Lindsay to the tales of Lois Lowry. The next year they were assigned by her teacher.

"OK. So what does it mean, *preordained*?" he said, still teasing.

Carly was silent and he could only see the back of her head against his knees. He poked her in the ribs. She elbowed him.

"Huh? What does it mean?"

"It means that everything that happens is already supposed to happen," she said and Nick could hear the clip of anger in her voice. "If people are going to die, they die. And there's nothing you can do about it."

He let it sit for a minute, silently cursing himself for setting a semantics trap that had hurt her and that had bitten him back.

"Maybe that's what that specific word means, baby. But that's not the way it is," Nick said, with authority, because he believed it.

Carly did not sniffle, did not even clear her voice. She simply remained silent while Nick stroked her hair.

"See?" she finally said, pointing her finger at the television screen. "The blond one is the smart one."

When the program was done, Carly got up and put her dishes in the sink and reminded her father that today her friend Jessica was having a birthday party and that he would have to drop her off in an hour.

Nick must have looked quizzically at her and she read his face and put a hand on her hip, just like her mother used to do to him.

"It's on the board, Dad. We talked about it on Wednesday, and you said fine, so we've got to be there by eleven."

"Right, right, right. You got it, babe. I didn't forget," Nick said, knowing she knew he'd forgotten. He tried to smile his way out of it. "Jessica's it is. Her mother's name is Ro. Her brother is Tyler. Her dad is Bob."

Carly frowned a frown that was filled with sarcasm but included that small twinkling humor in her eye.

"That would be correct, Dad," she said and he again marveled at her ability to be so damned quick and grown-up. Fast on the draw, just like her mom.

At ten thirty Carly was dressed and waiting by the door with a small wrapped present in her hands. Nick felt himself hustling to find his car keys. When they arrived in Jessica's neighborhood, he remembered exactly where to turn. He was trying to impress Carly, to show her that he was paying attention to her life. Without hesitation he spotted the Lipinskis' dominating two-story at the end of a cul-de-sac and he figured it made him look like a genius. He got out with Carly and went to the door instead of just dropping her off. Ro Lipinski welcomed them and when they stepped into the house, Carly spotted Jessica and two other girls back on the wide pool patio and with a flip of her fingers and a "'Bye, Dad," skipped away. Ro, an attractive woman with short blond streaked hair and a swimmer's athletic figure, asked if Nick wanted a cup of coffee.

"Bob's out with the boys teaching them how to play golf," she said.

Nick smiled and declined, his eyes following his daughter through the glass doors and the smiles and little-girl greetings. Ro watched the side of Nick's face.

"How's she doing, Nick?"

Her question brought him back.

"Good. I, uh, think she's good," he said.

The woman's face was showing concern, like a mom. She had been close with Nick's wife. Their kids shared schools and birthday parties. Both sets of parents shared cookouts and the occasional dinner out on weekends.

"The school counselor says that this Christmas should be easier than last year, but no guarantees. You know? They don't like to give you guarantees," Nick said, turning his gaze back out to where the girls were huddled around some new blow-up pool toy.

"Well, she's pretty good here when they're all together, Nick. I know it's still got to be hard over at your house when it's quiet," Ro said, her voice consoling, like it had been at the funeral and every time Nick had seen her since.

"Yeah, well, it's probably good for her to be around the girls instead of just me on the weekends."

Nick looked past the woman's eyes. Shifted his weight from one foot to the other. He hadn't moved off the flagstone in the entryway.

"And how are you doing, Nicky?"

"I don't know," he said. "It's been two years. I shouldn't still be dwelling on it that much. But I am, and you know something? I don't give a damn if I am."

Ro was looking in his face, nodding. Nick could feel his skin redden, caught clumsy by his own anger. He shifted his weight again and put his hand in his pocket and wrapped his fingers around his car keys. He wanted to run, leave his daughter here, giggling and playing and being happy, and just run.

"I know, Nicky. I know," Ro said, reaching out to touch his arm. "Look, when you come back to pick her up, come a little late, OK? Bob will be back with the boys and maybe you guys can talk, you know? Maybe you and Carly can stay for dinner or something."

"Sure, maybe that'll be a good idea," Nick said, even though he and Bob Lipinski had never been so close as to have heart-to-hearts about anything personal, and he doubted that that was going to change now. He started to back out through the front door.

"Yeah, I'll be back to get her about five, alright?"

She could see the look of lingering pain on his face and called after him. "She'll be fine, Nick."

He waved. "Yeah, sure. I know," he said and kept moving.

///

When Nick got back home, he sat at the empty kitchen table and began to make a mental list. He'd have to call Ms. Cotton early tomorrow to see about the collection of letters. If Hargrave got to her first, he could only make a request with the press officer to see what they'd come up with. Because the detective had loosened somewhat with information, Nick was holding out hope that the guy would share. It was still a give-and-take with him. He would also have to check out this OAS meet. If it was ten days off, Deirdre wouldn't get to it until this week. Daily newspaper editors rarely thought of anything more than a few days in advance and then jumped in with both feet when the show was just about to begin.

Nick caught himself mentally pissing and moaning again. It's just the nature of the biz, he told himself. That's the way it is. "Shut up," he said and the reverberation of his own voice stopped him. His wife would have looked over at him and shaken her head: "Talking to your-self again?" But she would have been smiling, knowing how he could get lost in his head and suddenly come out with statements and half thoughts so out of context that she couldn't help but laugh.

He'd also have to check on the list that Lori was putting together on sniper-related deaths in the state. Had she already sent that to him?

"Jesus, man. It's Sunday, Nick," he said, again out loud to himself. "Chill."

He went through the remnants of the Sunday paper, sorted out the sections that had nothing to do with news and got up and went to the couch in the living room. He'd been up late with Hargrave and hadn't slept when he did get in. Now it was quiet. The girls are gone. Take advantage of the day. He lay down with that thought in his head, then edited himself. Only two girls are gone, Nick, he thought. The third one needs you, man. Needs you to be strong. He held the newspaper up in front of his face. He'd stopped crying months ago even though the need was still with him. He focused on the sports pages. You can do this, Nick, he thought, repeating a mantra that had become very old for him. You can do this.

He tried to focus on a photo of Alonzo Mourning, started to read the paper's basketball beat writer opining about the star center's struggle and victory over kidney disease, but as he drifted off he saw his daughter sitting in the stands at a Miami Heat game, smiling and cheering. Lindsay, his dead daughter. His eyes came back open and he tried to clear them, and read about doctors still being amazed that Mourning had returned to the court, but he drifted off again and saw his wife's face as she closed the door on the girls' room. And he followed her vision into their room and there was candlelight flickering on the walls and the glow was warm and then her face appeared above him. She was whispering something that he could not hear. She was beautiful and her honey-blond hair was falling down in his face and she was straddling him and looking down and he could feel her against him, the warmth of her, and he could feel himself growing hard. She said something in his ear, a warning, but he did not want to hear it. He wanted the movement of her hips to continue and he could see the candlelight flickering in time to their rise and fall. And she tried to say something in his ear again, the brush and moisture of her breath both exciting and distracting him, and he turned his face away and let the sensation of sex take him over and then he tried to roll with her, but suddenly the warmth was gone and Nick woke with his eyes wide open. "Jesus," he said out loud. "What the hell was that?"

He was on the couch, the disorientation clearing fast. The newspaper had fallen to the floor. The light of late afternoon was slicing through the front blinds. He sat up and recalled the dream.

"Shit," he said, again out loud in the empty house. But it was not said in anger. He checked his watch: 3:40 PM. He had slept, or dreamed, or both, for almost three hours and it had been deep and not at all unpleasant. He sat up and realized he had to take a shower. Then he could go pick up Carly. Tomorrow he would sort out work. He was not embarrassed by his unconscious afternoon excursion and was in fact in higher spirits than he had been in a long time.

/ Chapter 18 /

On Monday Nick was back in the office, checking faxes and e-mails from a variety of law enforcement offices and from sources that he had scattered about South Florida and beyond.

There was a sheaf of fax paper on his desk, gathered from the machines in the newsroom over the weekend. Even though e-mails would be easier, police agencies still hadn't caught up with technology and still sent news releases out by facsimile machines to newspapers, television newsrooms and radio stations. They'd give a short synopsis of crime events. They might include names and dates and arrest numbers and a line of description of an armed robbery or gang shooting or multicar accident. If a newsroom had an interest, it was up to them to call and dig deeper. If the skeleton crew that manned the weekends missed anything worth writing about, Nick would have to pick it up on Monday morning. A two-day-old robbery was no good to him, the neighborhood already knew about it. A car fatality that happened over the weekend was old news by Tuesday's paper, which was what he was writing for on Monday. Unless there was a great hook—a thirteen-year-old gets in an accident while driving his pregnant mom to the emergency room for a delivery; a seventy-five-year-old grandmother shoots a burglar in her bedroom—Nick usually pleaded ignorant. "Hey, if we missed it, we missed it."

But today he was looking carefully for anything that might appear to be a random shooting, anything with a high-powered rifle involved, anything that might have a tie-in to a sniper working, no matter how peripheral. He recalled years ago hearing from a middle school education reporter of a sixth-grader being caught with a handgun. The kid told security officers at the school that he'd found the gun in the street on his way to school. They dismissed it as a lie. Later the gun turned out to be the weapon used to kill a prominent racing boat tycoon who had been assassinated as he sat in his car. Nick had learned years ago that stories are always out in the streets. The media only picks up on a fraction of them and the cops only a small fraction more.

When nothing in the weekend pile of faxes showed any promise, Nick started going through e-mails. He had one from the Bradenton Sheriff's Office giving him a number to call to reach the detective handling the shooting of the doctor who'd killed his wife. Another was from a Washington Bureau reporter whom he'd asked earlier to find out more about Fitzgerald:

Nick: I'll have to look further on the Secret Service guy. He's not their usual front man on State visits. Must be a back-roomer. I'll get back to you.
Rafael

The rest of the e-mail stuff looked too routine to bother with. Nick leaned back and started making his regular phone checks. Nick had been at the game for enough years to know who was plugged in and had an ear to the streets.

His first call was to the medical examiner's office to see if there were any fresh bodies from the weekend. A receptionist he knew answered.

"Hey, Margie. Anything new in the back room from the weekend?"

He heard Margie shuffling papers: "Nothing unnatural, Nick. Sorry."

Nick often wondered why they thought that the lack of violence would disappoint him. He didn't get paid by the number of dead people he wrote about. Sometimes he felt like a phone solicitor for Fuller Brush: *Got any death today? No? Sure? We're having a special for the front page tomorrow. OK, I'll check back with you later. Have a good day!*

His second call was to the Sheriff's Office communications desk. He was listening to the fifth unanswered ring when he heard a voice over the police radio near his desk. The dispatcher's voice was cranked just a notch above dispassionate.

"Kilo-nineteen, kilo-nineteen. Report of a man down on the side-walk. One hundred block of East McNab Road. Possible gunshots. Repeat. Possible gunshots."

Nick stood up and reached over to crank up the radio volume. He recognized the address as a corrections and parole office. He was listening to the radio with one ear, the ringing phone with the other. The phone spoke first.

"Broward Sheriff's Office, dispatch, Sergeant Sortal."

"Yeah, hey, Sarge. This is Nick Mullins from the *Daily News.* Anything going on today or over the weekend that we ought to know about?"

Nick always tried to sound friendly, like he and they were both on the same team, especially if he didn't recognize the person on duty.

"Nothing much over the weekend, Nick," the female sergeant said. She did not elaborate even though Nick knew that as the dispatch sergeant she was listening to the same radio traffic he was.

"So, this thing going on up at the DOC office in Pompano, what's that?" Nick said. Typically, the cops knew how to blow off the press if they could. It was always better to know a little bit going into the questions, like priming a stubborn pump.

"Well, I'm not sure about that yet, Nick. All we have so far is a man down with units on the way. Might be heatstroke as far as we know."

Nick figured this was probably bullshit since he'd already heard the call about possible gunshots.

"And it's not at a DOC building. It's a parole office in the center there," she said, using her knowledge to one-up him, but inadvertently giving him information that he didn't have.

"OK, well, I'll check back with you later on that. Thanks a lot."

"Have a nice day," she said and hung up.

Nick did not apologize for being a skeptic—it came with the job. As a daily journalist you want to know immediately what's going on, even if you discard half of it later. The government or business entities you cover do not share that enthusiasm. They want to spin things so they don't look bad, or, Nick conceded, they want to have all their ducks in a row before they tell you. Nick recognized this. He in fact held the opinion that everything eventually would come out. Even the identity of Deep Throat came out. Sure, it was thirty years after Mark Felt's information put an end to President Nixon. Still, a journalist's hunger to know is what drives the good ones, and Nick was too hyped up about guys dropping in the streets from unheard gunshots to wait. He called a friend at the city of Pompano Beach with the paramedic rescue unit.

"Hey, Billy. Nick Mullins from the *Daily News*. How you doin'?"

"Nicky! Hey, what's going on? Your girls going to get involved with the softball league this year or what? We really need Lindsay on the mound again."

Billy Matthews was a city administrator who oversaw the fire and rescue services for the city. His daughter had been on the same athletic teams that Carly and Lindsay were on. They were passing friends due to being fathers. Billy had obviously forgotten about Lindsay and Julie's deaths when he'd picked up the phone.

"I'm not really sure yet, Bill. I'm going to have to see if Carly's up to it yet, you know."

"Jesus. I'm sorry, Nick. Yeah, sure, see if she's up to it. It would be great to see you two back involved, you know?"

Now it was coming back to him, Nick thought.

"Yeah. But Billy, right now I need some help on a call you guys have going over near the DOC office. My sources say there might be a shooting victim out there and, you know, I don't know if I should run up there on it. Could you do a check for me and see how serious it is? I'd appreciate it."

"Nobody here has said anything to me yet. Let me check a second. Let me make a call and get right back to you."

Nick knew he now had the poor guy over a barrel. The man had forgotten about Nick's dead wife and daughter. Now he had to figure he owed him something. And hell, it was probably nothing. Maybe some guy did have heatstroke and some old lady passing by started screaming gunshots. It was South Florida, after all, filled with both heat and easily wigged-out retirees.

Nick sat back down at his desk with the police radio turned up even if he did know that the cops would switch over to an unmonitored tactical channel if they found anything good. He went back to his computer, called up a blank screen and typed in some times and locations on the radio call like he usually did on a breaking story. If the early reports eventually washed out, he'd just kill the notes later. Still better to put some facts down just in case. He stored the file and then went back into some earlier stuff. He had not yet been through all the research on statewide shootings involving high-powered rifles.

He scrolled through the listings. Lori had been thorough, as was her way:

A forty-eight-year-old man up in the central part of the state killed by fellow hunter. I.D.s on both of them. Friends since grade school.

A woman in Tallahassee shot dead by her common-law husband with a rifle during a domestic dispute involving allegations of infidelity.

A mysterious killing in the Keys in which police found a man dead in his boat with a gunshot wound to the head. The caliber of the gun that killed him was considered a large-caliber in early stories. Nick read the follow-ups, feeling a slight shiver in his blood. Forensics found the bullet lodged in the interior gunwales of the dead man's boat. An odd .303-caliber. Nick jumped three stories and found disappointment. The killing had been attributed to another fisherman, pissed because he thought the other guy had been raiding his favorite holes. The shooter had turned himself in after four days of speculation. Nick did not recognize the names. He moved on.

Four stories later was a story out of Sebastian, a city on the east coast up north near Daytona.

> Indian County sheriff's officials have released the name of a man found dead in front of a west Sebastian home Thursday as Martin J. Crossly, a 32-year-old house painter who had apparently been renting the home for some eight months.
>
> A medical examiner's report released over the weekend showed that Crossly, who was a former inmate at the Avon Park Correctional Institution in Polk County, died of a single gunshot wound to the head. Police said today that Crossly had an extensive criminal history and had apparently been living in the Sebastian home on the north side along Louisiana Boulevard since being freed from prison in December after serving three years on a conspiracy charge.
>
> Neighbors in the area near the FEC tracks said they were not familiar with Crossly and indicated that the home had long been used as a crack house before he moved in.
>
> "The victim was shot once with a large-caliber bullet from an unknown rifle," said Deputy Chief Larry Longo of the Indian County Sheriff's Office. "With the kind of background this guy had, I'm sure he had plenty of enemies."
>
> According to published reports, Crossly's prison stretch was the result of . . .

Nick did not need to read further. He knew Crossly's name, and knew his crime. Crossly was the delivery boy of a bomb that was sent to a small North Florida city meant to kill a woman who was turning state's evidence on a Broward drug dealer. Crossly's car was stopped by a Florida Highway Patrol trooper for speeding on an interstate near

Tallahassee, only forty miles from his destination. Suspicious of the man's answers to questions concerning where he was headed and the fact that he was driving a rental car, the officer asked Crossly to open the trunk. Inside was a box wrapped in birthday paper. The trooper asked Crossly if he could open the package. When Crossly said sure, the cop unwrapped a microwave oven and, looking through the door window, saw a package of some sort inside. When he opened the door, a powerful bomb rigged to the handle exploded, blowing the trooper into pieces. In the grisly aftermath a medical examiner's team had to do a step-by-step inspection of a forty-yard circle around the point of detonation to collect the trooper's remains.

Nick had written a huge story on the case and had quoted several street sources about the close personal link between the drug dealer who sent the bomb and Crossly. On the corners of northwest Fort Lauderdale, Crossly was known as the dealer's enforcer. There was no doubt among rival dealers and runners that Crossly knew exactly what he was carrying that day. In time, the dealer was arrested and charged with the murder of a law enforcement officer and sent to death row. But despite Nick's stories, which, as usual, were never allowed in court, Crossly was able to lighten his load by agreeing to testify against the dealer. Prosecutors offered him a conspiracy charge and he took it. He had been out on parole when someone shot him dead on his porch.

Dr. Chambliss.

Martin Crossly.

Steven Ferris.

All criminals with ugly homicides in their pasts. All subjects of extensive stories Nick had done for his newspaper. All killed on the street. Coincidence?

Nick had done hundreds of stories about criminals over the years, and no doubt other journalists would have done pieces on these guys too. But Nick had stepped up on these guys. He'd been both pissed and fascinated by their crimes, and to prove they were evil he'd checked more sources, dug into pasts, quoted more than the official side. He hated to admit it, but Deirdre had let him do the kind of extensive pieces on these guys that few reporters were allowed, bless her clompy shoes.

He started to scroll down the research list again, hungry this time for names that he recognized. He was about to call Lori's desk to get her to run another search, this time matching any names in the stories she'd sent him and his own byline. He was reaching for the phone when it rang just as his fingertips touched it, causing him to flinch.

"Nick Mullins," he said, finally picking up the line.

"It's Billy, Nick. Hey, this is all on the QT, right?"

"Yeah, yeah, Bill. I just need to know if I should run up there, you know?"

"OK. Rescue has a white male by the name of Trace Michaels, DOA when they got there. Single bullet wound to the head. It was actually in the doorway of the probation and parole office in that block. They didn't move the body because he was obviously dead when they got there. Guys said half his head was missing from the back. Ugly scene, Nick."

Matthews listened to silence for a moment.

"Nick? Did you get that?"

"Repeat that name for me," Nick said, his brain now flashing.

"Trace Michaels. M-I-C-H-A-E-L-S."

"Thanks, Bill. I appreciate it," Nick said.

"OK, Nicky, but remem—"

Nick hung up before the administrator could finish his sentence.

Three was too many. Four was impossible. Nick was up and on his way through the newsroom, his eyes glazed with remembering, when an editor called out his name.

"I'm going to a shooting in Pompano," he answered, snapping his notepad on the edge of the woman's desk as he walked by and left it at that. On his brisk walk to the elevators he was thinking, Trace Michaels, dead. Maybe they should give this shooter a medal.

/ / /

Nick drove north on Dixie Highway through the bedroom communities of Wilton Manors and Oakland Park, thinking about Mary Chardain's face, the skin on her left cheek and forehead whitened in splotches where the burned and crinkled skin had to be removed. Her thin arms, lying out straight on the hospital bed, were still gauzed and Nick had already been told by the nurse of the agony the woman would have to go through as those bandages were regularly removed, dead skin removed and then the new raw layer rewrapped. Trace Michaels had sloshed rubbing alcohol over the head of his lover of six years and set her on fire. "Jesus," Nick said aloud in the car, remembering the guy's face. A public defender had argued Michaels's case, claiming that both he and Chardain were drug addicts and the alcohol had accidentally spilled on Mary when they were cooking another dose together and had caught fire. Nick had done a story on Chardain and her daughter, a bright eleven-year-old who witnessed the incident and had jumped to her mother's aid. Michaels had gone down for attempted murder. But somehow—and Nick was thinking about the prison overcrowding that was forcing the release of model prisoners and the use of gain time, which cut their sentences down for good behavior—Michaels was back on the street.

When he got to McNab he turned east and as he went through the light at Cypress Road he could see the collection of cop cars and Pompano's yellow-green rescue trucks blinking in the next block. He pulled over into a small shopping center, parked his car and walked the rest of the way, watching, searching the rooflines of any building tall enough to give a sniper an angle on the offices where the largest knot of paramedics and cops were gathered. By now Nick had lost his skepticism. This was another one. As he approached he saw the paramedics reloading their truck, no one to treat or transport. A couple of deputies were standing just off the sidewalk, talking quietly, their backs purposely turned to the yellow sheet that covered a lump behind them. The body had not been moved and still lay mostly on the sidewalk, only its feet jamming open the door of the parole office. Nick stopped at the crime scene tape that was stretched around three parked cars, positioned to keep the gawkers at a distance. He was looking for a familiar face among the officers to signal to when he saw Hargrave step out of the building with a pen in his mouth and a leather-bound notebook in his hand. Nick stayed silent, watching the detective look down at the body. The ballpoint pen was between his teeth and was flicking back and forth like a metronome. He bent his knees and folded himself down like some adjustable ladder so that he was on the balls of his feet. Then he peeled back the yellow sheet, looked under it and finally turned his gaze to the sky, the rooflines. Nick knew he had been right.

"Detective?" Nick called out, as any reporter at the scene would.

But unlike any other reporter, he was summoned by a crook of Hargrave's finger and he raised the plastic tape and slipped under.

The beefy sergeant who seemed to run with Hargrave as protection, though Nick doubted that the wiry detective would need any in a street fight, stepped up to block his advance only a few feet from the body.

"It's OK, Tony," Hargrave said and the big man backed off.

The detective stayed in his crouch and Nick joined him. Hargrave said nothing and instead pulled back the yellow tarp and exposed the dead man's face. Nick was not squeamish and knew that it was not Hargrave's intent to shock him. In profile, the man's face had already gone whiter than normal. The dark stubble on his cheek and chin was unnaturally distinct, as if each follicle were raised in relief. Nick knew that the other cheek on the ground would be the opposite, growing dark purple as the blood settled at the lowest point. The man's exposed and wide-open right eye had already lost its glisten of moisture. Hargrave pulled the sheet back farther. The back portion of the man's head, behind the ear, had been ripped open by a heavy round.

"The woman in front of him opened the door and then dropped a set of keys. Our victim apparently had just begun to bend down to get them when she heard a 'slap,' as she described it," Hargrave said. "She's inside, trying not to look at the blood spatter all over her dress."

Nick stood up, not needing to see any more. Hargrave replaced the sheet and stood with him.

"Look familiar?" the detective said.

"Trace Michaels," Nick said quietly. "I did a takeout piece on him a few years ago. He's the guy who doused his girlfriend with alcohol and set her on fire."

"Good memory," Hargrave said.

"I remember them all," Nick replied.

They both went quiet for several seconds, maybe realizing what they both shared.

"I think we better step into the office here, Mr. Mullins."

Hargrave led the way around the body and into the reception area of the parole office. There were plastic chairs against two walls. A glassed window, slid shut, was in the middle of the third wall. They passed through a door into an interior hallway and Nick saw a small huddle of what he took to be employees sitting around a small break table in one room, talking quietly but in voices that were unnaturally high with anxiety and the breathlessness that goes with, "My God. I could have been walking in that door myself."

Hargrave opened the third door, checked for anyone inside and then nodded Nick in. The detective sat on the edge of a crowded desktop stacked with folders and what Nick recognized as Florida Statute books. With one skinny haunch on the desk, Hargrave's knee hung at a ninety-degree angle like a broken stick and his elbow was bent in the same geometric way while he stroked his chin. Nick had an unwanted vision of an erector set flash through his head.

"Mr. Michaels was coming in for his weekly visit to his parole officer," Hargrave began, opening his notebook as though he were checking the time. "A nine o'clock appointment. The PO says the guy had been consistent ever since he was released from his road prison gig last July. Hadn't missed a check-in and his spot urine had been clean of drugs every time."

"So how would our sniper know when and where he was coming in?" Nick asked, sitting down in the one chair that was probably meant for clients.

Hargrave hesitated at the question and looked Nick in the face. "Our sniper?" he finally said.

"OK, then, my sniper," Nick said, surprising himself with the tight anger in his own voice. He took a deep breath and then laid his findings out for Hargrave, how his research showed that now there were four felons or ex-cons who were dead of high-powered rifle fire and who had also been the subjects of major takeouts that Nick had written for the *Daily News*. Yes, he admitted the jurisdictions of the first two were different, then these two right here in his backyard.

"It's like he's working off my damned bylines," Nick said.

"Whoa, whoa, whoa," said Hargrave. "Paranoia we don't need, Mullins."

Nick pressed his lips together into a hard line. OK, he thought. Don't let your mouth get you into trouble again. This time he started out calmly, just the facts.

"Chambliss, Crossly, Ferris and now Michaels," Nick said. "I've done special takeouts on every one of them. Big, bylined pieces."

"So have half a dozen other reporters," Hargrave said.

"No, not in-depth pieces. Not the kind of coverage that really showed who and what these guys were. Hell, some of these psychopaths never got more than their five minutes of media infamy," Nick responded, again keeping his voice under control. "The *Herald* and the local city papers all did stories on Ferris. It was a big thing. But Chambliss wasn't local. No other paper down here followed that."

"And this guy lying out there on the sidewalk? Everybody else just treated what he did to his girlfriend like it was some domestic fight."

Hargrave was still perched on the desk like some kind of tabletop decoration, as if his stiff crane neck were going to dip his beak down into a cup of water at any moment.

"OK, say we inject your ego into the equation, Mullins," he finally said. "You friendly with any good snipers? You have any grand theories on which master criminal you've written about is next on the list to have his head blown off? Maybe he's just doing them alphabetically."

Nick stared at the detective, not realizing his own mouth was slightly open while he went through the names in his head and realized that the detective had already mentally sorted them.

"Speaking of lists," Nick said, figuring where the alphabet might fit in, thinking of the Secret Service man's list.

Hargrave might have smiled, but anyone observing would have been hard-pressed to testify to it. The detective opened up his notebook and removed a sheet of paper. Nick tightened his fist, resisting the urge to reach out and snatch it from Hargrave's hand.

The detective read, his eyes jumping from spot to spot on a page that Nick couldn't see.

"Since you never gave me Chambliss and this Crossly guy, I'm a little reluctant to be handing over internal documents to some reporter."

"They weren't in your jurisdiction," Nick said. "I figured you wouldn't care."

Hargrave just looked up over the top of the paper, his pewter-colored eyes static. Nick figured he was trying to think of something pithy. Or was he actually trying to decide whether he did give a damn? The praying mantis was not without some compassion, Nick thought. After another beat the detective handed the paper to Nick.

"Your copy," he said.

Nick flipped it over. There was no heading, just a typed list of names and dates and jurisdictions that covered a number of different states. Someone had put checkmarks next to Chambliss, Crossly and Ferris. Michaels was farther down, not yet acknowledged. Nick again started from the top, searching while his heart rate increased looking for more names that he recognized as subjects of his own writing. He stopped at a couple of last names that were familiar, but one was in California and the other in Texas. Doubtful, he thought.

"So these are the ones that Fitzgerald is checking out?" Nick said.

"At least they're the ones he was willing to give up."

"You think he's made the connection between these four and my stories?"

"Like I said about your ego, Mullins. Fitzgerald's looking for a threat to the Secretary of State. He's gonna tap anything he can, even if it's some vigilante offing assholes who burned their lovers or raped little girls. A psycho is a psycho. Who knows their motivations?" Hargrave said. "But our guy isn't some paid political assassin. Our guy is a whole different breed. Frankly, I don't know what the hell he's capable of."

"OK, so we've got Charles Bronson playing sniper from the rooftops of Broward County."

"You might put it that way, but my name better never show up agreeing with you," Hargrave said. "Besides, the Bronson character was being a hell of a lot less discriminating than this guy. Our guy's obviously doing some planning, lying in wait, leaving no sign other than the damn bullet behind."

"You match them up with forensics?"

"I just shipped this one," Hargrave said, jerking his thumb behind him toward the front where Michaels's body was cooling on the street. "And we'll have to get the others from those cases of yours out of our jurisdiction if they ever found or kept them. Believe it or not, every department doesn't exactly follow *CSI: Miami*'s television protocol."

Nick knew that crime scene technicians rarely did so much as a fingerprint check on ninety-nine percent of the crimes committed in their territory, much less ballistics and supposed laser scans. Only the high-profile murders would warrant that and this group of dead criminals were far below priority, though he had a feeling that was about to change.

Hargrave had gone quiet and Nick had the sense that this meeting was through.

"So what's next?" he asked.

"To the morgue," Hargrave said, standing up. "You want me to get your CD back from Dr. Petish while I'm there?"

Jesus, Nick thought, what doesn't this guy know?

"No, that's alright. I'll just get it later after you get done," he said, grinning.

They were at the door when Hargrave suggested that Nick go over the list that he'd given him and let him know if any of the names came up familiar on second reading.

"And speaking of lists," the detective said, mocking Nick again. "Ms. Cotton claims she doesn't have any kind of sympathy letters that she kept from the time after her children were killed."

Nick didn't know how to react. He was wondering why the woman would recant such a thing.

"But she's not a very good liar," Hargrave said. "She stonewalled me early this morning. Why don't you take a visit and see if she'll give them up to you?"

"Yeah, OK," Nick said. "But I'm also going to need some information and quotes from you on this thing for tomorrow's paper."

Hargrave held Nick's eyes for a moment and then seemed to give in to something he'd probably prided himself on for a career.

"Yeah, alright. Here's my cell number. Call me when you need it."

Nick took down the number and watched the detective pick his way through the office and leave. Then he stopped at the room where the employees of the parole office had gathered.

"Excuse me," he said and they all looked at him in anticipation. "I'm Nick Mullins from the *Daily News*. Can anyone tell me about what happened here?"

/ Chapter 19 /

Nick was inside with the parole office employees for a good forty minutes, taking down quotes and names and spending extra time with the woman whose dress was still spattered with blood, when Hargrave's sergeant at arms came in with a disgruntled look and gave him the thumb.

Nick nodded, thanked the group and left the offices. Outside, there were a few television trucks around the circumference of the crime scene and the body of Trace Michaels had been removed. One of the Channel 7 guys was about to do a standup with the scene as his backdrop when his cameraman spotted Nick coming out the door and maybe mistook him for a detective. He gave his TV reporter the high sign. When the guy turned and recognized Nick, he passed the microphone and came over to meet him, lifting the crime scene tape as if he were doing Nick a courtesy.

"Nicky, hey, what the hell, man? You're obtaining special access these days?" the reporter said, nodding back toward the crime scene.

"I don't know about that, Colin. I got here early and they were still scrambling a little. I guess I kinda slipped through," Nick said, giving the guy a little wink as though only they knew what that meant.

Nick was not into the "breaking exclusive" anymore. He'd been on the beat for enough years to have lost the instant competition shit that goes on in the news business. He wasn't one to give away the farm, but he didn't mind helping someone out with information he knew they were going to get from the press officer anyway. And it always helped to be one of the guys, us against them. He also often got a kick out of this chap's British accent and breathless delivery of a particularly heinous crime. He pulled out his notepad and went through some of the basics for him: Trace Michaels's name and date of birth, the fact that he was showing up to report to his PO when he was shot just outside the door and a little taste of what the employees were feeling on the inside, including a description of the woman who'd been just in front of the ex-con when he went down.

"Jesus. Did she see anything when it happened, you know, a drive-by or something?" the Brit said.

"No. She didn't say," Nick said, thinking of a way to move on without acting like he was keeping something important to himself. "She did get some of the guy's blood spattered on her dress. You know, she was pretty upset."

Nick could see the light go on in the guy's head. "When it bleeds, it leads" was the unofficial motto of his station. He'd spend half the day out here for the chance to get a shot of the stained dress on a weeping witness.

"Christ, thanks, Nicky," he said. "She's still inside, then?"

"Yeah, probably be coming out soon. I can't see them keeping the office open after all that."

Nick shook the chap's hand and walked away, only feeling a tiny bit guilty.

/ / /

When he got to his car, Nick called the city desk and filled them in on the shooting of Trace Michaels, another criminal gunned down by an unknown assailant. He told the assistant editor on duty that he would continue working the story from the streets and that he would be in to write in a couple of hours. He also let them know that somewhere in the archives they would have a photo of Michaels to run with the story, as he had done a major piece on the guy before.

"OK, Nick. Great. But let me ask you something, though," the assistant said. "This is like the one last week you did? The jail shooting?"

"Yeah, kind of," Nick answered, knowing what was coming.

"So, you know, Deirdre was asking if we have some kind of a trend thing going here? I mean, maybe you could put together a trend piece or something for midweek?"

Yeah, thought Nick, a trend piece: Subjects of reporter's stories being killed one by one at the hands of a serial sniper.

"Sure. Maybe. Let me get this one rolling first and tell her I'll get with her later, OK?" he said instead.

"Great, Nick. See you when you get in."

Nick could see the wheels working: Deirdre standing up at the noon editors' meeting offering up the story, sketching out a real "reader" for the folks before she knew a goddamn thing. Nick shook it off. "Way of the world, man," he whispered to himself and then started the car and headed west toward Margaria Cotton's.

On the way he dialed Ms. Cotton's number twice on his cell but only got an unanswered ring. He was trying to piece together why the woman would lie to Hargrave about the box of letters she'd kept from the time of her children's death. She'd been far too open with him to have made something like that up and Nick couldn't see a reason to keep it a secret from the detective. He was debating whether he should leave a note in her door explaining what he wanted when he finally turned the corner onto her small street and saw her old Toyota in the driveway. He pulled up on the patchy grass in front of the house and called her number one more time, getting the same unending ring as he walked up the cracked sidewalk.

Again the small figure of Ms. Cotton opened the front door before Nick had the chance to knock. And again the interior of her small home was dark and cool behind her.

"Hello, Mr. Mullins," she said in her deceptively soft but strong voice. "I figured you would be coming."

Nick stepped in, his thoughts tossed off-balance once again by this tiny woman.

"I tried to call ahead, Ms. Cotton. To see if you were in."

"Yes, I'm sorry," she said, motioning him to the sofa. "I didn't mean to make you think I was some sort of psychic. I do have caller I.D. on the phone. I just don't like to answer it all the time. Better to talk to folks face to face, don't you think?"

"Yes, I agree," Nick said, thinking that the line could have come from his own mouth. Maybe she was psychic.

He sat down and on the glass-topped table before him was an old shoe box with a piece of string tied at its center. Ms. Cotton sat opposite him, the same as she had during his previous visit. When he looked up into her face, he saw that she too was looking down at the box.

"These are the letters?" he asked, stating the obvious. The woman only nodded.

"So would it be alright if I took them with me, Ms. Cotton?" Nick continued. "I'll certainly return them, but I'd like to go through them carefully, you know."

Ms. Cotton nodded again. "You can keep them, Mr. Mullins," she said and clasped her fingers as if to show that she would not pick up the box again.

"I, uh—no, ma'am," Nick stammered, not understanding, or perhaps not wanting to. "I'll get them back to you."

"No, sir. I am finished with them, Mr. Mullins," she said, rising to her feet again.

"OK, well. Can I ask you, Ms. Cotton," Nick said, treading carefully, "why did you tell the detective that you didn't have these?"

The tiny woman looked down at him with a quizzical expression on her face, like she was surprised he didn't understand.

"Because they aren't for him, Mr. Mullins. He didn't lose his child. They're for you," she said as though the meaning were obvious. Again, Nick looked into this strange woman's eyes that were prying into the corners of his heart like she knew what lay there better than he himself did.

"I'm not sure what you mean, Ms. Cotton. What my daughter has to do with this," Nick said, stumbling into something personal, a major professional misstep.

"This is really just research, to see if we recognize any names or, you know, recognize any threats of retribution," he said, trying to recover, but seeing that odd, almost unnatural light in Ms. Cotton's eyes as if she knew something he needed to grasp.

"What's in them isn't for retribution," she said quietly. "It's for your forgiveness."

She was staring down now at her hands, almost as if in prayer. Nick was at a loss, the word *forgiveness* rolling in his mouth like a new taste that was so foreign to him he had to decide whether to savor it or spit it out.

"I don't know what you mean, Ms. Cotton," he finally said.

The woman looked up and held his eyes.

"You've got another daughter, Mr. Mullins," she said, "who's going to need that."

/ / /

Nick put the box of letters in the passenger seat of his car and started back to the newsroom, trying to sort out what the woman had said and then giving it up as the ramblings of someone who'd been knocked off her orbit of logic by her tragedies. But each time he was stopped by a traffic light he found himself glancing over at the lid of the box, the simply tied bow of string holding it together, and a nervous energy built in his veins. Was she warning him? Was she cursing him? What kind of forgiveness could be held in a box full of letters not even meant for him to read? A horn blew behind him and he accelerated through a newly greened light and then snapped open his cell phone: Things to do, not to dwell on.

He dialed in to the newspaper library using Lori's direct line.

"*Daily News* research," she announced when she picked up.

"Lori, Nick. Hey, can you run a name for me, please? I'm coming in from a shooting from this morning. The vic's name is Trace Michaels, common spelling."

"Got it. Another single gunshot wound to the head?"

"Yeah, but I gotta tell you, Lori, I'm not sure I like the fact that you're always ahead of me," Nick said with a smile at the corners of his mouth. He knew she kept an ear on what was happening in the newsroom during the day and that she also would have been required to be at the morning news editors' meeting where they discussed what might make the next day's paper.

"You have no idea how far ahead of you I am, Nick."

But before he could ask what she meant by that, she changed the subject.

"Did you do a piece on this guy in the past too?" she asked and he could tell from the slight lilt in her voice that there was more in the question so he didn't answer right away, waiting for the punch line.

"I did that comparative list for you," she continued. "Man, you ought to buy some lottery tickets quick, Nicky. If you did a piece on this morning's guy too, you're gonna be five for five. They're going to start calling you the Grim Reaper Writer."

"Five?" Nick said, and then tripped off the names to her from memory. "Chambliss. Crossly. Ferris. And now Michaels."

"Pretty good, Nick, for a reporter," Lori said. "But you forgot Kerner."

Nick did not respond. The name had slapped him, hard.

"Charles Kerner," Lori said into the silence. "Kerner was the boy-friend of Margaret Abbott, who helped him suffocate her own father while they were robbing him at his little mom-and-pop store for cash to go buy more crack," she said, obviously reading from some document or the screen of her computer.

"From the clips it looks like some overzealous prosecutor took Abbott's twelve-year-old daughter to trial first to get leverage on the adults and the kid got sentenced to life on a felony murder charge. You wrote a piece about how the daughter was just a tag-along in the rob-bery and that the justice system sacrificed her to get convictions on the other two."

Nick remembered the case too well. He had worked the story night and day. The daughter had been raised mostly at home by Abbott, who kept her near her side for company, like a doll or a confidante or maybe just some maternal reason to live. When the girl was ten she'd been sent out to the selling streets to buy cocaine, the adults knowing that even if she did get arrested she'd be a minor and wouldn't get too busted. It started out as a court story, but Nick couldn't let the thing go. He'd spent hours with the kid's older siblings, who had escaped the home. He'd interviewed teachers about the potential the child had and the corner drug sellers about the fear in her eyes when she had to approach them. The resulting stories detailing her upbringing—details which had not been allowed in court—had been pipelined to the appeals court in Atlanta where her conviction was being reconsidered. Her mother and the boyfriend, Kerner, had been sentenced to life.

"Nick? You still there? "

"Sorry, Lori," Nick said into the cell phone. "Yeah, I remember."

"Well, I included a short piece from the Birmingham paper about Kerner being shot in a possible drive-by while he and some other Alabama road gang prisoners were out picking trash along the highway. He'd been transferred up there by DOC in a state swap to put some other convict closer to family in Florida. I'll print all this stuff out and put it on your desk and get as much as I can on this Michaels guy, alright?" Lori said.

"Thanks. Yeah, I'm on my way in now."

Five, Nick was thinking. Or seven if you include my own wife and daughter. Maybe I am the reaper.

/ / /

When he got back into the newsroom, Nick cleared a pile off his desk. Included was a manila office-to-office envelope with Lori's name written on the most recent line.

He pulled out the list of sniper-style shootings that she had culled from archives throughout the United States along with the five names that had matched with stories he'd written for the *Daily News*. From his reporter's notebook, he took out the Secret Service list of deaths that Hargrave had somehow gotten from agent Fitzgerald. Then he untied the box from Ms. Cotton and tucked everything inside. When he used his fingers to open a space between the letters, he noticed that each letter and card had been stuffed back into its original envelope with the original postal cancellation mark printed over the stamp.

He was tempted to start pulling them, but what would he be searching for? More names? Some religious poem? Some envelope marked: REDEMPTION? His fingers had pinched a single letter from the box when a voice made him jump.

"Hey, Nick. How was it out there? Do we have a story or not?"

Deirdre had left her office bunker and was roaming the newsroom, her nervous energy and aura of supervision making everyone around duck and start clicking at their keyboards. Live by the day's lineup of stories, die by the lack of same.

"Yeah, sure," Nick said, clamping the top back onto the box and shoving it down in the knee space under his desk and then flipping open his notebook for effect. "Let's see. We got a forty-three-year-old male, supposedly coming in to the parole office up on McNab to check in with his parole officer for their weekly meet, and bam! Gets one in the head just as he's opening the door."

"Nobody else but the ex-con hurt, right?"

"No, but I did get some good quotes from the woman who was standing in front of him," Nick said, lowering his voice. "Got the guy's blood splattered all over her."

"We get a picture of that? Tell me we got a picture of that!" Deirdre said, not bothering to hide her enthusiasm.

"I don't know. I think you guys dispatched a photographer after I left," Nick said. But he did know the blood factor might get her off his back for a while.

"I'll check," Deirdre said, but she didn't leave. Instead she put an elbow on the top of Nick's partition and set a hip into the side of it like she was going to stay awhile.

"I was going to have you do a security piece on that State Department visit to the OAS convention, but this is sounding a lot more interesting," she said. "So what's the deal? Drive-by? Guy doing some other felon's old lady?"

"I can't say the detectives are that far along yet, Deirdre."

"But you got the guy's background, right?"

"Sure," Nick said, again looking at his pad even though he didn't have to read it. He was just relieved that Deirdre was pulling him off the OAS gig. This was what he needed to be doing.

"Trace Michaels," he said, as if he'd finally found the name. "He was in for attempted murder after he set his girlfriend on fire. He's been out almost eight months according to the research files. Plenty of time to make more enemies, I suppose."

Nick told himself he was not really trying to steer Deirdre away from the similarities in the sniper story.

"But it's a long-range shooting, right? And it was a large-bore bullet wound, right?"

"Yeah," Nick said. She wasn't so stupid.

"So we have a serial sniper running around the city shooting ex-cons and bad men, right?"

Deirdre's language always got tougher as the excitement of a good story got up her nose. After all, she had been a reporter before she joined management.

She leaned over his partition and lowered her voice. "Nick, do we have some serial killer out there doing a Son of Sam thing to scumbags on the streets? Are you working that angle or what?"

Nick looked away and flipped through a couple of pages in his notebook like he was searching for an answer.

"We've both been at this game a long time, Deirdre. You never say never. But to tell you the truth, right now I'm not focused on speculation and screaming headlines," Nick said, getting hot. "I mean, shit, since when does two dead jump to serial killer? Christ, Son of Sam had five shooting scenes and a ballistics match in before they started calling Berkowitz a serial killer."

The heads of other reporters and editors started peeking up over their cubicles. Even with Nick's reputation the tension level of his voice was rising too high for the modern newsroom-as-insurance-office protocols. Nick went silent.

"Instead I'm looking into any connection between this guy and the one from last week, but as of this minute, I don't have anything," he began again, quietly. "Research is running some driver's license history to see if they ever even lived in the same area. And I'm trying to get the probable-cause affidavits from their prior arrests to see if they were ever listed as running together on any of their earlier crimes."

The investigative theory, Nick knew, was to find out if any of the victims had something in common that might be a motive for their killer, and by now Nick and Hargrave were both on that page.

"Alright, alright. Do what you're doing, Nick," Deirdre said and started to walk away, but stopped. "And hey, send some of your contact numbers with the Sheriff's Office over to the national desk so they can assign someone to that OAS security story."

Nick nodded and she spun on her heel again, but not all the way around.

"And hey, why not check the DOC files too. See if these guys ever spent prison time together, you know, for midweek. But not today. Today," she said, looking at her watch, "we got deadline."

As she left, Nick was cursing himself. OK, OK. I didn't tell her about the other sniper shootings out of our area, or my byline connections with these guys, five now, just like Berkowitz, smart-ass. But you are not the story, Nick. You are not the story. Hargrave had already given him shit about that theory being an ego trip and he sure wasn't tossing that ammunition to Deirdre.

He turned back to his computer and started clicking keys. But that was good about the DOC files. Why didn't I think of that?

/ / /

By seven o'clock Nick had finished the Michaels shooting story. He had not been able to track down the girlfriend that the ex-con had set aflame. His contact, a social worker in the hospital where the woman was treated, could only tell him that the burn victim and her daughter had moved out of state. The attorney who prosecuted Michaels would only say things like "What goes around, comes around" that were off the record. The public defender that represented Michaels had moved on to another lawyer job.

Nick ended up laying it out in simple news style:

> A 43-year-old construction laborer was shot to death outside a Pompano Beach parole office early Monday morning, just as he was entering for a weekly appointment.
> Trace Michaels, who worked part-time with Hardmack Construction, was declared dead at the scene in the 100 block

of McNab Road, police said. He was shot once in the head, police said.

The shooting of Michaels, who had recently served five years in prison for attempted manslaughter after setting his girlfriend aflame during an argument, was the second time in two weeks that an ex-convict has been murdered in Broward County. But sheriff's detectives investigating the shootings say they have yet to find any evidence linking the two cases.

Nick had then run out the story with quotes from the office employees at the scene and from Joel Cameron, who had given the basics of the "ongoing investigation" to all the media. While he was constructing the piece he had typed into the file some of the linkages with the lists that Hargrave had given him from the Secret Service agent and his own research from the library but had then deleted the information off his screen. If the only thread in the cases was that he had written extensive stories about the shooting victims, he wasn't going to go there. A journalist wasn't supposed to be part of any story, and he sure as hell wasn't going to go there without a lot more factual evidence.

Before he wrapped up the piece, he gave Hargrave a final call. He went through the basics of what the next morning's story would say. Hargrave only listened and gave an occasional grunt of assent, or maybe just of boredom.

"So what else do you want, Mr. Mullins?"

"It's the serial killer thing, Detective. You and I both know the other newspapers and TV are going to start pounding the hell out of that line whether they have any facts or not," Nick said. "My editors are already on my ass about it."

Hargrave again went quiet, deciding something.

"We've got a ballistics match on the bullets used in both Michaels and Ferris," he finally said. "But that's not a public fact yet, Mr. Mullins. And I don't want it to be public yet."

Nick had been in on such negotiations before. Official sources and reporters played the game every day.

"OK. Give me something else," he said. "Something that's going to benefit both of us, because you know and I know the stories I'm going to have to write if these names keep matching up."

Again silence. But this time Nick knew the detective was being thoughtful instead of uncooperative. They both knew what the accuracy, efficiency and technique of the shooter meant. Unlike the Beltway shooter, this wasn't some kid in a trunk shooting people for some insane reason. This shooter was a professional, either military- or law-enforcement-trained. Without either one of them naming it, or its purpose, they collaborated on a message in the form of a quote:

> "We will investigate both shootings as we would any illegal killing. The victims' pasts don't open up an avenue for them to be gunned down in the streets. That's not how law enforcement works in a democracy. That's not how this country operates," said Broward sheriff's homicide detective Maurice Hargrave.

The quote went high in the story.

"Maurice?" Nick had said on the phone after asking for Hargrave's full name.

"Shut up," the detective had answered.

/ Chapter 20 /

On the drive home Nick paid little attention to the traffic rules. He was in the passing lane of I-95 northbound doing well over the sixty-five limit. He had promised his daughter that he would no longer show up from work after her bedtime and that he would no longer be the father who was absent from his family's dinner table, even if it was just the two of them. And because he missed her. His wife was gone. Lindsay was gone. All Nick had left was this dry, document-chasing, linguistic-game-playing pursuit of the truth that he called work, and Carly. There was no competition. Carly would win hands down, he told himself over and over and over again.

He skipped up the driveway and walked through the front door, dropping Margaria Cotton's box of letters on the couch out of sight. Elsa passed him with a basket of laundry and said good evening in a professional manner and her strict avoidance of eye contact screamed that he had fucked up again.

Carly was at the kitchen table doing homework. Dinner was done. The dishes cleared. Nick fought the mood with a chipper "Hi, sweetheart, whatcha' doin'?"

His daughter did not look up. He pulled out the chair next to her and sat. He studied her hair, the hues of blond the sun had put in it, the glisten, just like her mother's. She used her left hand to pull one long, loose strand and tucked it behind her ear and he still stared, now at the exposed profile.

"What," she finally said, without moving her eyes from the page, "are you looking at?"

"A pretty girl," he said. He got not a crinkle of response in the corner of her eye or flinch of a smile at the corner of her mouth.

"One that is *trying* to get her homework done?" she said instead and the exasperation in her voice was much too mature for a nine-year-old and even though it was a good approximation of a pissed-off adult, it didn't quite work.

"No. One who cannot hide her wonderful heart," Nick said. "I'm sorry I'm late, babe. I got kinda caught up at the office."

"I know," she said, still not looking up. It had been his standard excuse for years.

"I know you know," he said, pushing back his chair, the wooden legs screeching on the floor.

The noise seemed to startle the girl. She jumped, just slightly, and then she pushed her own chair back and rose as Nick pivoted and she climbed into his lap and he could feel the wetness from her eyes against his neck and he held her and could think of nothing to say but kept repeating, "I'm sorry, honey. I'm sorry, I'm sorry, I'm sorry . . ."

After he had dried her tears, after they put the homework away, he waited for her to get ready for bed and this time laid down next to her and read some of her favorite Shel Silverstein poems from *Where the Sidewalk Ends*. When her eyelids fluttered and she yawned, he stroked her hair and told her he promised never to come home late again and then stared up at the ceiling thinking how often he had made that same promise to his wife. Don't go there again, Nick, he told himself and then tried to block out everything but the sound of his daughter's breathing. When it became deep and rhythmic, Nick slipped out of the room and retrieved the box of letters and sat it on the kitchen table.

He started randomly. The first letter was dated a week after the killings and was from another mother of two who scribbled condolences and then copied a psalm that included something about lambs and innocence and God's love. Nick slid it away.

Another was from a parent at the school where Ms. Cotton's girls had attended sporadically. She had known the children "both of them bright and beautiful and I cannot comprehend your anguish." No, you can't, Nick thought and flipped that one into a growing pile.

After a dozen, he started from the back of the box and became more systematic in his search, not knowing what he was searching for. He first concentrated on the place, the postmark and the date sent. Then he studied the name to see if it sparked even the slightest memory. Then he scanned the contents, getting the gist of each letter without focusing on the words. The messages were familiar. He had thrown out a similar pile a month after the death of his wife and daughter without reading or even opening the majority of them.

He was more than halfway through the box when he picked up a long envelope, business-sized, with no return address. Ms. Cotton's address was typed on the face of it. Inside was a folded sheet of stiff stationery. No card. The message was also typed: *Condolences on your loss . . . a complete and utter lack of justice . . . we failed you and your children . . . something must be done, and will . . . the elimination of those that threaten civil society . . .*

Nick jumped to the bottom of the page where the name of the writer was not signed, but simply typed, in an uncapitalized format:

yours,
mike redman

The name was so out of place Nick recognized it immediately. Redman. The SWAT team member. Five killings in the line of duty. A professional with a sniper rifle.

Nick had written an extensive story about a SWAT shooting that took place in Deerfield Beach a few years ago. His editorial board had taken the opportunity to chastise this guy Redman for killing an armed man, one of a group of guys who were selling weapons out of some motel room and then tried to shoot their way out when the team busted them. Nick had been so incensed over the editorial, he'd gone out and interviewed every team member, including Steve Canfield. He was allowed to view the video- and audiotape of the bust and heard, with his own ears, the *whumph* of the door breaking down, the shouts of "POLICE, POLICE, DON'T MOVE" and then the scuffling of feet and the sound of gunfire. He'd pulled schematics of the parking lot setup, measured the distances himself and sat in the room where this Redman guy had been acting as sharpshooter and cover man. He'd even gone out on a training day to see how the team was trained. He'd come away impressed and wrote a detailed Sunday story called a tick-tock that gave a second-by-second unfolding of the drama. He had not been allowed to interview Redman, who was still waiting to be cleared by a shooting board investigation. But Nick remembered him. Six-foot. Muscled. Close-cropped hair. And strange eyes, the kind that seemed to absorb everything around him and give nothing back. Nick had read somewhere that his partner had been killed in a SWAT operation years ago. When Redman was eventually cleared, Nick had felt a personal vindication. No one from the editorial board ever said a word to him.

He flipped over the envelope and checked the postal cancellation date. One week after the trial that found Ferris guilty of rape and murder, but long before his sentencing was overturned. Redman. Hell, when was the last time Nick had even heard the name? Last thing he could remember was the pressure of moving the guy off to another division in the Sheriff's Office after the newspaper's editorial board pissed all over the guy.

He looked down at the letter again and first thought about copying it in his home office and then second-guessed himself. He took out a reporter's notebook and a pencil instead and then turned the page, using only the tip of the eraser to touch the paper. He then copied the message word for word into the notebook, and sat back, staring at the collection on the table in front of him. He was fighting an urge to call Hargrave and tell the detective to get the hell over here. "Chill, Nick," he actually whispered out loud.

There was nothing in the letter that said the writer was intending a specific act or what form of "something" would be done. It was also some three years ago when the thing was written. Ferris had been in jail most of that time and Nick didn't even know where the hell this Redman guy had been. He knew that a cop writing to the victim of a crime was unusual because of legal considerations. But after a case was adjudicated? He'd never heard of it, though that didn't mean anything. Coincidence again? Redman writes a vague letter to the mother of two dead girls. Their killer gets shot by a sniper three years later. Redman is a sniper. He must be the avenging shooter. It was the basic logic progression you used to construct in school, always of course in a vacuum. But Nick had learned long ago that logic rarely includes the spins that unpredictable humans can put on it.

He got up from the table and opened a kitchen drawer and took out a large plastic freezer bag from its carton. Then, using the eraser, he pushed both the letter and the envelope it came in into the bag and then sealed it. He'd watched *CSI* too. He then put the bag aside and looked at the box of letters. Only halfway through. Be thorough, he told himself. Go through all of them. Don't jump to conclusions. But as he did, he only skimmed the rest of the notes with less and less interest and kept looking for another plain envelope lacking a return address.

/ Chapter 21 /

Elsa woke him in the morning, partially with the scent of fresh-brewing coffee, then fully with a careful pat on the shoulder. Nick had fallen asleep on the couch fully dressed and with a jumble of unanswered questions and barely connected trails of victims and prisoners and violence that spun him enough to twist his shirt around his middle and cause his pants to shift a quarter turn around. When he finally stood, he had to adjust his clothes before he could walk to the kitchen counter and rescue his muddled brain with Elsa's Colombian coffee, black, no sugar.

It was nearly seven and he could hear Carly shuffling and moving in the girls' bathroom that she had taken over since the accident. She had insisted on saving Lindsay's bath oils and bottled fragrances, especially the ones they'd concocted together. And even two years later he couldn't bring himself to toss them. Even in the master bath Nick had not had the heart to put away the makeup tray where Julie had kept her perfumes. He used to foolishly pick up a spritzer and squirt a cloud of her scent into the air and just stand there, breathing it in. It used to make him cry. He'd tried to break the habit. Her side of the vanity remained spotless. He used the other sink and a small kit bag in the corner that had always held his shaving stuff, deodorant and a toothbrush. Julie had joked that he was always packed and ready to go. But it had not been funny near the end and they had both known it. Still, he never changed.

When Carly was ready for school she came out for breakfast and Nick moved his coffee to the table.

"Hey, sunshine," Nick said. His face was dark and slack with fatigue, but he was trying to cover it. "What's on the agenda for today?"

"Just stuff. But we are going to get to do some more clay sculpture in art and it's going to be way cool. I'm finally going to put the legs on that angel I told you I was working on. Then we might actually get them in the kiln this week. Do you think I should paint her, or just leave her with the clay color—I mean, you can see the details and stuff without the paint and that's what counts and it's kinda weird to paint them all white and silver and stuff when nobody really knows what angels wear anyway and so what, you can do what you want, right?"

Elsa came over and set a bowl of cream of wheat in front of the girl and smiled that smile at Nick that said, *She is wound up this morning, eh?*

"Absolutely," Nick said. "Art is in the eye of the beholder and you're the beholder. Do what you want, babe."

Carly rambled on about her teacher and how she'd already figured out how to manipulate her. "I can just play around with my own ideas and she'll still give me a good grade."

Nick listened, and thought, When did these kids get so smart?, and then they heard the car horn outside and his daughter jumped up, kissed him on the head, said, "'Bye, Dad," kissed Elsa and thanked her for the half eaten breakfast and then blew out through the front door, leaving a fragrance and an energy wafting behind.

Nick sat for a moment, sipping his coffee. When he finally rose, Elsa looked him in the face.

"You look like the sin, Mr. Mullins," she said with her thick accent and shaking her head as one might at a shameful sight.

"Thank you, Elsa," Nick said. "I'm going to shower and then I'm going to work. Please make me some more coffee."

/ / /

He'd gone over the scenario too many times to count during the night and it was still in his head. Nick was trying to decide whether to turn the letters over to Hargrave, including the one with Michael Redman's name on it, still in the plastic bag, right on top. The box was sitting on the passenger seat next to him. He couldn't help glancing over at it, like some snake crate about to pop open and let loose a beast that would rise and start spitting venom in all directions. He knew it could be evidence, that wasn't in question, whether it *could* be. But his reluctance through the night had been twofold.

First, he'd called Lori in research before he left the house and she punched Redman's name into the local and national media database and came up with nothing. The last reference had been Nick's own story on the weapons-dealer shooting and the editorial before it. As far as he could tell, no media had any idea what the guy had been doing for the last few years or whether he was even still with the Sheriff's Office. In Nick's head, linking Redman to the recent shootings was premature.

Second, if he gave the letter to Hargrave, then it would be in their house. Could Hargrave keep it under his hat? Would he have to tell Canfield, who Nick knew was Redman's supervisor back in the day? Would anyone be able to contain it if it leaked? Tell two people and three will know. Once there are three, there will be four by the end of the day. Rumor was always exponential. He could see the *Herald*'s headlines:

FORMER SWAT SNIPER INVESTIGATED FOR RECENT KILLINGS

**MODERN-DAY GUARDIAN ANGEL GUNS DOWN BAD GUYS
IN THE STREETS**

Once the television guys and the *Herald* got the story about the letter, they'd be knocking on Margaria Cotton's front door, dredging up all the ugly memories. Yeah, Nick thought, like you already have?

"Christ!" he said. He was driving south on I-95, trailing behind some late-model Chevy Cavalier. He looked over at the box and then at his speedometer. Fifty-four. OK, he might have been driving blind for the last twenty minutes, but it was putsy blind. He wasn't a speeder when his head was tied up. By instinct he instead tucked in behind another car and followed without paying any damned attention. He punched the gas and passed the blue-haired old lady piloting the Cavalier and pushed it up to the normal sixty-five. Eight miles later he got off the interstate and then crawled with morning traffic into downtown. When he parked in the newspaper lot he left the box of letters on the passenger seat and locked the doors.

The newsroom was, as usual in the morning, quiet. Nick headed for his desk, snatching up a copy of the day's paper and glancing at the front page as he went. His story on Michaels was below the fold, in the bottom right-hand corner.

SECOND FELON ASSASSINATED IN FIVE DAYS

POLICE LOOKING FOR CONNECTION

Nick's lead paragraph had not been changed. And they had also left Hargrave's quote on the front before the story jumped and was continued on a deep inside page. Nick sighed a bit in relief, but the respite was short-lived. When he logged into his e-mail file and scanned the dozen or so names there, Deirdre's was high up with a capitalized subject field: *SEE ME!*

No, thank you, Nick thought. He started down the list, looking for someone familiar. Hargrave, Cameron, anyone. His eye instead settled on *commiekid@computrust.net* and the subject field read: *you're a smart guy, nick. m.r.* The initials had already been branded into his head overnight. Michael Redman. Nick pulled up the message: *meet me behind super saver at ten.*

He checked the time the message was sent. Almost two hours ago.

The morning paper, displaying Hargrave's paragraph, had been out since dawn. He then looked at the clock in the middle of the newsroom: nine forty-five. Fifteen minutes . . . if it was the old abandoned Super Saver Market three blocks away, he could make it.

Nick closed out the message screen and then punched Hargrave's cell number into the phone while he stood. He looked around the newsroom, where he could see only a few heads. After three rings on Hargrave's cell, there was a heavy click and a recorded answer kicked in. Hargrave's voice, in a clipped tone, said, "Leave a message." Nick's head was already dwelling somewhere else and he quickly came up with a stumbling message:

"I might have gotten a response from the sniper. I'm going to meet him. I'll call you later. Oh, the e-mail account he used to get the message to me was from an account called *commiekid@computrust.net*, so maybe you could find something out about that. I'll call you later."

Nick punched off the phone and started around his desk on the way out. He took the long way around the assistant editors' pod so Deirdre would not spot him from her office. But Bill Hirschman caught Nick's eye from his desk in front of the city editor's glass window and started toward him. When the education reporter came near, he stopped at an empty pod partition like he didn't want to get too close to Nick and catch whatever he had.

"The vultures are out after your ass, Mullins," he said, just loud enough for Nick to hear. He tilted his head back toward Deirdre's office. "They've been in there for an hour. The boss, the managing editor and the man."

Nick looked past Hirschman's shoulder, but the angle on Deirdre's floor-to-ceiling window was too severe to make out the occupants.

"Best I could hear was something about you and a vigilante story you were supposed to be working."

Nick nodded, checked his watch and said thanks.

"I'll be back, I gotta go check out a lead."

/ Chapter 22 /

Michael Redman was on the seventh floor of the parking garage attached to the Riverside Hotel, once a quaint two-story historical jewel that had been transformed into a huge chunk of lime-colored concrete block like any other modern-day structure that had gone up in the city over the past fifteen years. He was wearing navy blue chinos and a light blue short-sleeved shirt. There was a simple baseball cap, without a logo, on his head, and in his hand a zippered jacket. He could be security. Or a parking attendant. Or even a guest. He'd simply punched the PUSH HERE FOR TICKET button and then yanked the ticket and jogged in long before the wooden arm even rose. He put the card in one pocket. In the other he'd carried the spotting scope and at the moment was watching the sidewalk below, scanning the empty back lot of the closed grocery store, waiting for the arrival of Nick Mullins.

Redman had been out on the street three minutes after the *Daily News* vendor dropped a dozen papers into the honor box. He'd then sat at the kitchen table of his new condo and read and reread Mullins's story. He'd felt a warmth rise to his cheeks when he read the quote from Detective Hargrave, someone new that he'd never met during his time with the Sheriff's Office: *The victims' pasts don't open up an avenue for them to be gunned down in the streets. That's not how law enforcement works in a democracy. That's not how this country operates.*

Redman wasn't stupid. He could spot a setup when he saw it. Hargrave and some dip from media relations had slipped that one to Mullins and he'd stuck it in there. It was meant for some hothead who'd boil over at the quote and do something foolish. They didn't have a clue who they were dealing with. But the attempt to rattle him had made up Redman's mind on one point: It was time to do the last one. He'd finished his list, but he had saved one last ex-con. Now he had to talk to Mullins, face to face so that he would understand, so that he would know, and would get the story right.

When the library opened that morning at seven thirty, Redman walked in like any civilian and took a seat at the public terminals. He scrolled through some websites just to look busy. He'd visited the library several times, culling info he couldn't get from his computer at home or to track back on archived stories that other journalists like Mullins might have done on the people on his list. Sometimes he'd take the dates and addresses straight to the courthouse, walk in like any other member of the general public and use their terminals or pull the cases he wanted to look at. He'd get the probable-cause statements and take down victims' and arrestees' addresses and check the file updates to find inmate numbers to cross-reference direct with DOC. Getting information was the easy part. Staying below the radar was only a bit harder. Now he had to come up from undercover. He had to make contact with the world again and he'd already planned it out.

In the library he'd tagged a familiar mark, the kid with the earring and the Karl Marx T-shirt, who was working the computer a seat away. Redman had seen him before, probably went to the community college around the block. The kid thought he was a radical, but he did the same thing over and over. Human beings with their patterns, Redman thought.

This morning the kid sniggered a couple of times after typing something into the terminal where he was sitting and then hitting the enter key. Then he got serious and walked back into the stacks and came out with a book or two and sat back down. Redman passed behind him once and confirmed that he was using his own Internet account, probably sending messages to some girlfriend. The next time he got up and went into the aisles, Redman slipped into the kid's chair and quickly typed in Mullins's e-mail address and sent him a message and walked away.

Now he was in the parking garage, waiting to see if the reporter would take up the offer. The morning's news clipping was now in Redman's file with all the rest that marked the deaths of those deserving few on his list.

That's not how law enforcement works in a democracy. That's not how this country operates.

"No shit, bubba," Redman whispered. The courts give a child killer like Ferris another bite at the apple to see if he can knock his sentence down instead of getting the death penalty. The country goes to Iraq and indiscriminately kills anything it sees in the name of retribution for 9/11 even if the skinny woman in the burka walking down the alley wouldn't know the Twin Towers if they fell on her. The spotter tells me to kill her, I kill her. No questions asked. There's your democracy.

At least Redman knew who his spotter was now, and he would show up. He looked at his watch—9:57—then raised the spotting scope. Redman knew he'd show up.

/ Chapter 23 /

Nick looked at his watch—9:58—and kept moving. He was walking along the river, yachts and sailboats tied up along the seawall to his right, the new, monstrous condos on the left. He'd been trying to recall Redman's face since reading the e-mail and all he could conjure was the intensity of the guy's eyes when Nick had done a day of reporting on the SWAT team's training. Sharp, clear and blue. Eyes that did not flinch even after twenty minutes of hard focus. There were few people on the street. A couple of guys rubbing the brightwork on a fifty-foot double-masted schooner. A blond jogger trotting by. A delivery truck pulling into the service entrance of one of the condos. Around the curve of the river the back lot of the grocery store came into view, the exact opposite of the high-priced luxury he'd just passed. The lot was empty. The ground was covered with gravel and patchy weeds. The rear delivery doors were padlocked. Nick knew that the city had tried to save this chunk of land for a park along the river. But when the grocery chain went under, the prime real estate went to the highest bidder, another condo developer. It had been sitting unused and decaying while lawyers argued. On occasion a rumpled fisherman would be camped at the seawall, a line tossed into the New River. But it was empty now and Nick took up the spot where the fisherman would have been. He'd done this kind of thing before, met with sources who did not want to be identified and did not want to be seen with a reporter. He wasn't thinking of safety, hadn't even considered himself a target, but as he turned yet another three-sixty, scanning the back of the building and the hedge of ratty trees and sea grape that walled off the other side, he felt an uncomfortable itch on the side of his head, just above his left sideburn, and raised his hand to touch the spot with his fingers. If this guy was who Nick figured he was, there wouldn't be such a thing as safety. If he wanted to take you out, you'd be dead.

/ / /

Redman caught the movement in his spotting scope and grinned. There had always been a rumor in sniper circles that there were targets that had such premonition that they could actually feel the spot of death on their skin before you took the shot. Redman had caught Mullins in his lens as the reporter walked up the sidewalk and then followed him to the seawall, where he stopped and waited. Redman took an extra few minutes to scan the area. He knew where the stakeout people would be if Mullins had called the new detective, Hargrave, and alerted him to their meeting. From his vantage point Redman could see up all three entry streets to the river. No cop cars within two blocks. No unmarked Ford Crown Victorias that any idiot would know carried plainclothes officers. He was going to give it another five minutes of all clear when a voice behind him called out:

"Excuse me, sir. Can I help you with something?"

Redman turned and slipped the scope under his jacket all in one motion. At the ramp leading down to the next level stood a uniformed security guard, a young guy, hair cut high and tight, eyes clear and sharp, not lackadaisical and bored.

"Well, I was trying to get my bearings," Redman said, looking back out over the retaining wall and then returning to the guard. He then slipped his hand into his pocket and watched the guard approach, unwary. Not an undercover, Redman thought. No real cop would let some guy go into his pockets without reacting.

As the guard came closer, Redman continued to dig around with his fingers and then pulled out the parking ticket he'd punched out of the machine and acted as if he were examining it.

"I thought I was on the west side of the sixth floor, but I can't seem to find my car."

"This is seven, sir," the guard said, scanning Redman's clothes, but not in a suspicious manner.

"No shit?" Redman said, looking around, trying to act the part. He turned and pointed at the number seven that was painted on the front of a nearby column. "Man, I gotta get my eyes checked." He hung on to the parking ticket, waving it but not offering or letting him see it too closely.

"You can take the elevator over there down," the guard said, pointing in the direction of the center column. "But you were right about the west side."

"Yeah, well, I guess I'm not all stupid this morning," Redman said and started walking. "Thanks."

The young guard just nodded. "Yes, sir. Have a good day."

Redman took the elevator to the ground floor, convinced that his meeting with Mullins was clear.

/ / /

Nick looked at his watch—10:08—but he did not move from his spot. A lesson from years of street reporting: Don't leave the scene until you've got everything you can get or your deadline is screaming in your face. At this point in the morning there was plenty of time to write, and knowing that Deirdre was waiting with a harsh *SEE ME!* was motivation to stay away as long as possible.

He looked out onto the river, the water a dark impenetrable brown color. He recalled a description of the same spot, recorded by Fort

Lauderdale pioneer Ivy Stranahan in the late 1890s, of a river so clear you could watch the fish swimming below. Growth of the area killed that vision, as it did her husband, Frank, who committed suicide by strapping weights to his body and throwing himself into the river in a spot not fifty yards away from where Nick now stood. Nick was thinking about ghosts when he picked up on the rustle of branches off to his left and saw a man coming through the sea grape hedge.

Michael Redman did not suddenly appear like some stealthy ninja warrior. He even stumbled a bit extricating himself from the brush. At first Nick thought the man might just be a fisherman, but he was carrying nothing but a dark jacket. He was dressed peculiarly, like some gas station attendant. There were no furtive glances to see if they were alone, the man simply walked over with a confident stride and when their eyes met, any doubt was immediately dissolved.

"Mr. Mullins," Redman said and it was not a question. He stopped just within handshaking distance, but did not offer his hand.

"Michael Redman," Nick replied. He was studying the man's face, older than he remembered, cut with deep crow's-feet and lines across the forehead, sallow skin that accented the dark pouches that hung under his eyes. Not a man who slept well, Nick caught himself thinking.

"I've read your stories, Mr. Mullins," Redman said in a clear, conversational tone. "You've always impressed me with your knowledge of certain events and people."

Nick wasn't sure how to react. But being cavalier, considering the circumstances, was out.

"I believe you've made some of those stories, Mike. Especially some of the recent ones."

Nick wasn't sure that the familiar use of Redman's first name was appropriate. Redman only nodded his head, a noncommittal bob.

"I believe the now-silent subjects of those stories created those situations on their own," Redman said.

Nick didn't reply. He was assessing the man: clean clothes and freshly shaven, not living on the streets. Eyes clear of any obvious drug tinge. The man's forearms were big for his otherwise thin frame, cabled with muscle that rolled in an almost dangerous way at the slightest turn of his big-knuckled hands.

"Yeah, sometimes," Nick finally said and believed it. "Can I ask where you've been the last few years, Mike? The last time I remember seeing you was after that crazy shoot-out at the Days Inn."

The look in Redman's eyes slipped to memory and he let just the slightest twitch raise one corner of his mouth—a suppressed smile?

"Wasn't anything crazy about it," he said, extinguishing the look. "It was by the book, just like you showed in your story. Too bad your editorial board doesn't talk to you."

"Is that why you left?" Nick said, thinking instinctively about the reporter's notepad in his back pocket, but then dismissing it.

"No. Hell, I understand a little about the politics of offices like yours, and like the ones I used to work for," Redman said. "No, I stayed for a while after that and then went to hell."

Nick hesitated. Man goes to hell. What does that mean? He gave it a second thought, but he rarely pulled punches at interviews and wasn't going to start now.

"What? Alcoholism? Rehab?" he asked.

Redman laughed, outright and pure, and the softness it suddenly gave his face nearly made Nick smile.

"No, man. Though there was plenty of that over there and plenty of rehab is coming down the road for the guys that will come back," Redman said. "No, Mr. Mullins. Iraq. I went to Iraq."

He lost the laughter quickly.

"There is no hell like war," he said.

"General Sherman," Nick said quickly, a lesson from a Civil War history class jumping into his head.

"'It's glory is all moonshine. It is only those who have never fired a shot nor heard the shrieks and groans of the wounded who cry aloud for blood, for vengeance, for desolation. War is hell,'" Redman quoted. "Ol' William Tecumseh, he got that one right, didn't he?"

Nick let the silence take hold. Sometimes it was the best way to keep them talking, just say nothing, let them tell it on their own. He was watching Redman's eyes as they went out onto the river. Post-traumatic stress? Just plain nuts? The quiet held too long.

"Is that what it is you're doing, Mike, waging war?"

"No, Mr. Mullins. That's not it. I did that for a lot of years with the Sheriff's Office, warred against the criminals. Sometimes it worked, sometimes it didn't. Sometimes you were second-guessed, as you know. But those editorial writers were the ones who never fired a shot or heard the groans, right?"

Nick did not disagree.

"No, this is just a list, my friend. One that's got to be cleaned out before I go."

"What list might that be?" Nick asked and he could hear the anxiety in his own voice, thinking about his byline list, the Secret Service list, the cross-reference list of both.

"My list," Redman said, turning back to again look straight into Nick's face when he spoke. "Just mine. That simple."

"But what does your list have to do with me, Mike? I'm not a soldier. I'm not in a war. I haven't fired a shot or heard the groans."

Redman would not move his eyes and they burned with some internal heat.

"Yeah, you have, Nick. You've heard the worst groans, the ones that ripped your guts, man. You took the heaviest losses. You're owed."

Nick's mind was racing, but illogically, he was trying to second-guess the words without just asking the question, every reporter's downfall. Find the guts to just ask the question.

"Is it me? Am I on your list?"

The question seemed to break Redman's intensity. The three lines that creased his forehead deepened and then he grinned.

"Well, hell, no, Mr. Mullins. You're not on the list. You're the architect of the list, man. You're the spotter," Redman said. "And I just wanted to meet you, properly, before we finish."

Redman then reached out his hand in such a formal and courteous way that Nick's muddled reaction was to take it. It was Redman's muscled forearm that gripped and raised the handshake one time and then let it fall. When he turned to go, Nick found his voice.

"Wait. Wait a second, Mike. What do you mean, finish? You mean you're going to kill someone else?"

Redman kept walking and Nick didn't follow. It was against his years of work and instinct to chase after an interviewee, even this one. He stood and called out instead:

"Mike, come on. What are you doing? Why? How many more on your list?"

Redman turned before he disappeared back into the sea grape.

"One more, Mr. Mullins," he called back. "Like I said, you're owed."

/ / /

Nick stared after the bushes, dumbstruck. What the hell did that mean? I'm owed? I don't do anything but write the stories. Then he pulled the notebook out of his back pocket and knelt right there, next to the seawall, and wrote down everything he could remember of the conversation, the exact words.

The now-silent subjects of those stories created those situations on their own. Yeah, alright, Nick thought.

War is hell. Goddamn Sherman quote. But if Redman had gone to Iraq, he either joined up or went as a guardsman. A lot of guardsmen from Florida went over there. Nick had done several stories about locals who packed up and shipped out, leaving families behind. That would be easy to check out.

This is just a list my friend. One that's got to be cleaned out before I go.

OK, his list. He's working his own list. Would it be a physical thing? Or all in his head? And was it the same as any of the samples Nick already had, the one with his byline all over it?

You're not on the list. You're the architect of the list, man. You're the spotter.

That can't be right. What's that mean? I'm the spotter. Nick knew enough about SWAT operations and snipers to know what a spotter was. He's the guy that calls the shots in a two-man team. I'm not on this guy's team. How the hell did I get on this guy's team?

One more, Mr. Mullins. Like I said, you're owed. Nick scribbled down the last quote, the final words Redman had used.

"I'm owed?" he said out loud. Why am I owed? I'm not the subject of my stories. I have never been the subject of my stories. Your career, your journalism is not supposed to be about you, it's supposed to be about other people.

The sound of Nick's cell phone caused him to jerk and he had to put his hand out on the rough concrete to keep from tumbling into the damn water. He looked at the readout and the calling number was blocked.

"Nick Mullins," he answered.

"Mr. Mullins," announced Detective Hargrave's quiet voice. "You have a flair for the dramatic that I didn't expect from you. I got your message about going out to meet with a homicide suspect on your own and tossing me an Internet research assignment as a bone. This is exactly why we don't bring amateurs in on investigations, Mullins. They always tend to do stupid things."

Nick said nothing. The guy was right. What do you say?

"Can I assume that you have already met with your possible sniper, or are you standing around in some open field waiting for him to put a round through your head?" Hargrave said in a muted, conversational tone.

Nick looked around at the open lot.

"No. I mean, yes, I met with him. It's Michael Redman, one of your own, a former SWAT guy for the Sheriff's Office. But I'm not a target. At least that's what he said. I think it's the subjects of my stories that are his targets and he said he's going to do one more before he goes."

"Might I suggest, Mr. Mullins, that you come in to the Sheriff's Office as soon as fucking possible?" Hargrave said, pronouncing the expletive in such a calm manner as to make it seem nearly inoffensive.

"Absolutely. I will get there as soon as possible," Nick said, almost adding a *sir* to the end of his sentence and then listening as the hang-up tone on the cell bleated out over the river water.

/ Chapter 24 /

When Nick got back to the newsroom, the place was starting to warm up to the day. He took advantage of the fact that the editors were having their early news meeting and he could slip in and out without being noticed by the powers that be.

He walked the long way around to his desk and started gathering up his notes and printouts from the research library. But he wasn't invisible. His desk phone rang.

"Nicky, man. Your ass is in the stew, brother."

Nick instantly recognized Hirschman's voice.

"Yeah, has been for some time," Nick said.

"No, no. Not like this time."

Nick sat and booted up his computer.

"What do you have, Bill?" he said and looked around the corner to see the top of Hirschman's head bobbing just below his partition. It was the norm these days in newsrooms and other offices. Employees didn't get up and go talk to each other, they called you from fifteen feet away or sent you e-mails. Nick had learned long ago that the company could scan the contents of every e-mail sent either in or out of the building, so he rarely used it. And this clandestine technique of calling the guy next to you was as distasteful to him as interviewing people over the phone.

But it was what it was and you didn't ignore information even if that's the way it was spread.

"They're gunning for you, man," Hirschman said, using a low, conspiratorial voice. "From the stuff I overheard, they're going to fire your ass for some kind of insubordination or keeping some kind of story away from Ms. Clompy Heels or some damn thing. The words *human resources* were definitely used and you know what that means when they're pissed at somebody."

Yeah, Nick knew. That and *due to economic considerations we are forced to separate certain employees from the company.* Christ, they couldn't even bring themselves to say you're fired. It had to be couched in some damn lawyerese. Hell, if he wrote something like that in the paper, he'd deserve to be fired.

"Thanks for the heads-up, Bill," he said. "I'll expect all of you to pull together in this time of eight percent profit margins instead of the usual twelve percent," he said.

"Ha!" Hirschman answered and hung up.

Nick only smirked at the long-standing criticism of a newspaper industry that earned higher profits than almost any other business in the country and started cutting employees long before that margin came anywhere close to flat.

At his desk he slipped a rewritable CD into the computer and called up a list of contacts he'd put together over a decade and copied it. He did the same with all of his notes on the sniper case. He also copied every e-mail address that he'd recorded. All of his personal stuff he could leave. If they ended up sacking him, they couldn't deny him those, but he knew they could confiscate his computer and all of the files in his desk drawers and claim them as work products that belonged to them. He slipped the CDs and notepads into his briefcase and made it halfway down the hallway to the elevator when an assistant editor came swinging out of the break room with a cup of coffee in one hand.

"Hey, Nick. There you are, man. Hey, I think we've got a big pileup on 95 up near Hillsborough Beach Boulevard that we're going to have to check out. You know, no fatalities or anything, but photo got some pictures so we're gonna need some cutline information at least."

Nick slowed but did not stop moving as he turned to sidestep the man.

"But other than that I think we're pretty clear, so what's the word on this vigilante thing, because, you know, Deirdre's going to get out of that meeting pretty soon and she's going to want to see you. . . ."

The editor's scattergun spiel started to slow as Nick kept backpedaling and he first noticed the briefcase in Nick's hand.

"You're not taking off again, are you, Nick, because, you know she's really gonna be pissed, and—"

"I'll call you, man. I need to make this meeting with the cops and I'll just have to call you. Alright?" Nick said and now he was walking backward with the editor following him. "I've got my cell. But I can't miss this meeting. Tell her that, OK?"

He joined several other people at the elevator and saw the door to the conference room open at the end of the hallway. The editors' meeting was breaking up. He ducked into the elevator and watched the doors close, perhaps on his career. He could stay and fight with Deirdre or go out to work a shooting that hadn't yet occurred, but would, all because the shooter thought Nick was owed something.

/ Chapter 25 /

This time they met him in Canfield's small office and they weren't nearly as accommodating as in the last round. Hargrave was standing, leaning against a bookcase jammed with big tutorials with titles on the spines like *Bomb and Arson Specialties in the Field* and *The ATF Field Guide to Indeterminate Explosive Devices* and three of the middle volumes of the Florida statutes that Nick knew as those that dealt with felony arrests.

Canfield was in the chair behind his desk but stood when Nick and Joel Cameron entered.

"You can sit, Mr. Mullins," he said, indicating a chair positioned in front of the desk. It was both a greeting and an order. Cameron took a step back but also remained standing and Nick got a flash scene in his head of some damned interrogation in a gulag described by Solzhenitsyn.

"Let's start with you telling us about this meeting with Mr. Redman this morning, Mr. Mullins. And then we'll go from there," Canfield said and Nick swallowed any idea of holding out on them, though that had not been his intent when he came in. After all, he had agreed to work with them. He just hated the feeling of being bullied.

He took the reporter's notebook from his back pocket and flipped the page.

"Assuming everybody now knows Mike Redman, I got an e-mail from him that the timing signature said was sent at seven forty-five this morning. I didn't read it until two hours later when I checked my computer at the office. I already gave Detective Hargrave the information on the e-mail account that it was sent from," Nick began, hoping to first show that he had indeed tried to keep them in the loop, sort of.

"The tech guys that do computer crime and Internet porn investigations are running down the *commiekid* account," Hargrave said. "Looks like some student type, on the surface. They're going to get an address and we'll go from there."

Nick couldn't tell by his tone whether Hargrave was defending him or just making a verbal report to Canfield. The detective wouldn't meet his eyes, so he went on.

"The message was signed 'm.r.' in lowercase letters and asked me to show up for a meet at ten, so I really didn't have a lot of time to, you know, alert anyone other than to just call the detective and tell him what I was planning to do, to meet with the guy."

He was dancing, but it was truthful dancing.

"Description?" Canfield said like he knew what Nick was doing and wasn't swallowing it.

"I'd say he looks just like he used to when you used to work with him only a little more worn," Nick said, putting it back on the former SWAT supervisor. "Clean-shaven. In pretty good shape. Tanned. Same blue-gray eyes. He was wearing some kind of uniform like a maintenance man, you know, blue work pants and a light blue short-sleeved shirt."

"Carrying anything *you* could notice?" Canfield said, slightly emphasizing the *you* as if Nick would not have the kind of powers of observation that a trained law enforcement officer would.

"He had a navy jacket draped over one arm, so he could have had something wrapped in it, but nothing as long as a McMillan M-86 or even a broken-down MP5," Nick said, using what little he did know to defend his ground. "He might have had an ankle holster, but I really couldn't tell."

"OK, OK, boys," Hargrave chimed in. "Enough of the pissing match."

Canfield looked down, even though he did officially outrank Hargrave. Nick took a deep breath and nodded in assent.

"What the hell did the guy say, Mullins?" Hargrave said.

Without realizing it, Nick was sitting on the front edge of the chair, like he was ready to pounce on something, or run. He sat back, took in another breath and flipped another page in his notebook.

"First of all, he never clearly said that he killed anyone," Nick began. "I mean, he was being real careful about the exact words, like he thought I might be wearing a wire or something."

Nick saw both Canfield and Hargrave raise their eyebrows at the suggestion.

"Oh, is that why you guys wanted to see me before I met with the guy? To wire me up?"

"Don't go Hollywood on us, Mullins. We don't wire anymore. We usually just put a microphone inside your cell phone. That gets most of them," Hargrave said with that grin in the corner of his mouth, his way of leaving a doubt in the veracity of every statement.

Canfield just made the motion of a wheel turning with his hand. "Go on."

Nick looked at the notebook. He was about to continue when he heard the door behind him open without a knock and all heads turned. Fitzgerald, who Nick now knew was working with the Secret Service, stepped in and said, "Excuse my lateness, gentlemen. I hope you haven't begun without me."

Canfield kept a straight face. "Just some preliminaries. Nothing pertinent," he said. "We were just going into Mr. Mullins's contact this morning with Redman."

The look on Fitzgerald's face said he didn't believe a word of it. He also never asked who Redman was, so Nick figured he'd already been briefed. "Go on, then," he said as if they needed his permission.

"Redman said he'd been in Iraq. I was going to check that out," Nick continued and then looked up with his eyebrows raised, a silent question.

"Yeah, he was," Canfield said. "It was while he was still on the job. They called up his reserve unit and he went over there as a specialist. He was working as a sniper with some other military group because of his skills, according to his reserve CO. But he's been back for over a year."

Nick turned his head and saw Fitzgerald take out a small notebook of his own. For some reason it pissed Nick off.

"Like I said, he was being very careful. I was trying to draw him out a little about the recent shootings and he said the victims brought it on themselves, like he'd convinced himself that they deserved to die. But he never said in any specific words that he shot them," Nick said.

"And you didn't ask him?" Fitzgerald said, using the same incredulous tone Canfield had used.

"It wasn't an interrogation," Nick snapped. "I'm not a cop. I talk to people, I don't grill them."

Hargrave jumped in to keep things from derailing again.

"Did he say anything about what's next, Nick? What his plans were?" Hargrave asked.

Nick smiled. Now Hargrave was on a first-name basis.

"He said he had a list that had to be cleaned out before he left," Nick said, reading from his notes. "He called me his spotter—'the architect of the list' are the words he used. Then he said I wasn't personally on the list but that he was going to do one more because I was owed."

The room went silent. It was a good fifteen seconds, a vacuum quiet enough to imagine the wheels turning in each man's head.

"Did he say anything about hating the war and the man who sent him there?" Fitzgerald said, his professional focus made obvious.

"He used the phrase 'War is Hell,'" Nick said.

"Christ!" the agent said.

"But he didn't say anything about the Secretary of State," Nick said, trying to cut him off. "Not a word."

Fitzgerald's mask of professional decorum cracked at the mention of the secretary. His lips went into a thin hard line and he stared at Nick and then at Canfield.

"But he called you his spotter. Which dovetails into the list, our list, of those convicts you've personally written about that are now dead," Hargrave jumped in. "So if he's working off a list he made up from your bylines, who else is there? Who else have you done a piece on who was a blatant asshole like these other guys who he figures deserves to die?"

Nick had been running the same question through his head. He couldn't remember every one of the victims he wrote about. He used to be able to recall their faces, before his own family took their places.

"I've done dozens of stories like that," he said. "I'd have to go through them all."

"So go through them all," Fitzgerald said.

"Hey, it's not like you just put my byline and the word *asshole* in the search field," Nick said, getting irritated by someone telling him what to do again.

"OK, Nick," Hargrave said. "Just do a search with your byline and the word *killed* or *raped* or *abused*, something you know would be in the real bad ones. We could start there."

"Start with the ones that have ranked politicians or their cabinet members in them," Fitzgerald said and all eyes turned to him and Nick let the order go this time. "The Secret Service is here for a reason, which you all now appear to know," he said, again cutting his eyes toward Canfield. "Intelligence has indicated a sniper on the wing in this country, gentlemen, and it's not a threat that we think is idle. We have credible reason to believe the gunman we're looking for is somewhere in Florida and with the political climate as it is, we're not turning away from any leads, no matter how thin. The fact that you have possibly identified a suspect who has a military background and was recently in Iraq raises that profile."

The room went quiet, with each man running the possibilities through his own head.

"I'm doing my job, gentlemen," Fitzgerald said before anyone else could speak. "We have been tracking this for over a year now. Does that not coincide with your Mr. Redman's return to this country from a position in Iraq where he could have easily come in contact with people who are a danger to the command decision makers within our government?"

Nick was weighing the possibilities: Redman targeting the Secretary of State? Redman killing someone for Nick that might be considered a favor? The two possibilities had no tie-ins. But Fitzgerald had the floor. Don't fuck with him now, Nick thought.

"Our information is that this man, this threat, is a trained sniper. Does that not coincide with the skills of this Redman? The Secretary of State is scheduled to speak at a conference being held not eight miles away from where we are and within a ten-mile radius of the three killings you are now investigating yourselves. You might think I'm paranoid, but it is my job to be paranoid, gentlemen. And if your Mr. Redman is a threat, then he is on my screen and I expect any information you turn up to be immediately forwarded to me as a matter of national security. Clear? Gentlemen."

Fitzgerald's little speech was directed at everyone in the room, but the last part was specifically aimed at Canfield, who was the ranking officer. Nick was just a civilian. He didn't have to respond, so he stayed quiet.

"Yeah. Clear, Mr. Fitzgerald. Whatever we've got, you'll have," Canfield finally said.

Fitzgerald came *this* close to saluting before he left the room, Nick thought, and when the door closed, Canfield looked at his shoe tops for a beat and then took control.

"OK, Detective," he said to Hargrave. "If you will work with Mr. Mullins here and see if you can come up with a viable 'final target' for our sniper based on their conversation, I'll get in touch with all the SWAT team guys who were around when Redman was here, see if they've heard from him. We can also pull his file and try to make contact with a family member. I know the guy wasn't married, he was all about the job, but his parents or a sibling might still be around.

"And like the man said, everything comes through me first," the lieutenant said, winking at Hargrave. "Then I decide what gets passed on for national security reasons."

Hargrave got up and Nick followed him. Cameron slipped out the door first, not even waiting to ask if anything that had been said in the room was to be distributed to any other member of the media.

Out in the hallway he said, "I'll just assume that all of that was off the record."

Nick just looked at him, and Hargrave said, "Jesus, I would hope so."

/ Chapter 26 /

Nick followed Hargrave down to the detective bureau and as they were about to pass through a door, the receptionist stopped them.

"Detective, you're going to have to sign this visitor in," she said.

Hargrave stopped just as he was about to put his badge holder against the electronic lock scanner.

"Yeah, sorry, Mary. It's Mike Lowell, he's a CI."

The woman didn't move.

"A confidential informant," Hargrave said, raising his eyebrows.

"He's still going to have to sign in on his own," she said, pushing the clipboard across the shelf that separated them.

Nick caught Hargrave's eye and then stepped over and signed the name Mike Lowell as his own. The woman thanked him and buzzed them both through.

Hargrave again led on, forcing Nick to catch up.

"The Marlins' third baseman? That's the best you could do in a pinch?" Nick said.

Hargrave did not turn around, but Nick again saw that twitch appear in the corner of his mouth that must pass as the thin man's only smile in life. They walked past three rows of office pods that looked way too much like those in Nick's newsroom and then through a door against the wall that led into Hargrave's office.

The room was half the size of Canfield's and it held two desks. Hargrave took his black suit coat off and hung it on a coat tree. The guy's white shirt was crisp. Not a sign of sweat stain, like he'd just gone down to the cafeteria for a cup of coffee. He sat down in the desk chair to the left, so Nick took the one on the right.

"Make yourself comfortable. Meyers is on vacation until the eighteenth," Hargrave said over his shoulder.

While he tapped into the computer in front of him, Nick took out his cell phone. He'd turned it off before going into Canfield's office and when he powered it back up the screen showed that there were four new messages. He looked at his watch. The daily budget meeting was coming up, when all the assistant editors met with Deirdre to pitch the day's stories. It had to be driving them crazy not to have heard from him. Never mind the fact that he had blown her off earlier in the day. He dialed into the research library instead and asked for Lori.

"Lori Simons," she said after Nick was transferred.

"Hey, Lori, it's Nick. You know that search I asked you to do that matched up my bylines with that list?"

"Jesus, Nick," she said and her voice went low and conspiratorial. "Where are you? I mean, the rumors are flying over here that you're big-time in the shit."

"Yeah, yeah, I suppose I am."

"No, really. Hirschman was over here and said Deirdre was bouncing off the walls."

"Yeah, that wouldn't surprise me, Lori," he said. "But she hasn't fired me yet and I need another search if you can, please?"

"Sure, Nick. I was just worried about you."

Her voice sounded sincere. It always had. Nick just hadn't been paying attention to his allies, especially Lori.

"Thanks, Lori. Really, I'm OK. But this story is really starting to roll up on me and I think I've stuck myself into it so deep now, I'm going to have to finish it."

"And finish it your way. Even if you get fired."

Christ, when did she get to know me so well? Nick thought. The comment was something his wife might have said three years ago.

"I put that other list on your desk," Lori said into the silence. "So what do you need?"

Nick explained how he wanted to look for his byline and all the stories he'd done that included homicides or rapes or incest. He didn't need the full stories, just the initial page that contained the doer's or arrestee's name.

"That's going to be a lot of stories, Nick. You want to narrow it down some, maybe by years?" she said.

"Yeah, yeah," Nick said and then covered the mouthpiece and asked Hargrave, "When did Redman start with the Sheriff's Office? What year?"

"Eight years ago," Hargrave said without turning around.

"Eight," Nick said into the phone. "Oh, and also pull anything that I've written that included the U.S. Secretary of State's name. It's a long shot, but it might come up in one of those stories I did on local soldiers who were wounded or killed in Iraq."

Nick waited, like he could hear Lori scratching the request down on paper, like he'd watched her do so many times before.

"OK, anything else?" she said.

"That's it. See what we get and then I need you to e-mail everything to . . ." He looked up at Hargrave, who was already scratching down something on a business card, which he handed over.

"To *maurice69 at kingnet.com*," Nick read and looked up at Hargrave, who had already turned his back on him.

"Nicky, that's off-campus," Lori said.

"Yeah, I know. I owe you."

"Yes, you do," she said, but there was something light in her voice. "I'll get it to you soonest."

Nick hung up and was flipping the business card with the e-mail address between his thumb and forefinger and wearing a bemused look on his face when Hargrave turned around.

"Year I graduated from high school," Hargrave said.

"Huh?" Nick answered, playing dumb.

"It was 1969."

"Personal e-mail?" Nick said, now smiling.

"I don't want that stuff coming through the department system or the fax," Hargrave said, staying serious. "We've got a thing here you might have heard about, called an Internal Affairs Division?"

"OK," Nick said, going instantly sober. Nick knew the newspaper had its own form of IAD, they just never gave it a moniker. He remembered the employee upstairs who was rumored to be logging in to pornographic websites during the day. Management had his screen monitored by the computer techs through remote access. They caught him and canned him the same day.

He didn't see how the research he was doing would be considered off-limits to his story enough to push Deirdre to fire him, but the doubt must have shown in his face.

"You're not even supposed to be here, Mullins," the detective said. "Your participation is on the QT. No one outside of that room back there knows about you. And I doubt that you, as a professional journalist, would want your cooperation to be broadcast material either."

Nick was about to say that he doubted that he was going to be employed as such by tomorrow, but held his tongue long enough for Hargrave's phone to ring. He listened while the detective grunted some acknowledgments, picked up a pencil and gave two-word answers to whoever it was on the other end.

Nick looked around, as was his training, for family portraits or awards or plaques of recognition in Hargrave's work area. Nothing. Not a sign of anything personal. He spun around in the chair. The other detective's space was cluttered with softball trophies, photographs of what must be grandchildren and a prominently placed photo of a man and woman in their late fifties or early sixties, arms around waists, smiles on faces, Hawaiian leis around necks in a too-bright sun. Nick's eyes went to the now-closed door and a map of the city that was taped to the back. He got up and took in the four red stars that had been placed on the nearest cross-streets of where the sniper's victims had been shot. Hargrave had obviously lumped them together long before today. Nick was studying the map for some kind of pattern when Hargrave hung up.

"The SWAT team went in on *commiekid*'s apartment after they didn't get a response and found the guy in the sack with his girlfriend," Hargrave said. "His real name is Byron Haupt, if you can believe that one. He's nineteen, a student at BCC and says he was at the library from seven to ten this morning working on some project. Said he uses the computer terminals there to send information to the other kids in his project group and maybe, just maybe someone could have had access to his e-mail account while he was away from the desk.

"Canfield went in with the team and flashed an old photo of Redman and the kid said he might have seen someone who fits the description, but he really doesn't pay that much attention to other people unless they 'get in his space.'"

Hargrave rolled his eyes at the last part and Nick waited for him to say, *kids these days*, but it didn't come.

"They ran Haupt's juvenile record and he's clean. They're going to make the kid sit tight, but at this point Canfield's going on the assumption that Redman used the library terminal after the kid logged on. They're going to interview the girl too just in case she used the boyfriend's log-on, but it's looking like a dead end."

The two men sat in silence, but their thoughts were rolling around the same subject, the questions and scenarios spinning on such similar wavelengths they could have been having an unspoken dialogue.

"I don't know, maybe he could be setting up on the secretary," Nick said out loud.

"Pissed off at some sense of command, some buck-stops-here idea he got from Iraq? Somebody has to be responsible for what he saw over there," Hargrave picked up. "God knows what a guy sees in those damned rifle scopes just before he pulls the trigger. I couldn't do it."

"But it goes out of his pattern, his M.O., as you guys call it."

"No, you guys call it that, we just feed it to you," Hargrave said, but his attempt at levity didn't cut the mood.

"The man's about retribution," he finally said.

"So he blames a politician for Iraq?"

Hargrave put an eye on Nick. "Who else you gonna blame?"

Nick's cell phone vibrated in his pocket and he automatically pulled it out. The readout on the screen gave just the main switchboard number for the newsroom, so it could be coming from anyone's extension.

"Shit," he said.

Hargrave stood up. "I'm not you, Mullins, but you gotta take that call sometime. Why not get it over with?" the detective said. "I'm going to get coffee, want some?"

"Black," Nick said as Hargrave closed the door behind him.

On the fourth buzz Nick punched the answer button. "Mullins," he said.

"Nick. You need to come in off the street," Deirdre said, her voice unmistakable with a distinct commanding edge in it.

"I'm working a story, Deirdre," Nick said.

She only hesitated a second. "Yeah? What story is that, Nick? The serial killer story? The story that matches up the ballistics on the sniper killings? Or the story that shows that an assassin is somehow connected to your byline?"

"I'm not sure where you get your wild imagination, Deirdre, but I wouldn't say any of those stories is on my budget."

Nick was scraping, trying to figure out if she was just guessing. None of the information about the ballistics or his byline list matches had been in his earlier pieces because he'd deleted it.

"Well, I know it's not on your budget line because you haven't filed one today, and that's the first rule you've repeatedly broken, Nick. Secondly, don't think for a minute that everything you write on *our computers* doesn't belong to this newspaper and is available to those who have the clearance to see it, because that would be at your peril."

Nick knew that the newsroom computer system was an open setup. Because of the direct production link, every PC was tied in to the next level of the chain. A reporter's PC could be accessed by his editor. That editor's by the copy desk. The desk by the printing facility.

They must have been monitoring him. Nick knew that every time a reporter hit the save button—and you did it all the time to keep from losing everything in a crash—the editors could read exactly what you were writing without asking. They were probably watching his screen while he was putting in his notes, before he deleted them. He suddenly felt like Patrick McGoohan in *The Prisoner*. The thought did not scare him as it had the character in the old television serial, it only pissed him off.

"I want you in here, Nick. I've spent the day trying to cover for you, but I'm going to have to take you off this story if you can't level with me. I saw what you wrote. I know what you're chasing, but I can't argue for your stand on this without you. "

He so badly wanted to tell her to fuck off, but knew she didn't deserve it.

"They'll slap it up there in headlines, Deirdre. You know they will, even if it is all still speculation. It'll be a command decision and you won't stop them."

The line was still open, but Deirdre wasn't arguing.

"I'll be in to pick up my personal items tomorrow," Nick said. "Today, I quit."

The second he pushed the off button he thought of his daughter, and then checked his watch. Carly would be home from school. Elsa gushing all over whatever art project she'd brought home. The television would go on, tuned to whatever kid thing was in vogue. There wouldn't be any fighting now that she didn't have her sister to share the decisions with. Not that Nick had ever heard the fighting. He'd never been home, just heard about it later in the evening.

Now unemployed, maybe he'd make up for it, find time to argue with her himself about watching ESPN or *That's So Raven*.

Hargrave knocked, or maybe just bumped the door before he came in with coffee cups in either hand. Nick accepted one and looked into the dark swirling slick. There was a sheen of bean oil on top.

"Fresh," he said.

"No such thing in a cop shop," Hargrave said and then sat down in front of his computer and punched some keys. Nick sipped at the cup, saying nothing.

"OK," Hargrave said with the only hint of surprise Nick had yet heard in the man's voice. "You've got a better computer researcher over there than we've got here. The file is in."

/ / /

Hargrave printed out two copies of the newspaper list and ended up with a healthy stack. He handed one to Nick, then sat back in his chair. Nick immediately started to scan the first page and when he jumped to the second, Hargrave reached out and stopped him.

"Let's do this one by one, if you don't mind, Mullins. I've only been here a couple of years and a lot of these names are going to be completely foreign to me, so I want you to walk through them. Believe it or not, I might pick up on something that you could skip over."

Nick conceded it made sense and went back to the beginning. Lori had printed out just the first or second paragraphs of first-day stories Nick had written on each person. The headers on the top of each story held the date of publication.

Bobby Andreson, the kid who shot a deputy when the off-duty officer tried to stop the twenty-one-year-old and his sidekick from boosting the chrome rims off a Cadillac.

"But when they tracked Andreson down, he did a murder-suicide, shot his partner and then himself. DOA at the scene," Nick explained.

Stephen Burkhardt, killed a hooker down on South Federal. Went in for twenty-five to life.

"Doesn't seem like the avenging kind of case unless Redman knew the girl," Nick said.

"I'll check him with DOC and see if he's still in," Hargrave said, making a mark on his sheet. "Pretty graphic stuff," he said, continuing to read the story. "You see this body when it happened?"

"Yeah. Back then the road patrol deputies thought it was fun to have the print guys take a look. This girl was hacked into pieces and tossed into the Dumpster," Nick said, moving on to the next name. Hargrave just looked at him, studying the side of his face.

Damalier, the casino boat operator that Susan caught the scoop on by photographing the guy's license plate.

"Mob hit," Nick said and they dismissed it.

By the fourth page they realized that Lori had sent the file in alphabetical order, not by year.

"Falmuth. I worked that one," Hargrave said. "Scrap it. That guy died of AIDS while he was in lockup. Rapist. Deserved the worst and got it."

Ferris was next on the list and both of them set his story aside.

It went on like that for two hours. Nick's cell phone rang three times and he refused to answer after checking the number. Hargrave on occasion would be interrupted by a receptionist or a call directly into his office, which he answered with short affirmations or begged off because he had "something going right now."

The Kerner story stopped Hargrave and when he asked about it, Nick filled him in.

"Did you call anyone in law enforcement up there to check it out?"

"Not yet," Nick said, embarrassed that it had slipped his mind. "I'll do it tonight."

When they got to the last sheet, they found Lori had included only a name and a date and the charges against the arrested.

Robert Walker. Manslaughter. There was no bylined story.

"What's this one?" Hargrave asked, flipping the page over to see if there had been a misprint on the back.

"Nothing," Nick said, turning his head away, trying to hide the flash of anger in his eyes. Why the hell would she include that? "Not what we're looking for. A DUI manslaughter case that got negotiated down. Doesn't fit our guy at all."

"OK," was all Hargrave said and then he reshuffled his papers and set them down.

In the end they had narrowed the list to a dozen. Twelve possible targets if Michael Redman was truly judging and executing subjects of Nick's stories who might be considered worthy of death.

"Look, I'll run these through the DOC website, find out where these guys are, whether they're even alive anymore. The ones who are on the street we'll track down through probation and parole," Hargrave said.

Nick nodded. It was the same thing he would do if he went back to the newsroom, where he would have access to most of the sites the cops had, with the exception of FBI links.

When Hargrave went back to his computer terminal, Nick did not move. After a few keystrokes the detective turned.

"You're dismissed, Mullins," he said.

Nick got up to go. "You've got my cell. Keep me in the loop, OK? That's the deal, right?"

"Yeah. Go write your story," Hargrave said without turning.

Nick stepped out of the tiny office and took a deep breath of the stale air-conditioning and left the building. He wasn't writing stories anymore.

/ Chapter 27 /

When he walked in the front door of the house he had owned for nine years, the only family left looked at him simultaneously and then at their watches in dismay. The early hour, long before deadline, caught them off guard.

"*Querido?* Mr. Mullins. You are early!"

"Hi, Dad. How come you're home?"

He put a smile on his face, the one that, if he really thought about it, he knew never fooled anyone.

"I'm here to see my girls," he said, using a familiar phrase, and then quickly added, "Carly the Creative, and Elsa the Magician!"

The two looked at each other with a mix of humor and apprehension and waited until Nick crossed the floor and bent to kiss his daughter and said quietly, "I wanted to see you, pumpkin." She accepted that and took his hand and led him to the sewing machine, where she was putting together her latest fashion project.

"See how cool?"

While she explained the intricacies of double stitching, Elsa hung near Nick's shoulder, pretending to watch, but not too secretly smelling his breath. When she was satisfied that he was not drunk, she said, "I am going to do the dinner."

Nick asked his daughter several questions about her technique and reasons for color choices and aspirations for the skirt she was making. It was like an interview for a lively little lifestyle feature. Carly kept giving him sidelong glances but eventually got caught up in her enthusiasm for the creation and went into great detail until Elsa called them to dinner.

While they ate, Nick turned out one of his favorite and long-memorized stories of building a fort with his best friend in the field behind his house when he was a boy. He described how it was three stories high in the shape of ever smaller plywood boxes and how they'd put hinged trapdoors in the floor of each to get from top to bottom. Rocket ship, battleship, Foreign Legion outpost—it was whatever they cared it to be with only a twist of imagination. Carly had heard the story many times, but her father's enthusiasm in the retelling on this night made her laugh at the funny parts and groan at the hokey parts.

After dinner both Nick and Carly demanded to help Elsa with the dishes and then after they were done they convinced her to play a game of Pictionary with them. They sat around the kitchen table and with only three to play they were forced to rotate teams—Nick and Carly first, then Elsa and Carly. It had been a family favorite. But with Elsa's partial knowledge of English and limited background in Americana, the game quickly became hilarious.

"*No es* donkey. *Es un burro, sí?*"

She took the merriment in stride even when Carly doubled over in the kind of childlike laughter that is as pure as a jiggling bell. All of their sides were aching by the time someone finally won.

At bedtime Nick kissed his daughter on the forehead and tucked her in and as Elsa passed him in the hallway she whispered, "You are a good man, Mr. Nick." He only nodded and found his way to the garage, where he searched out a hidden bottle of Maker's Mark and in the dark silence formed his own whisper: "No, I am not."

For the next two hours he sat out by the pool in turquoise light and drank the whiskey alone, thinking of the times his wife and he swam naked after the girls had gone to bed, of the arguments when their own bedroom door was closed, of the fragrance of her hair that he swore still hung in her pillow even after he tossed the sheets and cases in the trash bin months ago.

He poured another drink and when he put the bottle down, his cell phone chirruped as if the movement had set it off. He fumbled with it, punched the answer button and took a deep breath, about to curse who he figured to be someone from the paper again trying to rouse him. But before the words got out, Hargrave's voice snapped out of the earpiece:

"Easy, Nick, easy, Nick, easy . . . Mr. Mullins," he said, modulating his volume with each repetition.

Nick swallowed his words and held the phone closer. "Hargrave?"

"Yeah."

"Sorry."

"It's alright. I've been bitched out enough on the phone to know what's coming after that deep breath, Mullins. You OK?"

"Yeah," Nick said softly. "OK."

"Look, I ran the rest of those names and we need to talk," Hargrave said, his voice kicking back to business mode.

Nick looked at his watch. It was almost two in the morning.

"Now?"

"Now."

"Uh, alright," Nick said. "Let me give you the address and—"

"I already have it," Hargrave interrupted.

"Yeah? OK, then," Nick said. He wiped at his mouth and tried to sound sober. "Come on over, I've got some of your favorite here."

"Yeah, I can hear it," Hargrave said. "I'll be there in ten."

/ / /

Nick waited out at the end of his driveway, watching a constellation up in the Western Hemisphere that he had either just discovered for the scientific community, or he was drunk. He had to steady himself with a hand on his mailbox when the headlights of Hargrave's car swept around the corner. When the detective got out, Nick explained that he did not want to wake his daughter and then led the way around the back, where they entered his pool area through a screen door. He had fetched another tumbler from the kitchen, and had also drunk two deep glasses of water to try to take the edge off the whiskey's effects.

Hargrave scraped a patio chair across the flagstone and sat, angled with a sight line of the pool and darkness beyond. He picked up the bottle of Maker's and poured himself a glass.

"You're welcome," Nick said as he retook his own seat.

Hargrave got the crinkles at the corners of his eyes. "Nice spot," he said.

"Yeah, it serves its purposes."

Hargrave took a sip of the whiskey and said, "Cameron tells me that some other reporter from your paper contacted him this evening for update information on the Michaels shooting."

Nick took a silent few seconds to pour two fingers of whiskey into his own glass, but remained quiet.

"In our business we'd call that being bounced off the case," Hargrave said, this time turning to look at Nick. "Are you off the case, Mr. Mullins?"

"I haven't been told that officially, but since I quit this afternoon, it's probably a good guess."

This time Hargrave simply held his glass near his face, letting the blue-green light blend with the deep red of the whiskey to form a color that seemed oddly cartoonish.

"Just because I'm not doing the story for the *Daily News* doesn't mean I'm not doing it as a freelancer," Nick quickly added.

"They're going to call you a material witness," Hargrave said, again with the official tone.

"My ass," Nick said, though it would only take a minute of sober thought to know it was true.

"Oh, what fun it would be to see a journalist up there on the stand like the rest of us when the real mud wrestling begins," Hargrave said, now actually grinning, no attempt to cover.

Nick let him enjoy his shot, for thirty seconds, then scraped his own chair forward. "The names, Detective. What did you come up with?"

Hargrave put his glass down. The grin was gone.

"Of the names we decided on from your stories, four are dead, seven are still in prison and two are out on probation, but I still haven't been able to contact their parole officers to find out where they are. Last record had one guy over on the Tampa side and the other up near Pensacola."

Nick didn't have to say the obvious: that this information didn't bring them any closer than they'd been.

"How about Canfield? Any luck talking with the SWAT guys?"

"No one's seen Redman but you," Hargrave said, emphasizing the *you*. "Far as they know, he's off the face of the earth. Canfield even checked with the managers of the firing range where Redman practically lived when he was with the unit. His parents are dead, of natural causes, mind you, up north somewhere, and he doesn't have any siblings. The lieutenant said he wasn't surprised no one had seen him. He said Redman had become isolated even before he left for Iraq."

"The goddamn editorials," Nick said.

"Yeah, I read up on those," Hargrave said.

Nick eyed him over the rim of his glass, reminding himself to never underestimate this guy.

"So what's his reasoning? What's Redman's motive for putting ex-cons in his target zone?" Nick said, thinking out loud even if the thinking was a bit clouded.

"Could be a combination," Hargrave said. "Public humiliation, death of his partner, post-traumatic stress from Iraq."

"Might even be enough to put the Secretary of State there," Hargrave said. "She's the one who sets policy, the one with the President's ear when shit hits the fan over in the Middle East. He already killed the man who killed his partner, maybe he just considers this a job undone."

"Jesus, Detective, you're siding with Fitzgerald now?" Nick said.

Hargrave shook his head and blew out a long breath.

"Now, there's a fed with some major responsibility pushing on his sphincter," Hargrave continued. "But the secretary *is* coming to town and it would be a hell of a venue to make a statement."

Nick took another drink, like he thought the booze was going to make things clearer. "OK, so you're following the theory that you can never say never, but I can't see it. I don't see a man like Redman targeting his own country's leaders. That's not who he's after."

Hargrave matched Nick's feat of emptying his glass and sat back like he had given up and was just staring into the pool. Then he said in a clear, matter-of-fact voice, "How about Mr. Walker, Nick?"

He let the question and the name hang in the night air, not looking to see the reaction in Nick's face like he would if it were a question posed to some arrestee in the interview room.

"What were Redman's words again, Nick? Do you a favor?" he said just as clearly. "This one's just for you? How about killing the man who put your family in the ground?"

Nick wondered if the detective could hear the sound of his heart, impossible to ignore with the way it had started thumping in his ears. The detective had not trusted his explanation for the last name on the list. Hell, he might have recognized it right off. Why wouldn't he have been briefed on Nick's background before they gave the reporter such access? Why wouldn't he see immediately that a name that starts with *W* fits perfectly with the alphabetizing of Redman's own victims list?

"Yeah," Nick finally said out over the glow of the pool. "How about him?"

/ Chapter 28 /

Michael Redman was working the rooftops in the predawn hours of his last week in Florida. No operation he'd worked had ever come off so smoothly. Targets identified. Intel right on the mark. Clean shots. Perfect regress and four confirmed kills. This one should be no different.

He had done reconnaissance on the target, just like the others. He'd mapped out the probable movements and used the sight lines from the street to pick two spots that his experience told him would work.

Today he was up top, checking out the closer of the two. He'd used the height of a Dumpster behind the building to gain access to the second floor and then jimmied a simple half-moon lock on the sash to get into a stairwell. The door to the roof opened from the inside and he used a piece of gravel from the tarred deck itself to wedge it open. If anything happened, there would be no evidence left behind. At the east roof edge he raised the night-vision goggles to his face and scoped the front of the target building. Firing from here would be nearly a six-hundred-yard shot. His optimum distance. Easily done. Sure and clean.

He knew that this detective Hargrave, Mr. This Is a Democracy, would be scratching his head after this one, trying to figure out how it came out of left field at him. But such was the way of statement killings.

There was a purpose to them. In Iraq they were the only targets he had considered true.

He recalled the recruiter, the Iraqi who intelligence knew was luring or intimidating Sunni men and boys into the insurgency. You watched him and he watched you during the days in the marketplace. You standing with your rifle slung across your arm while smiling dumbly at the people. The recruiter acting like he was just a local, moving about, slipping into conversations among groups on the corner or in lines where the real citizens waited for U.N. food handouts. When he left, you never followed him. Instead you followed the young men he'd talked to and then had an Iraqi CI follow them to a meeting place in one of the neighborhoods. Then you set up a spot not unlike this, and when the recruiter stepped outside . . . smoke check.

When word spread that the recruiter himself was not safe, those who had been willing to join him would quickly change their choice of the insurgent life. Statement killing. Mullins would understand this, Redman thought. Mullins had done his job as a spotter and deserved to be thanked and rewarded. Redman was sure he would understand without explanation because after this last shot, Redman would be gone.

A blinking of small lights and a far-off *bing, bing, bing* of bells pulled his attention to the north. Only in the early morning quiet would the sound carry this far and he watch with the scope as the Seventeenth Street Causeway Bridge dropped its barricades in preparation to open. Redman thought of his exit route. He had calculated traffic for early morning. It would be heavy, but most of it coming east on the bridge to the oceanfront while he would be going west. But he had not figured in the possibility of a bridge opening. He took one more look down the firing line and decided he would check the shooting nest farther back. An eight-hundred-yard shot would be technically more difficult, but he had done it before. He pulled back from the roof edge and went through the door, kicking away the blocking stone as he went.

/ / /

Nick was up at eight. After Hargrave left, he'd drunk a quart of water with his two aspirin, and the preemptive strike against a hangover that had worked for years in the past worked again.

The fact that he'd not learned to clean up after himself, however, resulted in a partially empty whiskey bottle and two glasses on the patio table. He gathered and hid the evidence in the garage. While he made coffee for himself, Elsa came out to make breakfast and did not say good morning to him, just looked with a coolly raised eyebrow at the kitchen clock. When Carly got up and sat down at her place to eat, she picked up on the frigid atmosphere and whispered to her father, "Is Elsa mad because we made fun of her last night at Pictionary?"

"No, sweetheart. It's a woman thing," Nick said. He knew Elsa had probably seen the bottle and the glasses before he moved them, and immediately regretted the remark. When Carly left for school, Nick followed her out to the driveway and hugged her a second longer than usual before waving her off to the bus stop.

On his way back he picked up the newspaper, wrestled it out of the plastic bag and only scanned the front page centerpiece story about the OAS meeting. When he flipped the paper over he was met by the headline:

VIGILANTE SNIPER

GUNMAN USING NEWSPAPER'S
COVERAGE TO SELECT TARGETS

The story ran two columns below the front-page fold and Nick stood reading it in the middle of his driveway.

By Joseph P. Binder, Staff Writer

A marauding killer, armed with a powerful but silent sniper rifle, is hunting ex-convicts and criminals in South Florida and sources believe he is using the *Daily News* to select the worst of the worst in his deadly spree. According to this newspaper's research, five men, each killed by a single bullet to the brain, were prominent subjects of *Daily News* stories that documented their heinous crimes at the time they wreaked havoc on citizens and loved ones and may be the victims of the serial sniper.

The story listed the names of Chambliss, Crossly, Ferris, Kerner and Michaels as the suspected targets of the sniper along with brief descriptions of their crimes and their recent deaths. The fact that the former M.E. and Kerner were not killed in South Florida was conveniently ignored to help boost the local angle. When he opened the paper and continued to read, Nick felt a sickness in his stomach and knew it had nothing to do with whiskey.

Broward sheriff's homicide detective Maurice Hargrave, who earlier said the dead convicts had been "gunned down in the streets" by the vigilante, is heading the investigation and has been using the *Daily News'* database to collect information on the sniper's next target, according to computer research and documents.

Hargrave was not available for comment yesterday, but sources say ballistics experts have matched the deadly bullets from the most recent killings as coming from the same high-powered rifle commonly used by highly trained snipers.

"Shit," Nick said out loud. Had they somehow tracked the e-mail from Lori to Hargrave's private e-mail account? They easily could have snatched the printouts off Nick's desk and made assumptions about the link between the five victims. A trickle of sweat caught enough gravity to cause it to slip down his back and Nick realized he was still standing on the concrete in front of his house in the direct morning sunlight. He went inside and sat at his kitchen table, laying the newspaper out in front of him.

They'd cribbed the partial quote from Hargrave off Nick's earlier story. But where the hell did they get the ballistics match? He scanned the rest of the piece—not a single named source other than a boilerplate quote from Joel Cameron saying "the investigation is continuing." Nick was trying to re-create his earlier stories on the first two shootings and recalled writing the vigilante angle and the bullet match in his notes but then deleting them when he put the pieces together. But as he knew, that wouldn't stop them. As he feared, they'd used their unrestricted eavesdropping in the editorial computer system. Cops would need a court order to listen in to a citizen's conversations or read that person's mail. But in a newspaper's offices, management could electronically watch a reporter write with impunity. Work product, they would argue. It belongs to us. You're just an employee.

Nick went back to the front page to reread the story. Every scrap of information was his, no matter how they'd juiced it up and delivered it. Poor Joe Binder just followed orders and had his byline slapped on it. Then Nick noticed he'd missed the "Interactive news" box on his first reading. Below the line that said "continued on 12A" was a shadow boxed teaser inviting readers to go to the newspaper's Web page and vote in a poll question: *Do you think the vigilante sniper is wrong for targeting former killers? Yes or No?* Jesus, Nick thought. I gotta get out of this business.

/ Chapter 29 /

The traffic on I-95 seemed incredibly heavy. Nick wasn't used to being on the interstate so close to the lunch hour. When he pulled off onto the Broward Boulevard exit he had a decision to make: Turn right and drive to the Sheriff's Office headquarters and talk with Hargrave, or turn left and go to the newspaper office to clear out his personal stuff and take the chance of letting his short fuse get him to the jailhouse in the back of a cruiser.

What the hell, he turned left.

When he parked in the employee lot, Nick was surprised that his staff I.D. still worked and automatically raised the barricade arm. He grinned at the little victory and purposely left the badge in his car in case they asked him to turn it in. But as he got off the elevator on the tenth floor, Jim, the security guard, was as vigilant as ever.

"Good afternoon, Nick," he said, looking at Nick's shirtfront. "Got your I.D. with you?"

Nick and Jim had greeted each other nearly five days a week for the past eight years. The guard had commented on Nick's stories, had even congratulated him when he'd bought a new car three years ago. Yet after 9/11 all employees had to wear a badge identifying themselves. The first time he'd misplaced his I.D. and Jim made him sign in, Nick joked about joining al-Qaeda after eight years as a staff reporter, but the look the guard had given him was scary.

This morning Nick just shook his head and signed in.

"Try to find it, Nick. Or you'll have to buy a new one," the guard said.

Nick looked up at him. "How did you know my name without it, Jim?" he said and walked away.

Down in the newsroom the usual din was running. Most of the reporters were out on their beats. But folks on the daytime copy desk were in their nose-to-the-grindstone mode. While he worked his way through the back of the maze, Nick kept his eyes down, trying to be low-profile. Get in, get your stuff and leave. Simple as that. He ducked into a back room where they stored supplies and picked out an empty cardboard box and then made it to his desk.

The computer he'd used for the last several years was gone. Even the monitor. The only thing left was a pattern of dust where it once sat. When he tried the drawers of his desk, they'd been locked. He tried his key. No go, as he had figured. Even the belly drawer, which only held pencils and paper clips and stale breath mints, was locked. On the desktop the documents that Lori had delivered to his desk were predictably gone, used no doubt to put together this morning's story. His personal dictionary, a thesaurus and a copy of Bernstein's *The Careful Writer* were still stacked on one corner. There was a clay sculpture of a green-and-blue dog that his oldest daughter, by three minutes, had made and given to him on a Father's Day several years ago. The family photo, showing the four of them, was lying face down, apparently knocked over during the hasty removal of his computer. Nick could feel eyes on him when he picked it up and, refusing to be emotional, he slid it into the bottom of the box and then piled the rest of his stuff in after. On his way out Nick avoided Joe Binder's desk, even though he could see the back of the reporter's head, bent low as if he were studying some newly installed hieroglyphics on his keyboard. Carrying the box, he took the back way to the research center and when Lori saw him she got up from her terminal and walked straight to him. Her eyes were red-rimmed when she stepped up to the counter.

"I'm sorry, Nick. Really, I tried to call you and—"

Nick reached out and touched her hand. "It's OK, Lori. I shouldn't have put you in a bad position. It's all on me. Please. You're the best," he said and then hugged her to him, longer than he needed to, but not as long as he wanted to. "I'll call you. I'd like to see you, you know, off campus."

He smiled at the joke as he walked away, somewhat mystified that a moment that should have been sad had somehow left a lightness in his head.

/ Chapter 30 /

They met under the shade of a bottlebrush tree, gathered at a picnic table that was set up behind the county's fire and paramedics warehouse. It was a short walk for Canfield and Hargrave. Nick needed only to take the short drive from the newspaper he'd passed on earlier.

The meeting place was suggested by the detective after Nick called him on his cell. It was eighty degrees in the shade and the lieutenant in uniform was sweating twice as much as the two in plain clothes.

"It's out of the pattern. It's out of the sequence of logic. And you two are out of your minds," Canfield was saying to both of them but looking directly at Hargrave, who, for the first time since Nick had laid eyes on him, was appearing unsure.

"What, you're going to call this ex-con Walker and tell him some sniper might be targeting him because his good friend Mr. Mullins has an angel of death killing the subjects of his stories?

"And, I might add," he said, shifting his focus onto Nick, "you didn't write the story about the death of your own family, did you?"

Nick felt the anger starting up from that spot deep in his limbic system, the source in the very top of his spine where it always came from and where he so infrequently got it to stop before it came tumbling out of his mouth. This time he held it.

"Why don't you tell him yourself, Mullins?" Canfield continued, unaware of Nick's struggle. "You tell this Walker asshole he's in danger."

"I can't," Nick said. "I'm not allowed to have any contact with the guy."

"Yeah, no shit. We've got that in your file too. Stalking this guy, Christ. Why even bring it up? If you're so convinced this sniper is going to take Walker out, let him," Canfield said. "I would."

Nick could take the fact that the lieutenant would have pulled a copy of the dossier they undoubtedly put together on him when they invited him into this mess. But the suggestion of letting Walker be shot down in the street was one that made all three of them shift their eyes and go quiet. Nick had spun that scenario in his head a thousand times. He even thought of doing it himself but dismissed the notion by thinking of Carly having to come on visiting days at the prison. He'd done jail-house interviews himself and had seen children, dressed in their Sunday best, standing fidgety and unsure while their fathers, dressed in blue prison garb, tried to coax them into a smile. Could you trade retribution for that?

Canfield finally shifted his weight, stood up. The heat had caused dark semicircles to form under the arms of his uniform shirt.

"Mo, I can't believe you're going for this," he finally said to Hargrave, using a shortened form of the detective's first name that had not been used in Nick's presence before.

Hargrave shook his head. "Hard to judge this shooter, Lieutenant, I think we can all agree on that," he said, his voice flat and deliberately lacking in emotion. "The fact that he contacted Mullins gives a hell of a lot of credence to the theory that he's picking victims from Mullins's stories. That leads into the logic that he's read Mullins's work and has some kind of connection to him and would know about the accident that killed his family. So I'm not convinced it's that far of a jump to figure that the statement Redman made to Mullins—'One more. You're owed'—could mean he's going to take out this Walker character."

Nick remained silent. He couldn't have put it any better.

"I'm sorry, guys. I just can't go for it. I've already got deputies all over this OAS meeting and the Secretary of State coming to town and now some goddamn public relations thing they're going to do. You want to tell this guy Walker what you're thinking, go ahead, Mo. But I can't authorize some kind of protective custody or some damn sniper watch on a theory. You want to make it part of your investigation, go to it."

Canfield started to leave when Hargrave stopped him. "Sir, how about our man Fitzgerald? Did he show any interest in the story Mullins did about the secretary?"

Nick was looking at the tabletop when he heard the question. His head snapped up like he had been yanked by the hair.

"What the hell are you . . . What story?" he said, staring stupidly at Hargrave.

The detective pulled a folded sheet of paper from his back pocket and handed it to Nick. "Your research person faxed this after you left," he said. "Remember you asked them to send you anything political you'd done that mentioned the Secretary of State?"

Nick unfolded the sheet and read the headline:

LOCAL GUARDSMAN KILLED IN IRAQ

REMEMBERED BY FAMILY, FRIENDS

Someone had highlighted certain lines in the story, including a quote by the dead boy's father blaming the Secretary of State for keeping his son overseas beyond his assigned date to come home.

"I've kept Fitzgerald in the loop on your investigation all along," Canfield said to Hargrave. "I'm not sure how seriously he's taking this connection between Mullins and the sniper, but he did seem interested in talking to Redman if we ever find him. But that mention of the secretary carried a lot more weight than any mention of this Walker character." He nodded at the clipping in Nick's hands. "I got the feeling that Fitzgerald was going to do his job protecting the secretary, but wasting manpower on Walker was not his inclination."

Hargrave remained sitting on the edge of the picnic table until Canfield disappeared around the corner of the building.

"Not his inclination," he said in a mocking voice just loud enough for Nick to hear.

"What?" Nick said, just finishing the story and flipping the paper to see if it continued on the backside.

"Nothing," Hargrave said and then pointed at the clipping. "What do you think?"

"Hell, I don't even remember that quote," he said, tapping the backs of his fingers on the sheet of paper. "I remember doing this story on the National Guard kid, but not that quote about the secretary. I mean, that's kind of reaching. Unless Redman somehow knew the guy or his parents."

The story had been written shortly after Nick had returned to work. At the time he was doing both the cop shift and some home-front stories about area soldiers who were shipped out to Iraq. Some of those stories were obituaries, like the one in his hand.

By Nick Mullins, Staff Writer

South Florida friends and family of Corporal Randy Williams gathered at his parents' home Friday to remember a young man "who never walked away from a pal and always covered your back," when he grew up here in Fort Lauderdale.

Williams, 28, was killed in Iraq earlier this week during a routine patrol according to the Defense Department. He had been serving with a National Guard unit based in Homestead and was sent to the Gulf more than a year ago. He had been scheduled to return home in January but a change in policy in which guardsmen were to serve only one year of active duty was altered.

"If the Secretary of State had honored her promise, my boy would be back here now, alive and safe with us. He did his job," said Williams's father, Vern.

Vern Williams later said he was referring to a speech made last week by the secretary that defended the military's controversial ruling.

"The interpretation of the contract for guardsmen is that deployments are to mean twelve months, boots on the ground, in the service of the country and do not include the months of stateside preparations and training they spent away from their homes and stateside jobs," the secretary said at the time. "We hope this clears up any confusion and we regret if those families of the soldiers protecting our nation misinterpreted that commitment."

The secretary's words did not mollify the Williams family.

"That's not what our son's commanders told us before he shipped out. They said he'd be home three months ago. If you make a promise to these boys and then ship them off to risk their lives, you should honor that promise," said Vern Williams.

Williams was a highly regarded member of his unit and was guarding the rear flank of his patrol in Iraq when he was killed by a single gunshot fired by an insurgent sniper.

"We still have not taken down his stuff in the barracks," wrote Josh Murray, a fellow unit member from Coconut Creek in an e-mail sent to the *Daily News* yesterday. "He was a special guy. Always watchin' out for us."

The story went on, quoting friends and other members of Williams's Guard unit praising the kid's intensity and loyalty both at home and in Iraq. But Hargrave had circled the paragraphs that held the secretary's name.

"And Canfield showed this to the Secret Service?" Nick said, working it in his head.

"You heard the man," Hargrave said.

"Do we have any connection between Redman and this guy Williams?"

"Checking. But they weren't with the same Guard unit, nor did their units work together over there as far as anyone can find," Hargrave said. "But then it hasn't been easy to nail down exactly what Redman was doing over there. The information officer with the Florida National Guard will only tell us that he was with a special operations group that was farmed out across the country. No specifics."

"So what? You're thinking Redman reads this piece by me and gets juiced up about avenging this kid's death by assassinating the secretary who justified keeping him over there?" Nick said, to himself as much as to Hargrave.

"Hell if I know," the detective said. "I showed it to Canfield, just like that tight-ass Fitzgerald asked."

Nick could feel the sun cooking the back of his neck. He folded the story and unconsciously slipped it into his back pocket. Hargrave noticed and extended his hand and flexed his fingers in a give-it-back signal. Nick shrugged his shoulders and returned the paper.

"So what do we do now?"

"We?" Hargrave looked up. "We?"

It was hard for Nick to look wounded; he'd made himself an expert at not looking wounded. "What, you're going to sit back and just wait for the next victim to drop?"

"No," Hargrave said. "I'm going to get a return call from the P.D. up in Birmingham on this Kerner shooting and keep all possibilities open."

He gave a nod in the direction of Canfield's departure.

"That's what he was saying, between the management-speak. That goes with his job, not mine."

The detective flicked a furry red blossom, which did indeed look like a bottlebrush, off the table with one finger and then stood.

"Speaking of jobs, Mullins. I see from the front page this morning that someone else has taken over your story."

You can tell a cop either accepts you or despises you by the tone he uses when he takes a verbal shot.

Nick grinned at the statement and answered with an edge of bravado. "No way, Mo. Nobody else has my story. Because I'm the only one who has the true one. This is no marauding killer," he said, thinking of the lead paragraph on Joe Binder's front-page piece. "This guy's got it all planned out."

/ Chapter 31 /

Nick stayed off the sauce all day, passing by the urge to stop at Kim's Alley Bar on Sunrise when he drove out to the beach. Three years ago he would have slipped in, had a couple just to relax after a deadline, just to paint over the stress of the day, just to wash out the vision of another body bag or charred home or mangled wreck. Those were the excuses he gave his wife back in the days when he stumbled into the house late, after the girls had already gone to bed. When he repeated the excuses now to himself, they rang just as hollow, and he kept driving.

On A1A he turned left and then parked at the curb along the ocean. He was well north of the once-infamous Fort Lauderdale Strip, once the world-famous bacchanal of college kids gone wild. But the backdrop of *Where the Boys Are* had gone the way of most things money-driven. When the profit on kegs of beer and cheap hotel rooms couldn't stand up to family resorts and high-priced boutique stores, out went the old, in came the new. Yet it was still a wonder to him that this stretch of beach, from the road to the horizon, was sand untouched. The city had somehow worked it into a legal legacy that no buildings would go up on this stretch of land. Nick got out of his car and walked down to the tide mark and let the surf slosh white and bubbling over his ankles and up onto his cuffs. He thought of Julie, always with her feet in the water.

His wife would pull the beach chair all the way down to the edge, even when she knew the tide was coming in, even when she knew she was going to have to change her position within the hour. The closer to the ocean you are, the less of the city you see behind you, she would say. It's more like being out there, floating, without a care in the world.

Nick had never experienced that feeling of floating. He had envied her that. Out on the horizon, the cobalt blue of the ocean water was meeting the azure of the sky, trying to meld, but unable to mix the line until dark. Nick felt the tingle in his right hand again and flexed the fingers.

When his cell phone rang the sound made him turn to look behind, like he'd been caught, like the truth had come out and someone would be standing there. He shook off the feeling and brought the phone out of his pocket. The readout on the incoming number was blocked.

"Nick Mullins," he said.

"I am deeply disappointed, Mr. Mullins," said a man's deep voice.

The tenor of the words immediately charged his nerves and Nick turned away from the ocean wind, cupping his hand over the cell to listen closer.

"Yeah? Maybe I am too," he said. "Would you mind telling me who you are and why you're disappointed?"

"You gave our story up, Mr. Mullins," the voice said. "I planned out a lot of possibilities, my friend. But I never figured you to give our story up to someone else."

Nick immediately turned and ducked his head and started back to his car to get out of the breeze so he could hear and think.

"Mike? Mike Redman?"

"I mean, come on, Mr. Mullins. A marauding killer? That guy Binder writes just like the rest of them. All flash and no substance. Although I have to give him credit for mapping out my use of your journalism to decide on who needed to be eliminated. But I have a feeling that was your work. Am I right?"

Nick opened his car, climbed in and closed the door to create a vacuum of silence.

"Christ, Redman. What are you doing, man? You're shooting people in the streets. That's not your training. I saw your work too. This is not what you do," Nick said, guessing at the words to use, trying to juggle what he knew with how he thought the sniper might be thinking.

"It's not what any of us were trained to do, Mullins. I went to war and killed innocent people, did everything the opposite of how I was trained. And now look at yourself. I've read every story you did on those scumbags over the years. You were the truth. And now you gave it up too. You handed it over."

Nick was silent. Had he copped out by quitting? Was the sniper right?

"OK, Mike. Maybe I did. But do you want to set it straight?" Nick said, scrambling to keep him talking, truly falling back on his training. "You and I could talk. We could do an interview. I'd get it out straight from you, tell the story the right way. The truth, like you just said."

There was the sound of a deep chuckle in the cell earpiece. The guy was laughing.

"See? You and I are a lot alike, Nick. You can't help but be the newsman. I can't help but pull the trigger. It's what we do," Redman said. "I'm not after publicity, Nick. I don't need any stories. Like I told you, I've got one more shot, tomorrow. One more piece of business, and it's for you. Then I gotta move on. Then I'm gonna get on with my life, Nick. And you can too. Don't you see? We're a lot alike, you and I."

Nick felt the conversation slipping away. He'd lost interviews before, had them stop before he had the answers he needed.

"Wait, wait, Mike," he nearly yelled into the phone. "What do you mean, for me? Who's for me, Michael? The Secretary of State doesn't mean anything to me, Michael. I only wrote that quote. It wasn't me that said it."

There was no response. But no dial tone either.

"Is it Walker? Do you know about Walker, Mike?"

Nick's voice was still rising, reverberating in the closed space and buffeting back on his own ears.

"Hey, don't put this on me, Mike. I'm not out for retribution. Mike!" Nick slapped his right hand against the steering wheel in anger and frustration. "Redman?"

Three electronic beeps and the line went dead.

Nick sat back in his seat and stared out at the horizon. And then dialed Hargrave's number.

/ Chapter 32 /

At six fifteen the next morning Nick was sitting in his car, parked next to the Dumpster, down the street but well within view of Archie's Tool Sharpening Shack.

After talking with Hargrave, he'd gone home last night and had dinner with Carly and Elsa and tried to put on a clear-headed, smiling act. But when he went quiet in the middle of a conversation about his daughter's science lesson on the African desert's effect on forming hurricanes, she looked up and saw his eyes staring out through the window. She turned to Elsa, but the nanny only shook her head and said, "It's OK, Carlita, he will be back."

They pretended not to notice and in a few minutes Nick was back, rejoining the discussion as though no lapse had occurred.

Later in the evening Nick helped with Carly's math homework and then gave her an early good-night kiss and went out to the patio. He slept in the chair and, almost as if an alarm sounded, he woke at five AM, took a shower and drove to this spot.

At six thirty he began to squirm. Walker was late and he had never been late so far. Light from the east was starting to glow and a dusty gray was rising into the sky. He was leaning forward, anticipating the headlights of Walker's car, when a sharp tapping of metal on glass caused him to jump.

At the passenger window was the face of a man, a long flashlight tube in his hand. Nick was confused for a second. No one had ever approached him before. The flashlight snapped against the window again and now Nick could see the badge displayed on the man's chest.

He hit the automatic button to lower the passenger-side window and only then did he realize a second man was on his side of the car, standing back a few paces at the rear panel.

"Please step out of the car, sir, and keep your hands where we can see them," the officer at the open window said. He was standing sideways as he bent to look in. A standard defense procedure, Nick knew, that gave less of a profile to hit if a driver was thinking of shooting a cop during a traffic stop.

"Yeah, yeah, sure, Officers. I'm cool," Nick said, exaggerating his hands up and fingers spread. "I'm just reaching down to open the door, OK?"

Nick had written about citizens being wounded by officers reacting to unpredictable and quick movements. He'd also written about cops being shot during traffic stops. Both sides needed to know what the other was doing.

He opened the door slowly and then pushed his upraised hands out first and then stood.

"Come around to the front here, please," the officer to the side said and Nick followed the instruction, only glancing at the cop standing behind him.

While Officer One ran his flashlight beam over Nick's clothes and finally his face, he could see Officer Two doing the same kind of search of his car interior.

"License, sir?" Officer One said.

"I'm gonna get it out of my front pants pocket. OK?" Nick said before reaching. He had always kept his wallet in his front pocket since some street hustler had tried to pick it one day. And he knew reaching oddly into a waistband area was a motion that would surely agitate a cop.

The guy nodded and Nick took out the wallet and opened it away from his body and slipped out the license and handed it over. The officer looked at the license and then at his partner and said, "Mr. Mullins, may we look in the trunk of your car, sir?"

"Yeah, sure, no problem," Nick said. "The button is right there on the left of the dash and the keys are in the ignition."

He turned his head to watch Officer Two lean in and take out the keys and then walk around to the trunk. Officer One said nothing and while they waited Nick took in the uniform badge and seal on the officer's shoulder. Fort Lauderdale Police Department. He knew that this was officially their jurisdiction, but had never even seen a sector car in this area before. A pair of cops doing foot patrol was way unusual, Nick thought.

"OK, Mr. Mullins," Officer One said after getting an all-clear sign from his partner, who slammed down the trunk lid. "Can you tell me, sir, why you're parked here so early in the morning?"

"Actually, I'm working on a story. I'm a reporter for the *Daily News* and I've got an early appointment to meet a guy here." Nick nodded toward the buildings across the street. "And I usually show up early to, you know, go through the questions I'm gonna ask and stuff."

"Yeah, OK." Officer One was listening and looking down again at the license. "I was in on that plane crash over at Executive Airport back in August. I was one of the first units responding and you interviewed me.

"Larry Jacobs," Officer One said and stuck out his hand.

"Yeah, yeah, sure," Nick said, pretending he recognized the guy, but definitely remembering the crash. A small plane nosedived right after takeoff and went face first through the roof of a car repair shop. The pilot was thrown through the windshield and then the plane engine crushed him right in the center of the repair bay.

"Grisly scene, man," Officer Jacobs said.

"Larry, yo," Nick heard Officer Two say from behind with an impatient tone.

"OK, Mr. Mullins. You'll have to move the car, OK? We've got a cordon going up because the feds are doing some political dog-and-pony show a few blocks down and they're setting up security. OK?"

Nick looked around and said, "Yeah, sure. No problem. Probably why my guy is late. I'll just get him on the cell and, you know, reschedule or something. I didn't realize they were doing anything this far from the convention center."

"Well, they were keeping it under wraps," Jacobs said. "But I'm surprised you wouldn't know." The officer attempted a wink, but Nick's head had already gone elsewhere and he just waved as he got back in his car, took one more look at Walker's empty spot and drove away.

Two blocks away, Nick pulled over and parked in a coffee shop lot that was still empty and stared at his cell phone, thinking. I'm surprised you didn't know? The cops always figure reporters know everything. Not so. But photographers usually do. He dialed Susan's cell number and despite the hour, she picked up on the second ring.

"Hi, it's Susan."

"Well, good morning, early bird," Nick said pleasantly.

"My ass," she grumbled back.

Nick smiled. This was the stuff he'd miss.

"What's up, young lady?"

"Goddamn early assignment," she said. "But what's up with you, Nick? I heard you cleared out your desk. You get that job down in Miami?"

"No. No. I think I'm getting out of the business," Nick said.

"No shit! Good for you, Nicky," she said. "Man, I'm gonna be the oldest one on this beat before long."

"So what's going on this morning?" Nick said, getting to it.

"You know. Some gig that has to do with that OAS thing down at the convention center. It's all that hush-hush stuff. We have to meet them at the center and then they're going to drive us to some secret location to shoot some VIP hand-grab photos."

"Is it the Secretary of State?" Nick said, working.

"I gotta figure. That's the biggest face down here."

"Is it up north of the center? Like, by Tasker Street? 'Cause I got stopped up here by a bunch of security guys doing a sweep."

"Could be, Nick. They're not telling us anything yet," Susan said. "But why are you poking around if you quit?"

Nick didn't answer.

"Ha!" Susan laughed into the phone. "Can't get it out of your blood, eh, Nick? Not even for a day."

"You know everything, Susan," he chided back. "Have a great morning."

Nick's next call was to Hargrave.

There had to be a reason Walker hadn't shown for work. The son-of-a-bitch hadn't been late yet. It was part of his goddamn parole agreement. He was breaking his parole!

Nick fumbled while punching in Hargrave's number and got one of those high-pitched three-tone wailing sounds in his ear and cursed. Then he stopped, laid the phone in his lap, closed his eyes and took a deep breath. Think it through, Nick, he told himself. So Walker's late. Lots of possibilities. What were you going to say to the guy anyway? *Hey, duck, you're gonna get shot!* Or maybe you were going to just sit there and watch him get shot? Watch the man who killed your wife and daughter bleed out on the street? If Redman is going to assassinate the guy because he has deluded himself into thinking you are his so-called spotter, why not let him? If he thinks he owes you by giving you this retribution, then maybe he's a better man than you are.

He opened his eyes, took another deep breath, dialed Hargrave's number and waited.

"Hargrave," the phone said.

"It's Nick, Detective."

Hargrave pulled the old no-question-no-answer routine that so many hardass cops seemed to work at and remained silent.

"I was calling to tell you that Walker didn't show up for work this morning at his usual time," Nick said. "Did you by chance warn him of the possibility that he could be a target after we talked last night?"

"A target? Well, I didn't really get that far," Hargrave said and Nick thought that was going to be it until he continued. "But I did get some intelligence that he left his house this morning in his truck at six."

"And where might this *intelligence* have come from?" Nick asked.

"I stopped him in his driveway," Hargrave said. "He is one ugly guy, by the way."

"Tell me something I don't know, Detective."

"I informed him that the Sheriff's Office had reason to believe that he may be in danger and told him maybe it wouldn't be such a good idea to go to work today."

"And?" Nick said, feeling the heat of anger crawl up his neck.

"He asked for an explanation and as soon as I got to the part that had to do with you, he told me to fuck off and move my car out of his way."

Nick stayed quiet.

"Frankly, I don't need that shit," Hargrave finally said. "Even if you're right about Redman wanting to kill this son-of-a-bitch, I don't need it."

Nick wanted to say he agreed and just walk away. But somewhere in the last few days the story had changed for him. It was now more about saving Redman from himself than it was about saving his targets.

"Well, Walker never showed up here."

"I know," Hargrave said. "I'm watching his truck from four cars back. We're stopped at a roadblock to warehouse row, they're checking all I.D.s of people entering because of some federal action at a Cuban nursing home that's supposed to go off at nine."

"I heard," Nick said.

"Oh, really? Fitzgerald told us it was supposed to be a need-to-know deal, highly secretive."

"Yeah, well, what good is a photo opportunity like that if you don't tell the press?" Nick said.

"Yeah, well, if that info is floating around, Fitzgerald's not going to be a happy man," Hargrave said.

"You talked to him?"

"Right after I hung up with you last night I called Lieutenant Canfield. Then he patched together a conference call with Fitzgerald. The guy sounded hinky. He was under the gun because they got some kind of intel that this sniper they're looking for is definitely a foreigner and has been in the country doing one of those sleeper things, laying low, for a year.

"But that obit of yours with the National Guardsman's dad blaming the secretary for his kid's death might have creeped him out. They actually ran some kind of itinerary on Redman's movements over there and he might have spent time with the dead kid's unit. You didn't know that too, did you, Mullins?"

"No," Nick said. "But doesn't that say something to you, Detective?"

"Like too many coincidences?" Hargrave answered. "Yeah, it talks to me. But I get the feeling Fitzgerald is sticking with the foreigner-on-our-soil theory."

"But what do you think? Who's Redman's next target?"

"I already told you. I'm on Walker's ass right now," Hargrave said. "But you must be close by if you know he's not at work yet, Nick. So where exactly are you calling from? And what the hell are you doing?"

/ Chapter 33 /

Michael Redman lay with the hooded binoculars up to his face for forty-five minutes, but still his eyes were not tired. His eyes had never been tired. He could hold this position, prone on the roof, forever if he had to because if that's what had to be done, he would do it.

A week ago Redman had followed Mullins one morning and tracked him. He thought he might approach the reporter. Let him know what his stories had meant to him, how he'd planned this out for a year, how he was going to be the sword to Mullins's pen.

But he'd held off and tracked Mullins to this street and then watched as the reporter tucked his car in behind a trash Dumpster and then just sat there. Redman had been intrigued by the behavior. Maybe Mullins was working some investigative story. Maybe he was having a liaison with some woman. Redman had read about the accident that killed Mullins's wife and kid. It made sense that the guy wouldn't be shacking up with a new lady in front of his remaining daughter. Mullins was stand-up.

Redman had watched the reporter until a Ford F-150 showed and parked in front of a tool shop. The driver, dressed in a work shirt and six-pocket fatigue pants, got out and unlocked the shop. Redman scoped Mullins at the same time and could read the hardness in his face.

This was who he'd been waiting for. But once the mark was inside, Mullins simply waited a few minutes and then drove away.

Intrigued, Redman stayed. He had no deadlines. His was a patient study of people and what they did or did not do. In an hour the street began to fill with traffic and working men and women and Redman was about to slip away when the man Mullins had been watching reappeared from the shop, got into his truck and left. Maybe it was the bush pants that caught his attention. Military? Ex-military like himself? Redman trailed the mark first to a coffee shop and then to a liquor store. When the man emerged from the store with a small brown paper sack Redman watched him climb back in his truck, unscrew the top of a pint to take a snort and then slide the bottle into the thigh pocket of his cargo pants before closing the car door and driving away. Nine-in-the-morning boozer, Redman thought. And a secret boozer, at that. He took down the license plate number to check. It was never a bad idea to know the players. It was only later, when Redman tracked the name of the plate owner, that he found another name to add to his target list.

This morning at seven he took the position he'd found that week and was now scanning the street below. Traffic was again building, but there was a difference in the pattern. He tilted his binoculars up to sweep farther down the sight line and saw that some kind of barricade had gone up three blocks south. Uniformed police officers were manning the orange-striped sawhorses, but he could see that they had their arms crossed and were talking out of the sides of their mouths to one another, the classic sign of guys who were doing a special detail job, not really giving a shit because it wasn't their beat. Inside the barricades there were some unusually expensive-looking cars parked in an area where they didn't fit in. Some dark-colored Ford LTDs that Redman knew from experience were the car of choice for the feds.

He swung the glasses back down when movement in the kill zone caught his attention and he saw Walker's truck turn onto the street and pull into the same place where he'd parked before. Redman set the binoculars aside and pulled the stock of his sniper rifle close to his shoulder and used the scope to zoom in. Walker got out of the truck. He was dressed the same way as before, uniform shirt, cargo pants. But today Redman could tell by his body movements that the target was agitated. Walker stepped out into the street instead of going straight into his building. He looked south toward the barricades for a moment and then swatted the air with his left hand as if to say, *Fuck it,* and then turned and went inside. Redman allowed it. That was not the shot he wanted. That was not the statement. He would wait. If he was the study of human behavior he thought he was, the guy would return and the plan would go down with perfection.

///

Nick was scrambling, working the numbers. What the hell had Canfield said when Nick was doing the SWAT story? When Redman worked SWAT, six hundred yards was his optimal sniper range, the one he felt most comfortable with.

He left his car at the coffee shop and walked back into the area, taking the back alleys and parking areas, the ones tucked behind the warehouses and industrial shops and delivery bays. He thought about Hargrave, tailing Walker. The detective would be watching from ground level. But Redman would be up high, like any good sniper. And that's where Fitzgerald's boys would be looking too if they were worried about a legitimate assassination attempt. But would they come this far out from the nursing home? This was way too far, probably a thousand yards, for even a great sniper to take a shot at the secretary. Nick was working the numbers. He settled on the block that figured to be six hundred yards from Archie's front door, give or take. From behind the buildings he climbed up a utility ladder like the one he'd made his move on at the very first shooting site across from the jail. The top of the building seemed clear when he poked his head over the roofline. No man lying prone at the edge walls. No one dressed in black. He duck-walked to the front edge and took a bit of cover next to a metal container the size of a squared-off suitcase and snuck a look over to the street below. He could see Archie's green door across the way, but it seemed impossibly small. How the hell could anyone hit even the door from here, never mind put a bullet in someone's ear? He looked up the line, farther south, and started to retreat. But when he used the container to push himself up, the box gave way and tipped sideways, clunking over and making a racket. Nick again ducked down, softly cursing. He stayed silent and unmoving for a full two minutes and then carefully shifted around to look at the box. He had inadvertently knocked over the cover to a video camera that was wired onto the roof to record what was going on in the parking lot.

"Shit. A lot of good that does if a guy with a gun is walking around up here and the camera is looking out below," Nick said out loud. "Yeah, like anyone would be worried about that but you." He moved to the back roofline and found the utility ladder and made his way down to the last four feet and jumped to the ground, landing awkwardly with a sick twist of the ankle.

"What the hell are you doing, Nick?" he again said out loud.

He was on one knee, rubbing at the ankle with both hands. He wasn't sure why, but Nick found himself thinking about Ms. Cotton and her letters. "Forgiveness," she had said. "What's in them isn't for retribution. It's for your forgiveness."

Nick looked down at the hand on his ankle and flexed it and then shut his eyes against the memory:

He and Julie, up late. Two days before Christmas. She had joined him at the patio table, the aqua light softening their hard faces but not their voices. They'd been at it for half an hour.

"No, I don't understand, Nick! Why does your job always have to be more important than our family?"

He had stood up, angry that his obsession had started this all again, the late night on a story, the booze on his breath, the vision of another body swimming in his head. He'd meant to walk away, end it by saying nothing. But Julie's words stopped him.

"Why for Christ's sake do you care more about dead people than you care about your own family?"

The sting went through him. Truth? Did she really think that? Did he? When he looked up, his mouth started to open, but Julie's lips had already formed a hard line. Without a word, she turned and walked into the house and closed herself in their bedroom. The question she asked would be the last words she ever spoke to him. Two days later, she and Lindsay were dead.

Nick got up off his knee and tested his ankle. He blinked the tears out of his eyes and walked south. At the back of the building he'd selected, he climbed atop a stack of metal barrels and then to a fire escape, a rusty contraption that you rarely saw in Florida. Halfway up, he started doubting the possibility that Redman had come this way. The rungs were cracked and weathered by the heat and salt air. The metal had oxidized and Nick's hands were soon stained a reddish brown from the rust. But he made the top and as at the other buildings he was greeted by an empty expanse of tar and gravel interrupted only by whirring air-conditioning units and no Redman. He again moved low to the street edge of the roof. Nothing. Archie's green door was closer but untouched, and when he looked south the three-story building next to him was blocking the nursing home building. He scanned the other rooflines. Nothing. No protruding muzzles. No spun-around baseball caps. Nick turned away from the roof edge and reassessed. Think like a sniper. Think like a countersniper. Think like Fitzgerald.

/ / /

Redman saw the movement out of his peripheral vision just as Walker stepped out of Archie's Tool. The man had only been at work for thirty minutes, but it was past his regular time and he needed that taste. So predictable.

Redman swung the scope over and watched Walker move to his truck, climb in and drive north. He took a right just as he had the last time. If he went to the same liquor store, he'd return in twenty minutes, Redman thought. When he gets back. When he steps out of the truck. When he stops to open the door to the tool shop and becomes stationary, that's the shot. It will be just like when Michaels had opened the probation office door. He'll be a still target for one special second.

Redman was running the scene through his head, rehearsing like he always did, when his ear picked up the *whump*ing sound. He took his eye away from the scope and looked to the south. Helicopter. Whatever the gig that was going down inside the barricades was warming up and Redman took up his binoculars and checked the helo. It was a small two-man craft and did not carry the logo of any news channels that the media shitbirds always carried.

There was the possibility that it belonged to the feds who were parked below. Who else used spotter helicopters? Redman's head was clicking. He knew that the Secretary of State was in town. He'd read the newspaper's front page. But that was supposed to be at the convention center, well south, down near the port. There was no way they would expand a circle of security this far. He knew the federal protocols wouldn't even spread a sniper sweep more than eight hundred yards. He shifted his mind to other scenarios and came up with the only possibility: a political field trip.

The goddamn publicity machine, he thought, is taking the secretary on some baby-kissing visit and it's going down near my goddamn kill zone.

/ / /

"I know that, Lieutenant," Hargrave said, keeping his voice in check. "But if nobody's seen Redman, and none of his SWAT friends have heard from him, it's impossible to put a motive on this guy so we *can* predict what he's going to do next."

Hargrave had badged his way past the police cordon and followed Walker's F-150 into a neighborhood of industrial businesses. When Walker pulled up in front of a corrugated steel warehouse and went inside someplace called Archie's, Hargrave parked across the street. First he tried to get Mullins on the reporter's cell. He was immediately forwarded to some message service. Then he called Canfield and for the next thirty minutes found himself trying to explain why he was following Walker around. Who the hell even cared?

"Wait a second," Hargrave said into the cell. "He's leaving again." The detective watched as Walker came out of the shop, looked around and then got back into his truck and drove north, away from where Hargrave now knew there was an "official visit" going down at a nursing home only a few blocks away.

"Look, Mo. Like I said, you do what you think needs to be done with this asshole Walker. To tell you the truth, nobody here in command—and not Fitzgerald either—gives a damn about yours and Mullins's theory. The priority has shifted to the Secretary of State and not on solving the deaths of a few cons that probably deserved to die in the first place," Canfield said when the detective came back. "I know how that goes against your ethic, but like I said, you're hanging your own ass out there."

"I appreciate the help, Lieutenant."

Hargrave pushed the end button and stared out his windshield as Walker's truck disappeared around a corner.

"I might add," he said to no one.

The detective opened his car door and stepped out. His inclination was to go back to the office and again try to track hotel and motel registries for Redman's name even though he knew that was fruitless. Instead he locked his door and started walking south toward the cordon that was set up a couple of blocks away. Maybe he'd shoot the bull with the uniform guys doing duty. Ask if the feds were any more antsy than usual. Try to spot Fitzgerald somewhere.

/ / /

Nick made it down again, thinking like a sniper. He'd always heard the SWAT guys talking about taking higher ground and the philosophy moved him to the three-story building next door. He crossed the alley that ran straight south, looking for some kind of box or board to get within reach of the first ladder rung, and settled on an old shipping pallet with the nailed crosspieces and leaned one end up against the wall and used it as a makeshift stepladder. He had to stretch to get a grip on the first rung and hauled himself up. Again, the metal had not been touched, probably in years.

But he climbed. Thirty feet up he slowly came over the roof edge. Again, there was nothing to see but tar and air-conditioning vents, though over to his left a square bunkerlike access room protruded up. From his angle he could see two sides of the structure. One side had a door.

Great, he thought, I should have just walked in, flashed my press credentials and walked up the damn stairs. His cynicism was back, along with his doubts that he had any idea what the hell he was doing up here. But he still moved low along the roofline to get a look around the third side of the access room.

He was circling when he saw, or heard, the beat of a helicopter and raised his eyes to the sky. It was a small craft, not the big Channel 7 chopper shooting pictures of his ass again. But as he watched the aircraft slide to his left, his line of sight crossed the top of the access room and from this new vantage point he noticed a stepladder leaning against it, and then an odd platform on top. It looked as if someone had mounted a sheet of corrugated metal across two sawhorses. Nick looked behind himself for space and then stepped backward, forgetting to stay low and going up on his toes to gain a few more inches of view. Between the open legs of the sawhorses he could now make out the dark curve of a man's head, bent, absolutely still, over the top of a black rifle barrel.

Maybe Nick panicked. Maybe he should have taken a minute to think it through. But he didn't.

"Redman!" he shouted. "Mike Redman!"

/ / /

Mike Redman was sweeping the rooftops with his binoculars and keeping his ear tuned to the sound of the helicopter in case it should expand its circle and come his way. He had cover in the form of a sheet of metal that he'd rigged to hide his shape from the sky. He was tracking left to right, and then back behind himself, using time to pick up anything odd in the landscape, and he stopped on a sight that was new. Three buildings north he spotted on a container about the size of a squared-off suitcase near the edge of the roof that had been kicked over. The sun glanced off its surface and drew his eye. He remembered it from his earlier reconnaissance, a rain cover for a video surveillance camera. Some owners used the covers to keep the pigeon shit off the units. But this time the cover lay on its side and the difference bothered him. In his experience, few people visited the rooftops in South Florida, too damn hot, unless they had a reason. He swept the rest of that building's roof, but saw nothing, no human, no evidence of one. He set the binoculars aside and was shifting the rifle scope to take a closer look when he picked up movement below and saw Walker's blue F-150 turning onto the street. He knew that son-of-a-bitch would be back and silently congratulated himself for that knowledge. He let his sights follow the back window of the truck and tracked it to the spot in front of Archie's. He could feel his breathing start to settle and become deeper and slower. Every shot, he reminded himself, is a study of concentration and focus. Excitement only gets in the way. When the truck stopped, he kept the crosshairs on the back of Walker's head and watched the man who killed Nick Mullins's family knock back one more hit from the pint of liquor he'd just bought. Walker shifted in his seat, one shoulder dipping, and then got out. Redman took one more breath and then let the air pass slowly through his nostrils and began to pull pressure on the trigger.

///

Detective Hargrave saw the truck up ahead of him as he was walking back from the cordon.

"The son-of-a-bitch came back," he said softly to himself with as much surprise as his composure would allow and then quickened his steps.

The guys at the police line had been unhelpful. *We just showed up where we were told to show up, Detective.* Looked like they had the place pretty buttoned up. Nobody was going to get close to the secretary without an invite.

Hargrave asked if any of them had seen Fitzgerald, but when they all shrugged, he knew it was worthless and headed back. Now Walker was coming back to work. Fuck it, Hargrave figured, I already warned the guy. It's on him to look after himself and it's not my problem.

He was about thirty yards away when Walker got out of his truck and then instead of going toward the shop the guy stepped out in the street. He appeared to be looking up into the sky. Hargrave kept walking but followed Walker's sight line and looked up as well.

///

"Mike Redman!"

Nick yelled the name a third time and was now waving his arms, like he was signaling some kind of aircraft. Finally the gunman swung around from his prone position on top of the stairwell structure and the barrel of his rifle swung with him.

"Mike! You don't have to, man! It's not worth . . ."

There was a beat, no, three beats of silence that confused Nick. He was staring into the dark eye of a target scope and he thought, on the third beat, Jesus. Is he going to kill me?

Nick dropped his arms to his side in disbelief and then felt something swat his still-moving right hand just as it passed in front of his leg and the impact sent his palm slapping against his thigh. He did not hear the report of the shot or see any kind of flash, just the splat of the bullet as it ripped through the meat of his hand and burrowed deep into his leg.

The impact shut his mouth and he looked back at the sniper in disbelief. Redman. Dark, almost black eyes with an intensity that might have been anger, or maybe just pure focus. Then Nick felt himself dropping.

/ / /

Mike Redman was already pulling pressure on the trigger of his PSG-1 when the target did something unpredictable. Walker got out of the truck but instead of stepping toward the green door of Archie's, he moved the other way, out into the street, and looked up. Maybe at the helo, Redman thought and refocused. He shifted the sight and was aiming for the sideburn, just in front of the ear, and started his pull as an unexpected voice ripped the air behind him. His name. Being shouted from the rooftop.

"Mike Redman!"

The words cut into his concentration and his own reaction jerked one shoulder as he fired. He automatically swung the rifle around to the sound of a rear attack and instantly put a man's figure into his sights.

It was Nick Mullins. What the hell? The man who had become truth to him was looking directly at him, repeating his name, screwing up what had been a perfectly planned operation to gain vengeance against the man who killed Mullins's own family.

Mullins was gutless. Someone deserved to die. Someone had to carry it out. If you couldn't do it on your own, Mullins, take my gift and shut the hell up.

But now you don't deserve it, Redman thought. He watched Mullins's eyes flatten with confusion and then fear, and then Redman dropped his sight down to the reporter's thigh and fired.

Mullins stared at him for a second before his leg gave way and he sank to the roof. Redman instantly swung his rifle back to the street. Mullins was down, but as he put Robert Walker's face into the scope sight, a body stepped in to block the shot. Redman pulled back. Some bystander had already gotten to Walker and was covering him. Others, cops from the nearby barricade, were jogging down to the scene. Regress, Redman instantly thought. He gathered his shell casings and his rifle and backed out of the shooter's nest and swept down the ladder. At the door to the stairwell he stopped, looked across the roof at Mullins sitting with glassy eyes and his hands on a bloody leg and said, "Sorry, Nick," out loud, knowing the reporter could not hear him. "Maybe another time."

/ / /

Mo Hargrave was deeply confused. He was watching Walker looking up in the sky when the man suddenly crumpled and went down in the street. "Christ!" he said and started running, forgetting that he was now in a wide-open field of fire. "Goddamn Mullins was right."

He covered the last twenty yards and then bent over the downed man. Walker was now curled on the concrete, his back bent and his hands grabbing at his left thigh. Blood was already oozing between his fingers, but Hargrave grabbed him by the belt and the collar and dragged him like you might some wallowing drunkard in a bar fight until they were safely behind the bed of the truck.

Walker's eyes were squeezed shut and he was keening in a high pitch through his nose. Hargrave listened for a second rifle shot, fully expecting to hear a bullet *wang* against the fender, but heard nothing. In the distance he could see the boys from the cordon beginning to move his way, probably because they'd seen a fellow cop yanking some guy across the ground.

"Are you hit anywhere else?" he asked Walker, who had started breathing in those short bursts that come with intense pain. Walker didn't respond and Hargrave did a quick search of the man's head and shoulders and back. No sign of any other trauma. He then took a more studied look at the leg, which Walker was still clutching with both hands high at the thigh. Hargrave could see a puddle starting to form on the street surface, but it too confused him. It could be a through-and-through wound, he thought, but the consistency of the blood was too fast and watery. He pulled the man up by the armpits to put him in a sitting position against the truck wheel and when he inhaled with the effort he took the odor up into his nose. Whiskey, Hargrave thought. And it wasn't as refined as Maker's Mark. He reached down to Walker's hands and pushed them off the wound to feel it himself and when he touched the bloodied cargo pants he could feel the broken glass inside the thigh pocket. The bullet had shattered the newly purchased pint bottle and then ricocheted down into the man's leg. The blood-and-whiskey mix was now running a gravity trail out into the street and Hargrave made a note of it before standing and waving the arriving cops to the side of the buildings and pointing up. It only took seconds for the street to clear, but the officers continued to move up using the overhangs as cover until they were beside the truck and Hargrave stood up.

"Probably ought to call EMS," he said to the first man. "You've got one gunshot victim down on the street. And you also better get on the tactical channel to the Secret Service guys and tell them they might have a sniper working north of the barricades."

At that the officers all looked up at the same time as they crouched next to Walker. But Hargrave remained standing and answered a ring on his cell phone.

"Hargrave," he said.

"Detective, this is Mullins. I'm gonna need some help up here."

/ Chapter 34 /

Two weeks later, Nick was at home, lying on the couch on a Saturday morning, waiting to take Carly on a field trip. He'd had plenty of time at home, unemployed and without a deadline. At first he wasn't sure he was going to be able to stand the open time, the lack of schedule. The slow cocktail of pressure and adrenaline and approaching deadline that had consumed his life was now over for good. But he quickly found that he did not miss it, or its hangover, at all.

On the morning of the shooting he'd called Hargrave on the cell for help and directed him to the top of the Marsh Storage Facility. Hargrave had come alone and in his own stoic way took command. While calling for paramedics on his cell phone, he simultaneously spun his handkerchief into a rope, put a knot in the middle and then stuffed it like a plug into the palm of Nick's hand and then wrapped it in place. Then he crouched there and assessed the leg wound. He stripped his shirt and folded it to form a pressure bandage and then held it hard against the seeping hole and then watched as news helicopters filled the sky like carrion vultures until the rescue squad got there.

"Goddamn snipers aren't such good shots after all," he said.

/ / /

The next day's headline had read:

**SECRETARY OF STATE SAFE, TWO CIVILIANS WOUNDED
DURING SHOOTING NEAR OAS CONFERENCE IN LAUDERDALE**

The *Daily News* and other media jumped all over a speculation that the shooting had been an attempt on the secretary's life gone awry and that when the sniper was interrupted by two civilians and sensed capture, he fled.

The Secretary of State immediately flew back to D.C. and a spokesperson issued a statement that the incident was "troubling" but that they would have no comment until the Secret Service had done a full investigation.

When Nick was interviewed by the feds he simply told the truth. On a news hunch, he was looking for someone on the roof when he inadvertently surprised the sniper, who turned and fired at him. The bullet was deflected when it sheared through his left hand and then struck his leg. He could not say that he heard another shot, and he saw no one else on the roof until Detective Hargrave arrived.

Later in the week it was directly from Hargrave that Nick learned that FBI crime-scene technicians had taken over the scene and confirmed his story after finding that the round that pierced Walker's leg and his whiskey bottle matched that found in Mullins's thigh.

Both the detective and the reporter had their own theories on what happened. If they ever sat down and compared scenarios, their versions would not have been much different, but they never did.

Hargrave only called Nick one more time. It was on the day that charges of violating probation were filed against Robert Walker for being in possession of and consuming alcoholic beverages. Hargrave had made sure evidence from that shooting scene was gathered by the Sheriff's Office, including Walker's blood-and-alcohol-soaked pants.

He'd also called in a request at the E.R. and had them take a blood-alcohol test immediately. And he personally canvassed all the area liquor stores within a ten-minute radius of Archie's until he found the clerk who'd been selling the whiskey to Walker, to use as a witness.

When Nick's name was released as one of the wounded, he was inundated by members of the media, including old friends, requesting interviews. The managing editor of the *Daily News* sent a written request, pointing out that since he had not gone through the final "separation from the company" process, he might still be considered an employee with certain obligations. That was a new one on Nick. He'd yet to hear of the management technique of both asking a favor and threatening legal action against an employee at the same time.

To everyone he simply said, "No comment," and meant it. Maybe, when his hand healed and he was able to type without pain again, he might put his own exclusive story together.

But this morning he and Carly were on the living room couch, reading and waiting for a visitor. At the sound of the doorbell, Carly jumped up to answer the door.

"Hi, Lori!" she said to the research assistant who had been the first newsroom person to check on Nick without asking for a quote.

"Hello, Carly," she said, walking in. "What are you and your dad up to this morning?"

"I don't know," the girl said and smiled. "You will have to ask Mr. Secrecy over there."

Nick got up, shaking his head and dangling his car keys in his right hand, a smile on his face. "We're going on a visit."

The girls looked at him and gave in. Both of them had already learned not to rush to help him walk or offer to drive. During the trip the girls talked about their mutual interest in paintings and photographs. Lori told Carly about the access she had to hundreds of photos through the newspaper's archives and her collection of museum tomes like the one about Van Gogh she'd given her.

"Awesome!" was Carly's sophisticated comment and Nick smiled.

After several minutes they turned into a neighborhood in northwest Fort Lauderdale where neither Carly nor Lori had ever been. Both of them looked out with curiosity at the streets and the small, sun-faded homes. On Northwest Tenth, Nick spotted the red geranium on the porch and pulled into the driveway.

"I want you guys to meet Ms. Cotton," he finally said. "She's a very nice lady."

The small black woman was waiting for them just inside the door and Nick made introductions as they were invited in. Ms. Cotton had made a pitcher of lemonade and Carly politely accepted a glass while they sat. Nick watched his daughter's eyes go immediately to the photos of the girls on the wall and stay there, like she was studying them. Their host noticed.

"Those are my girls," Ms. Cotton said directly to Carly. "Your father was very kind to them when they passed away."

Carly looked at her father, anxious over the mention of death, but hiding it well.

"What were their names?" she asked Ms. Cotton.

"Gabriella and Marcellina," she said. "They were artists, the both of them. Would you like to see some of the things I kept?"

Carly's eyes brightened and Ms. Cotton led both her and Lori to a small bedroom in the back. After a minute she returned alone.

"That child is lovely, Mr. Mullins. Is that why you wanted to come by, to show her to me? Because I already knew she was special."

"Maybe," Nick said, not really sure what his motivation was. "Mostly to thank you, ma'am."

He fumbled at his back pocket with his good hand and came up with a white, lace-fringed thank-you card, which he presented to her.

"Whatever for, Mr. Mullins?" she said, looking not at the card, but into his eyes.

Since the last time he was in this house he had not been able to rid himself of the feeling that this woman knew things about him that should have been impossible for her to know.

"For forgiveness," he said.

"Ah," the tiny woman said and turned away to step toward the portraits on her wall. As she did, Nick could see the stack of newspapers on her coffee table. He had no doubt she had read every story of his involvement with the sniper. "You gave some of it to me, in your stories. Now I give it back to you. Somehow, I believe, that is how it spreads."

Nick went quiet. No question had been asked. He didn't know how to respond.

She extended her hand to his, held the bandaged palm lightly and turned toward the interior of the house. "Let's go back, Mr. Mullins, and see what your girls have found."

/ Acknowledgments /

The author would like to acknowledge the excellent autobiography *Shooter*, by Gunnery Sgt. Jack Coughlin, USMC, and Capt. Casey Kuhlman, USMCR (St. Martin's Press, 2005), and *Sniper/Counter Sniper* by Mark V. Lonsdale (S.T.T.U., 2000), both books that greatly aided me in the writing of this novel. A debt of thanks is also owed for the years of law enforcement insight gleaned from those who walked the walk, including the late Fort Lauderdale Police Chief Ron Cochran, former Broward Sheriff's Office undercover detective Dennis Gavalier, police expert Doug Haas and FDLE agent James O. Born. Any errors or exaggerations in police or sniper procedure are purely the fault of the author.

Also a debt of gratitude is due to the many newspaper editors who helped influence the author's twenty-five-year journalism career, including Will Williams, John Parkyn, and Henry Wright.

As always, many thanks to the folks at Dutton: Mitch Hoffman, Erika Kahn, Kathleen Matthews Schmidt and Dave Cole for their support and the reading and correcting of the author's numerous errors and lapses.

As from the beginning, the author wishes to thank Philip Spitzer and Lukas Ortiz. Also of great help and contribution to this story were my early readers and friends Maren Bingham, Dave Wieczoreck and Jane Wood.

Last but not least the author wishes to thank Florida National Guardsman Jeremy Polston and Army Airborne soldier Mark Kaufman for their service in Iraq and their families' sacrifices at home.

/ About the Author /

Jonathon King is the national bestselling author of four Max Freeman novels, which have been published to critical acclaim around the world. His debut, *The Blue Edge of Midnight,* won the Edgar Award for Best First Novel. Formerly an award-winning journalist with more than twenty years of experience, King has reported extensively on crime and criminal courts. He lives in Florida.